PRAISE FOR OTHER TITLE
ALLISON

Allison's telling is deeply engrossing; his exuberant style illuminates what is human and deeply relatable in material known for the lofty and the grand.

— DANICA BOYCE, FAIR FOLK MEDIA

A captivating retelling... meticulously researched and expertly paced, this book is a spellbinding testament to the enduring power of Irish myth, reimagined for a new audience.

— SORCHA HEGARTY, CANDLELIT TALES

Daniel Allison is a myth-walker. Bound by his love of myth and a deeply curious mind, he walks the world with one foot in the mythical and one foot in the here and now... This is work that we need.

— CLARE MURPHY, IRISH STORYTELLER

Epic battles, formidable heroes, powerful magic, and deep emotions create a mythic landscape that is vividly alive. If you enjoyed Neil Gaiman's *Norse Mythology*, you will love this book.

— CSENGE ZALKA, AUTHOR OF *DANCING ON THE BLADES*

Full of action, wonder and melancholy leavened by sprinklings of humour, *Irish Mythology* is an approachable, concise, and gripping read by an author who loves the stories, writes with agility, and knows what he's talking about. Highly recommended.

— LAURA SAMPSON, AUTHOR OF *ENCHANTED TALES*

A tremendous read... no end of dramas, surprises & reversals of fortune... a rattling good plot... wonderful stuff

— FAY SAMPSON, GUARDIAN CHILDREN'S BOOK AWARD-NOMINATED AUTHOR

A thrilling tale that twists and turns as you eagerly turn the pages. It breathes new life into the creatures of Orkney's folklore for a new generation of readers.

— TOM MUIR, AUTHOR OF *ORKNEY FOLK TALES*

SCOTTISH MYTHS & LEGENDS: VOLUME II

CELTIC MYTHS & LEGENDS RETOLD

DANIEL ALLISON

HOUSE
LEGENDS

INTRODUCTION

I first floated the idea of writing a follow-up volume to *Scottish Myths & Legends* when I was driving through the Highlands with a friend. He nodded to my idea and said, 'So is this one the B-sides and rarities, then?'

His words underlined what was already extremely important to me: that this volume must not be B-sides and rarities. In the four years since I published *Scottish Myths & Legends*, I've been overjoyed by how positively readers have responded to it. I shouldn't have been surprised; I packed it with stories which I'd told at firesides for years and which I knew audiences loved. If I was to write another volume, the stories would have to be of the same standard. All killer, no filler. So I made a longlist of stories, told them wherever I could and resisted starting writing until I was absolutely sure of them.

Like its predecessor, this volume contains stories sourced from all across Scotland. There are local legends, ancient epics and everything in between. For the first time, I've included historical legends, both well-known and obscure. Anyone who has toured Edinburgh Castle or watched *Game of Thrones* or *The Hills Have Eyes* will recognise at least one of them.

I've also included for the first time a few extremely short stories, for want of a better term. These stories can feel somewhat unsatisfying to modern readers. They are over almost as soon as they start and don't contain the familiar rhythms and pacing that we are trained to consider necessary to a story. Yet they are a vital part of Scotland's folklore tapestry, and can be a real joy if one develops a taste for them. Think of them as more akin to photographs than novels.

I've also included, for the first time, a Scottish folk tale which I've blended with elements of a few related stories to create something not altogether old but not altogether new. This is what storytellers have always done; it's the reason we have over five hundred versions of Cinderella. I consider it important that storytellers feel free to do this, so long as we are transparent and don't try to pass off our creations as ancient lore. *The Sea Maiden* is a splicing of Scottish and Nordic folktale elements with a dash of my own imagination. It is an offering from me to the tradition; a feeding of the fire just as my forebears did for thousands of years. I hope you enjoy it.

What kind of creatures and characters lurk within these tales? The well-loved selkies, kelpies and fairy folk return, and there is of course a Fianna tale or two. You'll also be introduced to some less well-known creatures, including the wonderful trowies of Orkney and Shetland and the deliciously sinister Baobhan Sith.

A huge part of an oral storyteller's work is to demonstrate to audiences that oral stories aren't solely for infants. The idea that folk tales are interchangeable with nursery tales is incredibly pervasive. You can advertise an evening of 'dark, gruesome, erotic and violent folk tales' and someone will inevitably bring along their six year-old. Yet the truth is that for 99% of the time humans have existed, oral stories were the only stories. And when oral stories were the only stories, everybody, young and old, listened to oral stories.

This book is intended for an adult audience. Though many of these stories make wonderful reading for children, some definitely don't. Particularly *Sawney Bean*. Even the light, humorous stories often contain darker currents. That said, there are stories here that I have told to children countless times, and I'd hate for yours to miss out on the fun. If you'd like to share these stories with your younglings, please read the book yourself first and then decide which ones to share.

Enough with disclaimers. Time for the tales.

THE WITCHES OF KINTAIL

I f you've ever driven to Skye from Inverness or Fort William then you will surely remember Loch Duich. It's a sea loch that stretches on for miles through Kintail, on the last leg of the journey before you reach Skye. By this point you are almost breathless with anticipation. You have to fight to keep your eyes on the road rather than gaping at the rows of mountains lining the loch shores. It's the kind of place which makes you wonder if perhaps all the strange stories you ever heard were true.

A young man named Donald once lived on the south shore of Loch Duich. He was a fisherman and a crofter, living off the sea and the land and bartering for whatever they didn't provide. He wasn't a rich man but he was a happy one.

One autumn day, Donald woke up and went outside to assess the weather. Snow mantled the mountaintops. The sky was a sheet of grey; not a breath of wind rode the air. Donald watched as an otter padded down to the shore and slipped into the still, silent water.

It was going to be a calm, quiet day. A good day for fishing.

Donald went inside and made a pot of porridge. After he had eaten he picked up his fishing rod and tackle, put on his coat and went down to the loch shore. He pushed out his boat and set off across the steely water.

Donald rowed until he was far out on the loch before stowing his oars. He hooked a wriggling worm, cast off and sat back to wait.

Nothing bit. No matter. Donald filled his pipe, struck a match and watched his smoke trail vanish into the vast sky. He was perfectly happy to pass the whole day in this way. The fish were in no hurry, and neither were the mountains, and neither was he.

Morning became afternoon. Donald caught one small fish but that wasn't enough to turn him homeward. He was glad it was past midge season; they would have devoured him on a day like this.

Midway through the afternoon, sleep tugged on Donald's eyelids.

Donald knew it was a bad thing to fall asleep on the boat. He'd done it a number of times and always swore he would never do so again. Loch Duich was a sea loch, and it was a fool who went out to sea without keeping an eye on the weather.

Yet the day was so peaceful. So perfect. As his eyelids grew heavier, Donald found that the thought of a storm didn't frighten him. Today was not a day for storms. It was a day that had somehow stepped aside from the march of time. If storms went somewhere to sleep and dream, that was where they would be today.

Donald's chin drooped as he drifted off, fishing rod in hand.

He awoke to black clouds and the hammering of rain.

THE LOCH WATER had gone from grey to black. It hurled itself against the boat as the wind wailed and moaned. A wall of storm clouds was rolling in from the west, and booms of thunder resounded like battle cries.

Donald seized his oars. He tried to turn his boat for home but it was no good. The point where he could match the strength of the current had passed. He abandoned his oars and clung instead to the sides of the boat as it sluiced back and forth on the rising waves.

Higher the waves rose, throwing Donald's boat about like a toy. He was soaked to the skin and water was gathering in the keel.

Things weren't looking good.

A towering wave darkened the sky. It smashed into the boat, launching Donald into the air. He couldn't swim, of course; it was known that a fisherman who could swim would one day have to swim.

This is the end, Donald thought as he hurtled towards the water.

He struck the water.

His feet touched the bottom and sank into the mud.

He had been blown all the way to the shore!

Donald scrambled out of the water, laughing and spluttering. He was alive! He had survived the storm!

His head was spinning, so he stood and waited for his mind to clear and his breathing to steady. Since he didn't recognise the landscape around him, Donald guessed that he had been blown all the way to the north shore of the loch.

Loch Duich was no puddle. Donald lived about halfway along her southern shore; to get home from the same point along the northern shore was a journey of many, many miles. He was soaking wet, his teeth were chattering and his fingers were blue and numb. There was no way Donald was getting home tonight. Indeed, if he didn't find shelter and warmth soon, he probably wouldn't see tomorrow at all.

'I shouldn't have trouble finding a friendly house,' said Donald to himself. 'I'd never turn a stranger away from my door, and I'm sure my neighbours to the north are the same.' So Donald set off, looking for a welcome. The problem was that he seemed to have washed up on an uninhabited stretch of shore. A dense oak forest lined the loch, the trees ancient and twisted.

'I've fished for miles up and down Loch Duich, east and west,' Donald said to himself as he made his way east. 'I don't remember a woodland such as this one on the north shore, and I would certainly know it if it lay on the south shore. Very odd.'

There was nothing to do but keep walking.

Rain poured down. Lightning split the sky. Donald walked onwards, cold to his bone marrow.

Finally, he spied firelight.

It came from somewhere among the trees, uphill from the shore. Donald whooped for joy; he was saved! He ran towards the light, tripping over roots and crashing to the ground before hauling himself up and carrying on. Branches scratched at his face and he ached from every fall but he didn't care. All that mattered was fire. Warmth. Life.

Donald halted before a house.

It was round and squat, with wattle walls and a thatched roof. The oaks pressed in close around it, their branches embracing overhead as if to protect it from prying eyes. It had two little windows, and from its windows came the glow of firelight. The house somehow seemed like a living thing, a predatory bird come home to roost in the shadows.

You might have expected Donald to call out a greeting or to rush in through the door, sure of the warm welcome that was customary in those days. But instead he stood still, knees knocking together, watching the house in the way you might watch a sleeping bear you encountered in a mountain cave. There was something very strange about this place. That much was clear even to Donald's storm-addled mind.

But he was in need. Dire need. So he crept forward and peered in through a window.

This is what he saw.

A hearth fire burned in the centre of the house. Three women sat around the hearth on wolf pelts, wearing cloaks of woven adder skins. One was old, one middle-aged, one young. None of them moved or spoke.

At the far end of the room, opposite the door, Donald spied some kind of altar. An enormous bear's skull sat atop a stone slab, surrounded by candles and draped in a veil of bats' wings.

Donald didn't know what this place was, but he was sure it was no place for a fisherman like him. Yet his need was dire.

He went to the door and called out his presence.

He waited. His knees knocked together.

The door opened.

The young woman stood there. She had golden hair and glittering, blue eyes. She smiled at him, drinking in the sight of him as if he were mead and honey. Wordlessly, she beckoned him in.

DONALD ALLOWED the young woman to help him out of his coat. She still hadn't spoken a word, but Donald made up for that.

'I'm so grateful I saw the light from your window. So grateful. It's a terrible storm, and it blew in so fast, didn't it? And then, do you know, I've never noticed this woodland before, and I've lived on the south shore all my life! Can you believe that? I had the croft from my parents, of course...'

The young woman beckoned him to sit with them by the fire. Donald did so, his stream of words vanishing into the cavern-deep silence. It was so quiet; even the fire did not crackle or sputter.

So Donald sat silently with the three women. Gradually he ceased shivering. Steam rose from his clothes. He sighed with pleasure as the fire's warmth reached inside him and banished the cold.

He was lucky to have found this place. Yet it was so quiet.

He realised he couldn't even hear the storm. Could he hear anything at all?

Yes. If he listened carefully, he almost thought he could hear the three women talking to one another, though their mouths did not move. He looked at the bear's skull and almost fancied he could hear it speaking too.

Hours passed. Donald was bone-dry now. He had no reason to fear dying tonight. This was a strange place, sure, but there was nothing wrong with a bit of peace and quiet. Most folk talked too much. All was well.

The only problem was his stomach. He hadn't eaten since his morning porridge and it had been an eventful day. He was hungry. Very hungry. Yet there was no sign of food anywhere in the house. No pot or kettle bubbled over the fire. Did he dare break the silence to ask for a morsel to eat?

He really was hungry.

'I... I don't suppose you have a bannock going? Or maybe some soup?'

A darker shade of silence fell.

'Soup?' said the young woman.

'Bannocks?' said the middle-aged woman.

'Bannocks and soup?' said the old woman. 'I think we can do better than bannocks and soup.'

'Oh yes,' said the middle-aged woman. 'We can do better than bannocks and soup. Much, much better.'

A terrifying suspicion took hold of Donald in that moment. *These women are witches!* he thought. *They are witches, and they are going to eat me.*

The young woman stood and walked over to a chest which

sat in the corner. She dug around in it, found what she was looking for and returned to the fire.

In her hands was a green flat cap, or a bunnet as they are sometimes called in Scotland. She passed it to the old woman, who put it on her head and said, 'Away to London!'

The old woman vanished. The bunnet landed where she had been sitting.

The middle-aged woman picked up the bunnet. 'Away to London!' she said, and she too vanished.

The young woman put on the bunnet. She smiled suggestively at Donald, spoke the same words and was gone.

Donald looked at the bunnet sitting on the wolfskin.

How could he not?

He put the bunnet on his head, held it in place and said, 'Away to London!'

Streaks of silver light enveloped Donald.

A moment later, he was in London.

So THIS IS LONDON, thought Donald. *Well, probably*. He couldn't be sure of where he was; he'd never been to London before. He knew it was somewhere in England, or possibly France.

He had arrived in a tavern, that was certain. It was bigger than any tavern he'd ever set foot in, and so noisy that his ears hurt. Tables lined every wall, all crammed with drinkers, while in the middle of the room stood a great crowd of people; probably more people than Donald had met in his life.

And what folk they were! It was mostly men but there were

a good few women. They wore strange clothes and talked in a way he could barely understand. In one corner a band played outlandish music on flutes and drums and stringed instruments. The bar was under assault from a mob of drinkers four men deep.

Donald himself was sitting at a table with the three women. By now he was quite certain they were witches. The young witch sat beside him, the older two opposite.

The middle-aged witch grabbed the sleeve of a passing barmaid and said, 'Whisky and ale, and four bowls of whatever's in the pot.'

'Right you are, love,' said the barmaid, or so Donald guessed. She really did speak strangely.

The food and drink soon arrived. Donald tucked into his steaming bowl of broth with delight, mopping it up with thick slices of warm bread. It was soon finished.

'Donald is still hungry!' said the old witch. She ordered more food and soon a plate of roast beef and potatoes arrived for him, along with a sweet and fiery drink called rum.

Donald ate and drank, talked and laughed. The hours shrugged off their skins and merged together. He fell into deep conversation with the young witch, who was looking more beautiful with every drink. Donald told her wild tales his grandmother used to tell him and she laughed uproariously. She sang him songs in a hushed, high tone which lit torches in the deepest caves of his mind.

The band played on. The tavern grew hotter, louder. More drink, more food, more drink. Donald was having the time of his life.

He noticed that his companion's cup was empty, and called out to the barmaid as she passed.

'Landlord says no more for you lot until you've paid,' she said and carried on her way.

The three women shared a look.

The young one reached into her cloak, pulled out the bunnet and set it on her brow. She flashed Donald another smile and said, 'Away to Kintail!'

She disappeared.

The old witch put the bunnet on her head, said 'Away to Kintail!' and vanished.

The remaining witch put the cap on her head, said 'Away to Kintail!' and she vanished too.

There was only one thing to do. Donald reached for the bunnet... and felt a heavy hand on his shoulder.

He turned around. The hand belonged to a large and unfriendly-looking man.

'Planning to pay for all that, mate?'

'Er... the thing is, I don't actually have any money...'

Donald stuffed the bunnet into his back pocket as he was hauled out of his chair, out of the tavern and into the street. The large man dragged him to a building which he called a 'police station' where Donald was thrown into a barred room full of foul-smelling men. He kept his head down, wishing that he could put the bunnet on his head, but his hands had been tied behind his back.

At some point Donald curled up in a corner and fell asleep. In the morning, his head pounding, he was taken to a building called a courthouse. There Donald explained the whole story to the judge, from making his morning porridge to the magic green bunnet, happy for the chance to clear up the misunderstanding. But the judge shouted over him and pounded his hammer.

'For the crime of theft,' said the judge, 'compounded by your insolence in telling lies to the court, you, Donald Mackenzie of Kintail, shall hang. Take him to the gallows.'

Justice was dispatched quickly in those days. Donald was led out of the courthouse and into the back of a cart packed with condemned men. They trundled through the streets as passersby jeered at them and threw rotten vegetables.

'I don't think I like London,' Donald whimpered as a putrid cabbage struck his face.

Soon the cart arrived at the square where the gallows waited. Donald watched in terror from the cart as a condemned man was led through the crowd by a black-hooded executioner. They climbed the steps and the hangman put a noose around the man's neck.

The executioner and the condemned man exchanged some words which Donald couldn't hear. Then the executioner gave the prisoner a push. He kicked and writhed then fell still, eyes staring upwards as the crowd cheered.

'I don't like London at all,' muttered Donald.

One by one, the men in the cart took their turn to swing.

All too soon, it was Donald's turn.

The hangman seized his shoulder and shoved him through the crowd to the gallows.

'Up you go now.'

Donald climbed the little ladder and looked around. So many faces, young and old, all clamouring for his death.

The hangman put the noose around his neck.

'Any last words, mate?' he said, standing behind Donald on the block and leaning forward.

Donald thought for a moment.

'No? Alright, then—'

'Hold on! I don't have anything to say, but I do have a last request.'

'Last request? What do you want, mate, a kiss goodbye?'

'No, thank you. But do you see the green cap in my back pocket? I'd like you to put it on my head please, so I can die looking respectable.'

'Fine.' The executioner pulled the bunnet from Donald's pocket and set it on his head. Without another word, he put his hand on Donald's back and shoved.

Right as he did so, Donald shouted, 'Away to Kintail!'

He crashed down onto the floor of his own house by Loch Duich. The noose was still around his neck, and he brought with him the crossbeam of the gallows and five dead men.

Donald buried the men in his garden that day. He was sorry that they'd died in such an ugly way, but they made for wonderful fertiliser. Donald used the crossbeam of the gallows to build himself a new boat, and he used the ropes for all sorts of things throughout the long years of his life. *

---

* I first came across a version of this story by Sheila Douglas in a collection called *Tales on the Tongue* published by the Scottish Storytelling Centre. It's a very popular story among Scottish storytellers and I'm surprised that it hasn't been further adapted.

One version of the story has cats in place of the witches. A variant from Skye names the hero as Topsy-Turvy' (*But-ar-scionn* in Gaelic), while another from Harris has a tailor as the hero.

If you'd like to look deeper into beliefs around witchcraft in Scotland, *Witchcraft and Second Sight in the Highlands and Islands of Scotland* by John Gregorson Campbell is an excellent source.

FAIR MAID'S TRESSES

The island chain of the Outer Hebrides runs for over a hundred miles from north to south, shielding Scotland from the full fury of the Atlantic Ocean. At the very southern tip of the shield lies the Isle of Barra.

Barra is small, low-lying, inconspicuous; you could walk around it in a day. It's quiet, serene and easily overlooked. No gnarled cliff stacks; only soft white sand dunes. No sky-piercing mountains; only undulating marshy fields. The wind whistles through the dunes as history happens elsewhere. Yet strange things have occurred on Barra, such as the tale I'm about to tell you.

There once lived on Barra two sisters named Sorcha and Finola. Sorcha was the eldest by two years. She was golden haired and good-natured, with a smile and a kind word for everyone she met. Finola was her opposite in many ways: dark haired where her sister was blonde and as quiet as Sorcha was brazen. She preferred her own company to the company of other children. Sorcha would ask Finola to come out to play or go beach-combing with her friends, but Finola usually refused.

Finola preferred to wander alone. She liked to sit on shore-side rocks and listen to the music the wind made as it danced over the water. She sometimes fancied she could hear voices on the wind and see dancing figures in the ever-shifting surf. She would pass hours in this way, wrapped up in her little cloak, knitted extra thick by Finola's mother to keep her warm on her long vigils.

Life went on in this way for Sorcha and Finola, the years rolling in and out like the tides, until the day their father went fishing and never came back.

He had gone out alone on a calm summer's day. A storm blew in without warning and claimed him like so many fishers and fathers before him. Splinters of his boat washed up on the white sands.

His wife and daughters grieved hard for him, as did all the folk of Barra. They were few in number and every life was precious. Everyone pulled together in their long-practised way. The afflicted family were gifted fresh fish, smoked fish, turnips, kale, potatoes. Clothes 'no longer needed', clothes newly spun. Sorcha and Finola's mother gladly accepted it all; she had been on the other side of that old arrangement more than once. She knew, as every island woman knew, the cost of such gifts to those who gave them. Barra was beautiful, but she had never been bountiful.

So the family set to work. The mother had a gift for spinning, knitting and weaving, and she ensured this was passed on to her girls. Childhood fell from them like a shed skin as they sat indoors, working to stay alive.

The offerings from their neighbours came gradually less often, though they did not stop entirely. One person who regularly stopped at their door, claiming his catch was too much for his own table, was a young fisherman named Callum.

Callum and Sorcha had been friends since childhood, when they had been two cubs in a scrawny pack that roamed the beaches and moors. Now Callum was a young man, red-haired and broad-shouldered, with a quiet, gentle nature. As a boy he'd been in awe of Sorcha, often bringing her shells he'd found and trinkets he'd made. Now he came to her door with fish to keep her from starving.

As a child, Sorcha had nursed a soft spot for Callum. Now that she was a young woman, that softness grew into something more: a warmth, a fire fanned by his kindness until it burned fiercely for him. Every day Sorcha hoped Callum would come by, and happiness stole back into her heart as she saw in his eyes that he loved her too.

Sorcha's mother was delighted.

Finola was furious.

FOR AS LONG AS Callum had loved Sorcha, Finola had loved Callum. On the rare occasions that she had played with the other children, she had done so to be near him. She would steal glances at him, hoping to catch his eye, hoping he might look at her in the same way that he looked at Sorcha.

Callum always did his best on those days to include Finola, to be kind to her and ensure the others were kind to her too. But she was a cat among dogs and everyone knew it.

So Finola grew up apart, watching Callum from afar, crafting fantasies in which he led her away and asked for her hand, saying she had always been his true love. She spent so many years alone with these dreams that she forgot they were only dreams. As Sorcha approached marrying age, and Callum started inviting her out for long walks around the island, it seemed to Finola that Sorcha was stealing her lover away.

Callum's visits grew more frequent. Those walks went on longer, sometimes late into the evening. Finola remained at home with her needlework or went out alone, sometimes watching the pair from afar.

One evening, on the beach at Traigh Mhòr, she watched them kiss.

The wind caressed her ears. Her knees buckled; her heart turned to ash.

An idea blossomed like a black flower in her mind.

In an isolated cove in the southwest of the island lived an old woman. She knew the secrets of herbs and wildflowers; she could read the landscape of a life in the circling of carrion crows. Such a person was of no small use to an island community. Many made the journey over the rocks to learn from her the best day for planting a new crop, or to locate a missing possession, or to look into the pattern of their coming years.

Yet dark words were spoken of this woman. Rumours flitted across the island of demonic familiars, of arcane knowledge bought with blood. A few folk swore she had put a curse on them. Thus many islanders stayed away.

One of those was Finola.

She had spoken to the old woman a number of times over the years. Once, the old woman had approached Finola, sidling up to her as she sat alone by the sea.

'You hear them speaking, don't you, little bird? You hear the hidden ones. Would you like to learn to speak back?'

Finola had been curious but frightened. There was something about the old woman which she didn't trust, so she kept her distance.

No longer.

FINOLA LEFT her home one evening in late summer. The day was dry; the wind had teeth. She wrapped her cloak tightly about her as she made the journey south then southwest across the island, arriving at the old woman's house as the sun sank beneath the horizon and turned the sea and sky to gold.

She called out a greeting and went inside.

The old woman's house was full of practical things: half-mended nets, drying bait, hooks and hammers and pots and rope. The old woman's hearth fire was at the centre of the room and she sat beside it, cutting a piece of leather. Seeing Finola, she grinned widely.

'Sit down, dear. You're very welcome. That net needs untangling.'

Finola set to work and the two of them talked.

'Were you looking for something from me, dear?'

'I was thinking to learn a song.'

'Far better singers than me on Barra.'

'It's a certain kind of song I'm looking for. I thought you might know one.'

'What kind is that?'

'One that will put someone to sleep.'

The old woman didn't respond. She and Finola went on working, the fire sending an endless stream of sweet-smelling smoke into the air.

'I might know such a song,' said the old woman at last. 'But the power isn't only in the song. Much of the power comes from the one who sings it.'

'Could you teach me to sing in that way?'

'It depends, dear. Who is it you wish to put to sleep?'

Finola looked up from her work. The old woman's eyes held her like a fly in a web.

'Maybe I'd rather not say.'

'Maybe I'd rather not help you.'

'It's my sister.'

'I see. And what has she done to earn such a song?'

Finola told the old woman the whole story. How she'd loved Callum for so many years and how Sorcha had stolen him away. It was the first time she had spoken her tale aloud, and all of her hatred and jealousy poured out like a river of poison bursting its banks.

Finola finished her tale.

The old woman continued to gaze at her.

'So will you teach me?' whispered Finola.

'Yes,' said the old woman, nodding slowly.

'Will it work?'

'Oh yes. It'll work.'

FINOLA RETURNED to the old woman's house four times over the next few weeks. She learnt the song and practised it until the old woman said she was ready. The only price the old woman asked was a promise that Finola come back to learn more from her. Finola had raw talent, and it was past time the old woman took an apprentice.

On the chosen evening, Finola invited Sorcha out for a walk.

Sorcha gladly accepted. She wasn't blind to her little sister's pain, and it had hurt to watch Finola grow ever more distant. Here, at last, was a peace offering.

They left the house and walked north along the western shore, past the Borve Stone and up to Traigh Hamara. Their footprints made winding tracks on the white sand. Autumn was settling in, the evenings growing darker.

Sorcha had hoped they would talk but Finola remained quiet. She was usually quiet, though, and didn't look hurt or angry; rather, she seemed strangely peaceful. Sorcha gave up her attempts at conversation, letting her words fall away into the quiet of the evening.

Onwards they went. Crabs scuttled out of their way; red-beaked terns screamed from their nests. Eventually they came to a place where seaweed-smeared rocks stretched out towards the sea beneath a wall of low cliffs.

'Let's rest awhile here,' said Finola.

Sorcha agreed. She sat down against a rock to watch the tide slowly make its way inshore.

'Your hair looks so beautiful in summer,' said Finola, kneeling down beside Sorcha and running her hand through her sister's hair. 'It's as if the sun itself were caught in it. It's like a golden fly got trapped in a spiderweb and turned the web to gold. Could I braid it for you?'

'Of course,' said Sorcha, touched and puzzled by her sister's sudden show of affection. She made room for Finola to sit behind her.

Finola took Sorcha's hair in her hands and began to braid it.

As she worked, she sang.

Finola sang and Sorcha sighed. She shifted. Her head nodded.

Finola went on singing. The sun sank slowly into the sea. All was blue and white and gold.

Sorcha was now softly snoring.

Hearing this, Finola began a new work. Wriggling out from behind Sorcha, she crouched at her side, her hands moving quickly. She took Sorcha's braids and bound them to the rock, around and around, weaving them as tightly as any fisherman's net.

Her task was complete. Leaving her sister's side, she climbed the short distance to the clifftop and sat down to watch.

The sea surged forward, inch by inch.

It reached Sorcha's feet.

Her knees.

Her breasts.

Her mouth.

Sorcha disappeared under the foamy water.

Finola grinned and laughed... then frowned. For swimming in from the open sea was a grey seal.

The seal made straight for Sorcha. It disappeared under the water.

Finola watched, mouth hanging open, not breathing.

The seal reappeared.

A moment later, another seal appeared at its side.

The two seals looked up at Finola, their eyes inscrutable. Then they turned and swam away.

Finola screamed, and her scream was a bloody knife slashing the sky.

When it was spent, she leapt from the low cliff. She tumbled downwards and as she fell, she took a new shape. Her bones shattered and mended; feathers tore through her skin; before she could hit the ground she became a cormorant, a black watchman of the sea. Finola beat her wings and flew across the water, searching for those two seals, singing her dark-throat song.

Cormorants and seals have known little love for each other since then. You will often see a seal barking and biting at a cormorant, and might think they are fighting over fish. But really it's because of what happened between Sorcha and Finola.

All this took place a long time ago. Ever since then, a rare kind of seaweed has grown around the shores of Barra. It's called Fair Maid's Tresses. Though it tastes sweet, nobody on Barra will eat it, in remembrance of Sorcha who lived on Barra so many years ago. *

---

* Another tale of witchcraft. I first heard this story from Linda Williamson, who included a version by her late husband Duncan Williamson in her book Land of the Seal People. In Duncan's version, the main characters are referred to as the light-haired sister and the dark-haired sister.

If you'd like to learn more about selkies/silkies/seal-people, I have an in-depth blog article about them on my website.

Barra is a beautiful island with a dream-like atmosphere; it is easy to imagine such things happening there. I haven't visited since before I heard the story, so I haven't had the chance to go looking for Fair Maid's Tresses myself.

AULD CROOVIE

There was once a young man named Jack who lived in a cottage with his mother. Their cottage lay on a highland estate owned by a rich laird, and Jack earned his living by minding the laird's sheep.

It was easy work but it was dull work. Jack would sit outside all day, in all weathers, watching a flock of sheep who rarely did anything interesting. Fortunately, the glen in which the sheep grazed was a bonny one. A river ran down the middle of the glen; oaks grew on one bank and birches on the other. Jack liked to sit with his back to the tallest and grandest of the oaks, which was known to the people thereabouts as Auld Croovie. It stood farther up the bank than all the other oaks, and from his high seat Jack could see all the way to the laird's castle, which sat at the end of the glen on the far bank.

One summer's morning, Jack was sitting beneath Auld Croovie as usual. The sky was grey, the air muggy. Everything was quiet and still, as if the earth beneath and the sky above were asleep and dreaming.

Jack noticed someone coming his way down the glen. The figure drew closer and he saw that it was Kate, who assisted the cook in the laird's kitchen. Jack was happy to see Kate, but nervous too, for he'd been in love with her for as long as he could remember. She came to see him often, bringing him sweets and cakes that she'd baked especially for him, but Jack guessed that she probably did that for everyone.

'Good morning, Jack,' she said with a smile. 'How are you today?'

'Same as always. Minding sheep. Bored of minding sheep.'

'You can't be bored today, Jack! It's a special day.'

'Why?'

'It's midsummer.'

'So what? Midsummer is just another day to the sheep, so it's just another day to me.'

'It's more than that, Jack, whatever the sheep might think. There's magic in the air today. Don't you feel it?'

'Ach, I don't know anything about magic. All I know is I'm hungry,' he said, eyeing the bag in her hand.

'Well, you'll see for yourself soon enough. Tonight, on midsummer's night, if the legends are true, the trees in this glen will rise up out of the earth and dance. Anyway, I'd best be going, Jack. It was nice to see you. It's always nice to see you.'

She gave him a handful of biscuits, smiled in a way that made him blush and left.

'Dancing trees indeed,' said Jack as he began on the biscuits. 'I never heard of such nonsense.'

AROUND MIDDAY JACK noticed another person making their way down the glen towards him. It was his mother, who mostly spent her days at home, knitting clothes from the wool which Jack gathered. She often brought Jack his lunch.

'There's your piece, son,' she said, handing Jack a bannock and a slice of cheese. 'Have you had a good morning?'

'Kate came to visit. She was blethering about magic, saying the trees would get up and dance tonight.'

'She's right, Jack. Many folk say that the trees in this glen dance each midsummer's night.'

'I don't know about that.'

'You'll see. But be careful, Jack. You and me are insects to an oak like Auld Croovie. You could get squashed if you don't watch yourself.'

'I'll be fine, Maw,' said Jack, rolling his eyes.

'Don't give me that look, son. And take this.' She handed him a length of rope.

'What am I going to need...' began Jack. But she was already off.

THE DAY CRAWLED BY. Jack never saw a glimpse of sunshine all day, but at least it wasn't cold or raining. He drifted in and out of daydreams as the sheep wandered around, chewed grass and stared at nothing in particular. When Jack got sore he would stand up and stretch or wander about for a while before sitting down again, his back to Auld Croovie.

The day wore on.

Jack picked up a twig, tossed it into the air and caught it. Magic? Dancing trees? Could it really be true? No. There was no such thing as magic. Kate and his maw must have got together and decided to play a trick on him. Some folk had too much time on their hands.

All the same... he'd heard so many strange stories about midsummer. Seal people emerging from the sea to dance. Sidhe-folk gathering at the old stone circles. If fairies and seal people danced on midsummer, was it possible that trees did too? And he had to admit that there was something odd in the air today. It was as if a storm had gathered far, far away but was even now racing towards him. It was as if something in the earth deep beneath him was slowly, slowly waking up.

Why was he thinking such strange thoughts? Jack tossed his twig away down the glen. Maybe he was going daft. There was no such thing as dancing trees, and he would stay here all night to prove it so.

With that settled, Jack leaned back against Auld Croovie and promptly fell asleep.

Hours later, beneath a dome of shimmering stars, Jack awoke as Auld Croovie shifted behind him.

JACK LEAPT UP so fast that he lost his footing and tumbled down the hillside. He halted himself, got to his feet and looked up at

Auld Croovie. The ancient oak was jerking from side to side like someone trying to kick off a tight pair of boots.

A moment later, he broke free.

Auld Croovie pulled a long, twisting root out of the earth. Another followed, then another, leaving great gaping holes in the earth. Once all his roots were free, he used them to walk down the hillside towards the river.

Jack dived out of Auld Croovie's way as he passed. Auld Croovie was huge yet he moved gracefully, almost cat-like. Jack could have sworn that he glanced at Jack as he passed, but without much interest.

Auld Croovie had other things on his mind.

Jack saw that all of the oaks had wrested their roots free and now made their way downhill. The ground shook with each step they took, yet Jack felt unthreatened by the trees. He followed them downhill.

The oaks reached the river and waded out into the water. They seemed to be gazing up at the far bank.

Jack followed their gaze to where the slender birches were pulling their roots free. When that was done, the birches made their way to the water. Their movements were lithe and elegant; they didn't shake the ground but glided over it like silver spiders.

The oaks moved to the centre of the river. The birches came to meet them. Every tree held out its branches to another. They came together as pairs, embracing one another with their branches.

Then, beneath the midsummer stars, the trees began to dance.

Round and round each pair went, oak and birch entwined together, the river rushing and bubbling about their roots. Some pairs danced sedately, or clung together like long-parted lovers; others twirled and pirouetted, throwing their branches up to the night sky.

Jack watched it all, full of wonder. It was like a dream, yet somehow he also felt as if he were truly awake for the first time. If he listened carefully, he could hear faint music, or even feel it rippling across his skin. He swayed as he watched, mimicking the dancing trees, his smile growing ever wider. If only Kate were here to see this with him.

Should he go and get her?

He looked up the glen, in the direction of home...

And saw the laird marching down the glen towards him.

The laird had a sack on his shoulder and a fierce, hungry look in his eyes. If he had seen Jack, he gave no sign of it. He drew close, turned uphill and headed towards the spot where Jack normally sat. The laird didn't stop to watch the trees dance for even a moment.

What was he up to? Whatever it was, Jack was worried.

Jack reluctantly turned his back on the trees. He climbed the hill, following the laird. He saw the laird reach the place where Auld Croovie normally stood, and then disappear.

Jack broke into a run and soon reached the spot where the laird had vanished. Gaping holes pocked the earth; light glimmered from within them.

Jack peered into one and gasped.

It was full of treasure!

Gold and silver coins, jewels, cups... Jack couldn't believe it.

The laird must have climbed down a hole to collect the treasure.

And why not? Trees had no use for treasure. Surely Auld Croovie wouldn't mind if Jack took one or two small items, perhaps a few coins...

His mind made up, Jack climbed down one of the holes. There was a little cave at the bottom with treasure stacked against its walls. Jack set to filling his pockets, all thoughts of restraint quickly forgotten. Very soon his pockets were stuffed. Well, he could only carry what he could carry. It was time to go. Unless he came back with a sack...

Just then, Jack heard a voice calling down to him.

'Jack! Come on, now! It's time to go!'

It was Kate.

Jack ran to the edge of the treasure cave to see Kate squinting down at him. 'Hurry, Jack! The trees are done with dancing. They're bowing to one another and saying goodnight. You'll get squashed!'

Jack took one last look at the treasure. It still sang to him but the spell was broken. He turned his back on it and climbed to the surface with a helping hand from Kate.

Out on the hillside, Jack brushed the dirt off his clothes as he looked downhill. The oaks were indeed heading their way. Some had already reached their standing spots and thrust their roots back into the earth. Anyone caught in one of those holes...

'The laird!' said Jack. 'He's still down there!'

They ran from hole to hole until they spied the laird in one of the deeper holes. He had three bulging sacks at his side and was busy filling a fourth one.

'Get out of there!' called Jack. Remembering the rope his mother had given him, he pulled it from his bag and threw an end down to the laird.

'Grab hold and we'll pull you up!'

The ground was shaking so hard that Jack was nearly knocked from his feet. He glanced downhill; the old oak was almost home.

'Now! Come on!' shouted Kate.

'No!' said the laird. 'I'm not leaving any of it!' He went on stuffing his sack, ignoring the rope.

Kate pulled Jack aside just as Auld Croovie arrived home.

They collapsed together as Auld Croovie thrust his roots back into the ground, one by one. As his final root entered the earth, they heard a muffled scream that was quickly cut short.

'That's the end of the laird, I suppose,' said Jack. 'I never liked him, but it's a bad way to go.'

It occurred to Jack in that moment that he and Kate were lying together on soft grass, their arms wrapped around one another. His pockets were full of gemstones and Kate seemed in no hurry to let go of him.

Kate caught his eye and grinned.

'Do you still say there's no magic in the air, Jack?'

Jack and Kate didn't come home that night. They spent the night beneath the branches of Auld Croovie as he swayed in the rising wind, remembering the feeling of a birch in his arms and cool water rushing around his roots.

Jack sold the gemstones he had acquired and used the money to buy the laird's castle. He married Kate beneath Auld Croovie's branches and the two of them moved into the castle, along with Jack's mother whom they gave her own wing. Every midsummer's night, for as long as they lived, they went to watch the dance of the trees and to give thanks to their favourite tree, Auld Croovie. *

---

* My version of this story comes from a version by the influential Traveller singer and storyteller Stanley Robertson. Supposedly Stanley's family would camp at a Traveller site near Lumphanan in Aberdeenshire when they were working on the flax harvest; Auld Croovie was the name of a tree near the site. In some versions, the trees dance only once every fifty years. The word 'Croovie' is from the Gaelic word 'craobh' for tree.

Stanley Robertson had a profound influence on many singers and story-tellers, including the celebrated singer Sam Lee who was his apprentice. You can listen to some recordings of him on Soundcloud.

THE HEDGEHURST

A woodcutter and his wife once lived in a cottage beside a forest. The cottage was small but well-maintained, with bright blue paint on the door and window frames. To the front of the cottage was a little field in which they kept their sheep, hens and geese.

Every day the woodcutter went to work in the forest while his wife saw to their animals. They weren't rich but they weren't exactly poor either. By selling firewood, wool, eggs and meat, they always had enough to get by. Yet in the wife's eyes they were as poor as anyone could be, for they had no children.

Ever since their wedding night they had tried for a child, at first with pleasure and then with a growing sense of despair. That despair eventually caused the woodcutter to retreat from his wife. His hand no longer reached for hers at night; he took to spending his evenings in the tavern. Yet as time went by and his paunch swelled, he started to see mockery in the eyes of his fellow drinkers. He knew what they must whisper to one another: that a man who could not father a child was no man at all.

He abandoned the alehouse, but home was no better. His wife's eyes held no mockery but were rife with pain and disappointment. So he went instead to the woods, working from before sunup to after sundown. The best solace he found was in the swing of his axe, the grim certainty of his own strength.

Disappointment turned to anger in the woodcutter's wife.

'You may have given up on becoming a parent but I haven't,' she said one day as she thrust his lunch in front of him. He usually ate his lunch alone in the forest but an autumn storm had forced him home. 'A child would keep me company! You're never here and when you are you don't say a word. The geese make better conversation than you.'

The woodcutter sighed and poured himself another ale.

'I don't need a whole clutch like some women in the village have,' she continued. 'Jean Fletcher, she has seven bairns. Seven! All I ask for is one. And they needn't be handsome, or clever, or strong. Why, I wouldn't care if they were as beautiful as a rainbow or as ugly as... as that hedgehog feeding in the garden there!'

The woodcutter glanced out the window. There was indeed a hedgehog feeding in the garden.

And there was another creature in their garden too.

Unbeknown to the woodcutter or his wife, a fairy man had come walking out of the forest as they spoke. Tall, slim and elegantly dressed, he had tasted the tang of their discord on the air. Intrigued, he had sidled up to the door and listened to every word.

'As ugly as... as that hedgehog feeding in the garden there!' he heard the wife say.

That gave him an idea.

The fairy man summoned his power. He shaped it into words of magic. As he spoke, though she did not know it, a fire awoke in the wife's belly.

The fairy man laughed to himself and wandered off in the direction of the village.

THE WOODCUTTER and his wife were utterly astonished to discover, several weeks later, that they were pregnant. There had been one or two brief, joyless couplings in recent weeks, so the news wasn't altogether miraculous, but it was shocking nevertheless.

The wife cried with joy, all day and every day. The husband held back. So many children failed to make it through the gauntlet of birth or the dangerous days, weeks and months that followed. Better to keep his heart clenched. Yet he had moments where he dared to hope, and his wife caught the look of joy that flitted across his face at those times.

Autumn passed, and winter and spring.

Early in summer, the birthing day came.

The woodcutter ran to the village and returned with the midwife. She arrived and set to work as the wife began to shudder and scream.

Hours later, the baby was born.

The midwife had seen a thing or two in her time. Yet when she held the child up to the light, she let out a scream herself.

She thrust the boy into his mother's arms. The woodcutter's wife looked at the boy and saw why the midwife had screamed.

Her child was not entirely human.

His long, thick hair did not end at his neck. It ran all the way down his back. His limbs were short and stumpy while his face was small and sharp, his nose long and pointed.

He looked like a hedgehog.

'I've heard whispers of such creatures,' said the midwife, her voice shaky. 'They're called hedgehursts. It's the custom when one is born to... well... I can take care of it for you, if you like.'

'You'll take care of nothing,' said the wife, recoiling from the midwife as she clutched the boy to her chest. 'Hedgehurst or no, he's my son. My husband will pay you.'

The midwife left, shaking her head as the woodcutter's wife stroked her son's bristly hair. So what if he looked like a hedgehog? She loved him. She loved him more than she had ever loved anything or anyone. He was beautiful to her.

Her husband was knocking at the bedroom, asking if he could come in.

Surely he wouldn't react as the midwife had. Surely he would see his son's beauty. He had a hairy back himself.

Yet when he entered the room, and looked at his son, his wife's hopes died.

THE HEDGEHURST GREW up in good health. His mother took him everywhere, talking to him endlessly whether she was shearing a sheep or plucking a goose. He learnt in time to walk, to talk and to go here and there on his own, investigating the world.

Wherever he went, his mother was always close by. She often told him that he was indescribably precious and must never come to any harm.

Things were different with his father.

The woodcutter's clenched heart had hardened into stone. In his eyes, some cruel god had chosen him to torment. The pain of those barren years! Then the pregnancy, the dreams he had allowed himself to dream... only for his wife to give birth to a beast. As if that wasn't enough, he was forced to watch the beast grow, waddling about his house, eating his food, taking all his wife's attention that should have been for him. If only he'd torn it from his wife's arms on that day and taken it out to the forest, axe in hand. But he had been too weak.

THE HEDGEHURST GREW OLDER. He learnt to stay away from his father, especially at night when he was full of ale. At such times the Hedgehurst would take himself out to the garden, the fields or the forest. He felt most at home when he was close to the ground, close to things with six or eight legs, which he often enjoyed as snacks. When his father stumbled after him and managed to find him, he learnt that it was best to curl up into a ball. When he did so, the hair on his back would harden into spikes. There was no touching him when that happened, as his father soon learned. The woodcutter would stand and roar curses at his son instead, while his wife screamed her hatred at her husband. The Hedgehurst would only curl up tighter.

His mother sent him into the village a few times to try to make friends with the other children. They were as cruel to him as his father was. His mother worried at that, saying every boy needed friends. But the Hedgehurst had all the friends he needed. The sheep were his friends; they liked him and never scampered away when he approached. It was the same with the geese and the hens, who would flock around him when he came their way. But his greatest friend was his cockerel.

The cockerel had been born around the same time as him. As he grew, it grew, and it never stopped growing. It had quick, clever eyes, shimmering blue-black feathers and glittering claws. The cockerel was devoted to the Hedgehurst and one day, when they were both around twelve years old and the cockerel had reached the size of a pony, the Hedgehurst climbed up onto its back.

The cockerel crowed with pleasure. It took off at a brisk trot, around the cottage, down the road and back again as the Hedgehurst laughed; something he rarely did. Seeing the world from the cockerel's back, he came to a decision.

That evening, over dinner, he addressed his father. The two of them rarely spoke.

'Father,' he began.

'I don't know who you're talking to. There's no father of yours sitting at this table.'

'Well, whoever you are,' said the Hedgehurst, 'I have something to ask of you.'

The woodcutter laughed and took a swig of ale. 'You've taken my wife from me. You eat my food and ride around on my cockerel. And now you want more from me? Go on, then. What is it?'

'I would like you to give me two sheep, two hens and two geese.'

The Hedgehurst's mother stiffened. Her husband rarely tried to hit her son; the boy had learnt to curl up quickly. Yet she knew that glint in her husband's eyes; he was wondering if he might get in a strike or two before it was too late.

'Furthermore,' continued the Hedgehurst, 'I would like you to make a saddle for my cockerel, or pay for one to be made if you cannot do so yourself.'

'Your cockerel, eh? And why would I do that?'

'Because if you do, I will leave this place. I will ride away upon my cockerel, with my flock behind me, and I will never trouble you again.'

The Hedgehurst's mother gasped. His father's eyes sparkled.

'In that case,' said the woodcutter, 'we have a deal.'

The woodcutter wasted no time. Within days he returned from the saddler's with a fine saddle, a perfect fit for the cockerel. He ushered their best sheep, hens and geese out in front of the cottage and even placed the saddle upon the cockerel's back himself.

As his wife wept in the shadowed doorway, he stepped back to watch as the Hedgehurst solemnly wriggled up onto the cockerel's back. He placed his feet in the stirrups, took the reins in hand and whistled to his flock, who lined up in pairs behind him.

'You won't see me again,' said the Hedgehurst to his parents. 'I am going far away from here to build a kingdom.'

'Your kingdom won't be worth a hog's arse,' said the woodcutter as his wife wailed and the Hedgehurst rode away.

THE KING LANDED with a splash in the murky marsh water.

He lay half-submerged, chest heaving, slowly sinking. Why bother getting up? He was so exhausted, his mind thick with fog. It would only be a few moments before he fell again.

Then he saw with his mind's eye his wife and daughter weeping over an empty casket. That was why he had to get up. He had to get back to them.

The king hauled himself up, marsh water dripping from his sodden clothes. A week had passed since he'd got separated from his huntsmen. Oh, he had been so stupid! He should have stayed put, waited for better hunters than he to find him. But no; he had gone marching off, sure he knew the way home. Instead, he had ended up lost in a marsh that seemed to go on forever. Perhaps it really did; perhaps this was the world's end, a marsh that stretched on into eternity.

He could turn back, but he'd done so a dozen times already. All he'd found was more marsh. He couldn't see the sun, had no idea in which direction he walked. But he had hope. Hope that he would see his daughter's bright smile, and the gleam in his wife's eyes that told him how dearly she loved him. Not to mention his kingdom, his people, his old hound that no longer hunted but instead waited by the castle gates for him to return home. His kingdom had known peace for years; no man could ask for a more blessed life. Although if he could have been blessed with a little more sense of direction...

The day wore on. The king splashed about, fell, got up and waded forward. Dusk was on its way and he dreaded nothing more than the coming cold night, huddled on a sodden bank without a fire to warm him...

A blackbird's song rang through the air.

He hadn't heard birdsong in days.

There it was again. The king frantically waded in the direction of the sound. As he did so, the ground beneath his feet grew firmer. He reached a dry bank. Another bird called out up ahead, then another.

He had reached the edge of the marsh.

A beech grove stood ahead of him. As he stared up, sunlight pierced the gloom and danced among the leaves. A pair of squirrels scampered up and down the branches.

If he could somehow catch a squirrel to cook...

Somewhere up ahead, a sheep bleated.

The king froze. There it was again. Another sheep answered, then another.

He ran forward, all thoughts of squirrel-hunting forgotten, then stopped and stared.

He had reached a fence. Beyond the fence was a field full of sheep, and beyond the field lay a grand house. Smoke rose from the chimney. There were more fields on either side of the house, some home to sheep, others to hens and geese. Beyond the fields lay forest. The sun shone down, the grass gleamed and the king thought that he had never seen such a picture of tidiness and order. It made his own castle seem rather scruffy.

The king climbed over the fence and crossed the field. The sheep eyed him warily and scampered out of his path. Everything was in spectacular order; not a blade of grass over-long, not a broken fence post, not a sheep with a shaggy coat.

He passed through a gate and made his way towards the house. Finding his way to the front door, he got another surprise there. Standing by the door, eyeing him with detached interest, was a cockerel the size of a horse.

The king cleared his throat. 'Good... good afternoon,' he called out. 'Whoever lives in this fine property. I am a king. I got lost in the forest and found my way here by accident. I'm looking for help to get home.'

'You are no king here,' said a voice from inside, 'for this is my kingdom.'

The door opened. The king gasped.

Out came a man with a long, pointy nose and stubby arms. He wore shoes and trousers but no shirt. Long, sleek hair ran from his head down the length of his back. His hair was coarse and stuck out almost like the quills... of a hedgehog.

The king had heard of such creatures.

This man was a hedgehurst.

'In that case, I apologise for not addressing you correctly, Your Majesty,' said the king. 'It is a fine kingdom you have here.'

'Thank you.'

'Really, I mean it! Everything is so neat and tidy. And your cockerel, what a wondrous creature! I am so sorry to come barging in here, all dripping wet and muddy, disturbing your peace. But I really am so grateful to have found you. I don't think I would have lasted much longer out there.'

'Hmm. Well. It is no trouble,' said the Hedgehurst, looking somewhat uncomfortable.

'Do you live here alone?'

'How could I be alone? You can see I have my cockerel, my sheep, my hens and my geese.'

'Oh yes, of course, of course. Well then... I am so sorry to trouble you, but do you think you could help me get home?'

The Hedgehurst gave the king a long, piercing look.

'I make you this offer. I will feed, clothe and shelter you tonight. Tomorrow, I will lead you away from here and back to your own kingdom. In return, you shall give to me the first member of your family to kiss you when you get home. Do you agree?'

The first member of his family? The king thought about it. His old hound always waited for him by the castle gates whenever he left home. She would surely be waiting there for him now, and she always licked his face when he returned.

And oh, how he loved her. He'd had her since she was a pup; he would never have dreamed of giving her away. But he was a king, and a king had to be in his kingdom. His wife was waiting for him too, and his daughter, his beautiful daughter who was on her way to becoming a woman and needed her father's guidance.

He had to get home. Besides, the Hedgehurst seemed to have a way with animals.

'Very well then,' he said. 'We have a bargain.'

The Hedgehurst nodded. 'Come inside then. And please wipe your feet first.'

THE KING PASSED a pleasant evening in the Hedgehurst's house. He was given a hot bath, and fresh clothes to wear, and after bathing he and the Hedgehurst sat down together to a hearty bowl of stew. The king had a second and a third helping, all the while trying to make conversation with his host, but not getting far. The Hedgehurst wasn't exactly rude but he certainly seemed ill at ease.

Too much time with only geese and sheep to talk to, thought the king.

The king collapsed into bed that night and slept deeply. The next day, the Hedgehurst mounted the king on his cockerel and led him away into the forest. They entered the marsh, which made the king feel terribly frightened, yet the Hedgehurst seemed to have no trouble finding his way forward. He sniffed and snuffled as he waded through the water, seeming to find his way by smell. The king felt very grateful to be sitting safe and dry upon the cockerel's back.

After only a single day of travel, the ground grew firmer beneath them. They emerged from the swamp, the forest thinned out and the king realised they were at the borders of his own kingdom. A little further on, he made out the distant turrets of his castle in the clear blue sky.

'I have upheld my end of the bargain,' said the Hedgehurst.

'And I shall uphold mine,' said the king.

'Then I shall return in a year for what you have promised me.'

The king climbed down from the cockerel's back. The Hedgehurst took his place and rode away into the forest.

'What a strange fellow,' said the king to himself, watching the Hedgehurst go. Then he turned and continued on his way. His kingdom was not especially large and at dusk he reached his castle.

His faithful old hound sat outside the gates.

So did his daughter.

She saw him at the same time as he saw her. Letting out a whoop of excitement, she leapt to her feet and bounded towards him.

The king backed away, stammering at her to halt, but she was already upon him and laughing as she threw her arms around him and kissed him. 'Father! Thank the gods, we've all been so worried! Where have you been? Whose clothes are these? And why are you crying?'

He was crying, of course, because he would have to give his daughter to the Hedgehurst.

'I'm just so happy to see you,' said the king, wiping his tears away as his old hound ambled towards him on tired legs. 'Let's get inside.'

THE KING ATE with his wife and daughter that evening. As they ate he told them about his journey through the marsh and his meeting with the Hedgehurst. After dinner had been cleared away, he excused the servants.

'Nobody will believe this, Father,' said the princess as the servants closed the doors behind them. 'A real hedgehurst! I always thought they were only a story.'

The king gave her a weak smile. 'So did I. But they are real, or at least, this one is. He is a hedgehog in some ways, but he is a man in many ways too. He lives in a house, he has animals he takes care of, and he... he is in want of a wife.'

The princess laughed as the queen gave her husband a sharp look.

'A wife! Are there hedgehurst women then too?' asked the princess.

'Well. The thing is...' the king sighed. 'I made a bargain with the Hedgehurst in order to get back here.'

'What are you saying?' said the queen, her tone implying that she knew exactly what he was saying.

'I... I promised the Hedgehurst I would give to him the first member of my family to kiss me when I got home. I thought that would be my hound, but it was our daughter.'

The queen and princess gasped. 'I'm sorry,' said the king. 'The Hedgehurst shall visit us in one year's time, daughter, and I have promised that you shall be his wife. He's a decent man, if a little odd. And he's a king, or so he says. A lonely one at that. I believe he will treat you well.'

'You are joking, Father.'

'No.'

The conversation grew more heated after that. The queen and the princess railed at the king, calling him all manner of names, telling him to refuse the Hedgehurst or even to go to war with him. But he would not be swayed.

'I gave him my word. What kind of king would I be if I broke it?'

Neither his wife nor his daughter spoke to him for days afterwards. But they both understood what he'd done.

Life went on. Winter came and went. All too soon, the day of the Hedgehurst's arrival was imminent.

The king found his daughter in the castle gardens one morning.

'The Hedgehurst should be arriving soon. Are you still happy to proceed?' he asked her.

She looked up at him with red-rimmed eyes. 'I am not at all happy to proceed. But I will do as I must, Father.'

He kissed her forehead and went away to begin the wedding preparations.

THE CASTLE EXPLODED WITH ACTIVITY. Rooms were readied, cartloads of food and ale were ordered, hunters set off for the forests while messengers rode out in every direction with invitations.

Amidst it all, the princess wept.

Finally a captain of the guard declared that a strange procession had been sighted on the road.

'Is it him? Has he come?' said the king.

'I think it must be him,' said the captain. 'Only... well, he's got an army with him. But it's an army of sheep and hens and geese, all marching along in perfect ranks. Better than our men could ever manage, forgive me for saying. He's a strange-looking man, I might add, and he's riding... he's riding a giant cockerel, sire.'

The king nodded. He had not shared news of the Hedgehurst's singular appearance outside of the family.

'Show him in when he gets here, and see that his animals are quartered.'

The captain saluted and ran off to see his orders fulfilled. Not long afterwards, the Hedgehurst rode into the castle court-yard where the king and queen awaited him.

'Your Majesty,' said the king. 'I trust your journey was not too wearying?'

'I am not easily wearied,' said the Hedgehurst.

'About our agreement—' began the king.

'It was your daughter who greeted you, not your hound as you expected,' said the Hedgehurst. 'I know. I am glad to see that wedding preparations are afoot. When shall the ceremony take place?'

'Tomorrow.'

'Very well. My rooms?'

The king nodded to a butler who led the Hedgehurst away to his lodgings.

'He's... he's not so bad, is he?' said the king to the queen.

'He's worse.'

THE PRINCESS STEPPED AWAY from her window.

She had watched the Hedgehurst arrive on his cockerel. Though she hadn't heard his words, she had noted the Hedgehursts's stiff manner, his unsmiling face. How could she go through with this? How could she marry such a creature?

The princess was no swooning girl who expected to ride into the sunset with a handsome prince. Her mother had schooled her to be realistic about her marriage prospects. She would marry for the good of the family and the good of the kingdom, not for love. If love arose, it would be a happy accident, or might perhaps be cultivated over time. But she would be a fool to expect it. All she had ever hoped for was to marry someone good and kind, like her father.

No. That was not true. She did dream of knowing love. But everyone dreamed.

She had always known she could trust her father. He would never have married her to a cruel man, or a drunkard, or some old lecher who might collapse dead on her at night. But now he had married her off to a hedgehog. A proud, cold-hearted hedgehog.

'It could not have been any other way,' she said to herself. 'The Hedgehurst knew what would happen somehow. It's not Father's fault.'

Yet anger still seethed in her heart and tears still rolled down her cheeks.

THE CEREMONY TOOK place the following morning.

The princess awaited the Hedgehurst in the family temple.

It was only half-full; word had got out that the princess was marrying a hedgehurst and some guests had apparently chosen to stay away. Those in attendance kept glancing at the door and whispering to one another until finally he arrived. He walked in with his head held high, wearing a loose-fitting cloak of rich blue velvet embroidered with the image of a cockerel's head.

The priest spoke the words that made them man and wife. All the while, the Hedgehurst did not once glance at his bride.

After the ceremony there was a feast that lasted all afternoon and into the evening, followed by dancing that went on late into the night. During the feast the Hedgehurst sat stiffly, accepting the congratulations and good wishes he was offered but saying little otherwise. The princess sat at his side and pretended to enjoy herself. She hoped that her husband would overcome his shyness and speak to her at some point, but she waited in vain.

'Do you prefer human food,' she said to him eventually as he ate the carrot and parsnip soup, 'or hedgehog food?'

'I enjoy both.'

The princess nodded. 'I see. And... have you had your cockerel long?'

'I do not "have" him. He is my friend.'

'Oh. Sorry.'

The Hedgehurst put down his spoon. 'Excuse me,' he said. He stood up and left the table.

The princess went on eating her soup, waiting for her husband to return, until eventually she got up and went outside. She walked through the castle and the gardens until she spotted him in a shadowy corner. He was sitting beneath a tree, curled up, staring despondently at a nearby wall.

He turned, saw her watching him and looked away.

The princess returned to the feast and busied herself with drinking wine. When her husband returned from the garden she said, 'I will go to bed now.'

'So shall I,' he answered.

The musicians were taking a break at that point. A few half-hearted cheers and whistles followed the departing couple, but quickly died out. They left the hall together in silence.

The couple climbed the stairs to the marital chamber, opened the door and went inside.

The princess looked at her husband. They had barely spoken a word besides the ones that bound their lives together. He met her gaze but did not speak nor smile. She could not read those tiny, narrow eyes of his, but she knew one thing for certain. Whatever was in his mind and heart, it was not love.

The princess turned away, undressed and climbed into bed.

She listened as he undressed.

He did not enter the bed.

Darkness fell; he had extinguished the lamps. Only the faint light of the dwindling fire lit the walls.

She heard a soft snoring.

The princess whipped round to see the Hedgehurst curled up in a ball in front of the fire.

Anger seized her. Was he trying to insult her? To tell her that even a hedgehurst would not desire her? Or was he so grand and mighty that she was beneath him?

Yet as she watched him, her anger burned away. There was

something peaceful about the sight of him curled up asleep in front of the fire. All of his pomposity seemed to have departed. All the same, this was not how she had imagined her wedding night in the hidden chambers of her heart.

The princess cried herself to sleep.

In the depths of the night, a strange thing happened.

The princess awoke to a shuffling sound. She opened her eyes and saw the Hedgehurst's shadow upon the wall. Her husband had arisen and was now undressing.

After he had undressed, he removed his skin.

She heard wet, sticky sounds as it came loose, revealing the profile of a man. When he had finished removing his skin, the Hedgehurst rolled it up and put it down before the fire. He took from the cupboard a set of clothes, donned them and quietly left the chamber.

The princess lay absolutely still, too scared to move.

Some time later, the Hedgehurst returned. Again she watched shadows dance on the wall as he undressed, covered himself with his own skin, donned his hedgehurst clothes again and curled up once more by the fire.

THE WEDDING FEAST continued the next day. The princess did her duty, mingling with the guests and even joining in the dancing when invited. Her husband made brief appearances but, according to her maid's reports, spent most of his time in the gardens. When he did appear at the feast, his discomfort was clear, and the few guests who attempted to talk to him soon gave up. He would sit and inspect the ceiling or the contents of his cup.

That night, they retired to the bedchamber as before. Again, the Hedgehurst slept before the fire.

The princess lay awake, waiting to see what would happen. Sure enough, her husband rose in the depths of the night and did as he had done on the previous night.

The following morning, she pulled her mother aside.

'We need to speak privately.'

The two of them slipped away from the feast and into an empty chamber.

The queen faced her daughter. The princess could see the guilt in her mother's eyes; she felt responsible for what had happened.

'Is he treating you well?' said the queen. 'Has he harmed you?'

'Yes. No. What I want to say is... something strange is happening.'

She told her mother what she had seen the previous two nights.

'It is too much. I thought I could bear this but... what is he doing? Could he be about some evil magic? And if he wanted to marry me but not to... what does he intend for me?'

The queen's eyes narrowed. 'I don't know. But it is past time we found out.'

THEY DONNED cloaks and slipped out of the castle. Instead of taking the road into the village, the queen led her daughter off the road and into the woods. There, they went by no discernible path until they came to a tiny hut which lay at the edge of a bubbling stream in a rocky glen. Hens roamed outside and a short, bent-over old woman stood watching them from the doorway.

The queen greeted the woman, using words the princess could not understand. They seemed to know one another. The woman gestured for them to enter.

Inside, they sat down on deerskins by the fire. Drying herbs hung from the rafters above them.

'Who are you?' asked the princess.

'This woman is a hen wife,' said the queen. 'She has knowledge of things beyond the ordinary. She may be able to help us in our predicament.'

'What predicament is that?' asked the hen wife.

At a nod from her mother, the princess told the whole story.

'So you have married a hedgehurst,' said the woman when she had finished.

'You know of such creatures?' asked the princess.

'I have heard of them, lass.'

'Then you know how to...'

A smile hovered at the edge of the old woman's mouth.

'How to what? Do you want him dead, is that it? Be wary, lass. Hedgehursts see much.'

'No! No... I want...' she searched the flames of the fire. What did she want from him? She could ask the hen wife to help get rid of him. Make him go far away and forget about her. That would be the most sensible thing to ask. Yet she knew in her heart that she wanted something else.

'I want to know who he really is.'

The hen wife gave her a wide smile. 'Then I can certainly help you. There's something you must do. If you've a good heart, this will be painful, but if it's a strong heart, you will see it done.'

THE QUEEN and her daughter returned to the wedding. The princess endured the celebrations as her husband roamed the garden.

Night came. She retired to bed as her husband curled up by the fire.

She waited.

The night hours passed.

Her husband rose, peeled off his skin, dressed and left the chamber.

It was time.

The princess climbed out of bed and approached the fire. There was the Hedgehurst's skin, neatly rolled up.

She knelt down and picked it up. Her hands were trembling. Could she do this?

She remembered the hen wife's words.

The fairy may have given him a blessing or may have given a curse. The truth of that is in your hands now.

She threw the skin on the fire.

The sickly-sweet smell of burning hair filled her lungs.

Tears sprang to her eyes and her chest heaved; somehow she felt as if she were committing some terrible act of destruction. She threw open the window to release some of the terrible smell, then stood by the window watching the Hedgehurst's skin burn. The spiky skin that had protected him ever since he was a child.

What had she done? How could this be right?

Be strong, she told herself. She had to trust the hen wife. This wasn't over.

She went to her bedside. A pail of spring water stood there. She picked it up and went to stand by the door.

Footsteps on the stair.

They grew closer. Closer. What did he look like without his skin? Was he angry, did he know what she had done? Would he become monstrous? Would he attack her, tear her own skin from her flesh?

Steady, she told herself. *It's almost done...*

The door opened.

The princess closed her eyes and threw the water over her husband.

He screamed. She heard two distinct thumps as the pail and the Hedgehurst hit the floor.

Opening her eyes, she saw clouds of steam rising from the shape on the floor. A man writhed and twisted before her, gasping and sobbing, his skin red and cracked as if he had been thrown into a fire.

But it was changing. Softening. Smoothing. Healing.

'You... should not... you should not have done this,' moaned the Hedgehurst. 'It was my skin. I need my skin...'

'No!' said the princess. She dropped to her knees and reached out towards her husband, but he pulled away from her touch as if it burned her. 'You do not need... I mean, perhaps, sometimes, we all might want... but I'm your wife. You don't need it with me. Please, look at me.'

His sobbing paused. He uncurled a little, opened his eyes and look at her.

It shamed the princess to see the terror in his eyes. How far this man was from the haughty creature she'd wed! She reached out again to take his hand; he flinched as if expecting her to strike him.

'Take my hand,' she said.

After a moment, he took it.

Their eyes locked. As they gazed at one another, she saw the man he was beneath his skin. Fearful, lonely, but full of love for those whom he trusted. She saw the deep well of strength he'd used to survive and to build his own kingdom. And though she was neither naked nor skinless, he could see in her eyes the truth of her. Her shame that she had destroyed that which protected him. The fear she had harboured, that he might mistreat her. And her hope, her desperate hope, that he would forgive what she'd done, and open his heart to her, and love her.

He knew then that he wanted her love. He wanted it more than anything. More than his spiky skin.

'Maybe I don't need my hedgehog skin,' he said. 'Maybe you can be a skin for me sometimes, and I for you.'

The princess smiled. A tear rolled down her face. 'I'd like that,' she said.

They got to their feet. Some of the king's old clothes were in the cupboard; she fetched them and helped him to don them.

'I'm sorry I never looked at you. Or talked to you, or danced with you,' said the Hedgehurst.

'So make it up to me. Dance with me now.'

They went downstairs and into the garden together. The sky was clear, the moon was bright, and beneath the moon the Hedgehurst danced with the princess. He was hesitant at first, as if unsure of how to be in the world without his old, spiky skin. But he found his ease in time, and he even began to laugh as they spun and twirled through the gardens.

They were still dancing the next morning. Most of the guests had been planning to make their excuses and leave that day, but seeing the bride and groom dance around the gardens together, they watched in wonder, and remembered when they had first known love, and decided to stay on.

The wedding lasted another week. The Hedgehurst was soon talking and dancing with everyone, and by the end of it all, the princess was convinced that there was no better man in the world for her.

The princess went to live with the Hedgehurst in his kingdom, where she reigned as Queen. They lived a long and happy life together, and they might just be living there still.[*]

---

[*] This story comes from Duncan Williamson's *Fireside Tales of the Traveller Children*. It bears some similarity to the tale of Hans the Hedgehog which was recorded by the Grimm brothers, which may explain why the story has the feel of a European fairy tale.

You may also be reminded of an episode of the Netflix series, *The Witcher*, which features a hedgehog man named Duny. It seems likely that Hans the Hedgehog inspired this character, who originally appeared in the *Witcher* books. I got quite a shock when I happened to watch that episode while working on a first draft of this story.

MACLEOD'S TABLES

Alasdair Crotach Macleod was a fierce, fighting man. Chief of the Macleod Clan of Skye, he had earned his nickname of 'Crotach', meaning 'humpbacked', during a battle with the Macleods' old enemies, the Macdonalds. A force of Macdonalds, led by Evan MacKail, had once landed on Aird Bay on Skye. Alasdair led a force to meet them and during the fighting, Evan MacKail brought Alasdair down with his great battle-axe.

Alasdair grabbed hold of Evan MacKail as he fell, pulling him to the ground. Despite the terrible wound Alasdair had suffered, he managed to get on top of his opponent, draw his dirk knife and cut his throat. He afterwards cut off Evan MacKail's head and carried it away as a trophy. He continued to suffer from the axe wound, and never walked fully upright again, but men did not fear him any less.

In 1536, Alasdair received a letter from King James V of Scotland. It contained an invitation for Alasdair to dine at the king's table in Edinburgh, in the company of chiefs and noblemen from both the Highlands and the Lowlands.

Alasdair considered his response. The winds of change had blown hard in recent years. The time in which highland clan chiefs exerted total control over their lands and people, having little to do with the faraway kings who supposedly ruled them, was gone. King James and his father before him had dedicated much of their rule to bringing the clan chiefs under control. Alasdair was one of the most powerful chiefs, a symbol of the old order. If he ignored the invitation, there would be consequences.

Alasdair accepted the king's invitation. He left his castle at Dunvegan and travelled over land and sea until he reached the city of Edinburgh and passed through the gates of Holyrood Palace.

The humpbacked clan chief was shown to his rooms. He washed and rested. Come the evening, he donned kilt, sword and dirk knife, and descended the stairs to the feasting hall.

Glittering, golden candelabras cast dancing light across a magnificent table resplendent with rich food. Above the hall rose a breathtaking, intricately carved ceiling, its higher reaches lost to sight. Around the table sat the great men of Scotland, with red-haired King James at their head.

Servants guided Alasdair to his seat. The feast soon began and he dutifully made conversation with his neighbours as he ate and drank. All the while, he scanned the table just as a general assesses a battlefield. Beneath the facade of friendship, the divisions were clear to see. The lowland nobles thought themselves above the uncouth, primitive highlanders, while the highlanders scorned the lowlanders as pampered princelings.

And as for the king himself?

Like Alasdair, he kept watch with shrewd yet subtle eyes. He was not here to enjoy himself; he cared only to observe and influence the balance of power.

Late in the evening, King James addressed Alasdair Macleod.

'Lord Macleod,' he said, raising his voice so that it carried across the table.

'Your Majesty,' said Alasdair as the hall fell quiet.

'I am so grateful that you could attend my feast. It must have been a long journey for you, over the rough sea and through the bleak lands of the west, all the way to this great city.

'And now that I see you here at my table, I cannot help but wonder. How does it feel for you to sit here, surrounded by elegance and sumptuousness, when you are accustomed to primitiveness? To barbarity?'

The lowland lords laughed as the highlanders bristled.

'Tell me,' continued the king, gesturing towards a golden candelabra. 'Indulge my curiosity, Macleod. Did you ever in your life see candlesticks worth as much as these? And did you ever dine at a table so large, or beneath a ceiling so magnificent?'

All eyes turned to Alasdair Macleod.

He took his time answering.

'It is a fine feast you have laid on, Your Majesty,' he said eventually. 'There can be no doubt about that. Those are fine candlesticks, this is a fine table, and that is a magnificent ceiling above us. But I will answer you honestly, for you deserve nothing less.

'And my answer is that back home on the Winged Isle, I dine at a table far greater than this. Surrounded by candlesticks worth more than these, and beneath a ceiling infinitely more magnificent.'

Uproar ensued. The cheek of the man! Many lowland lords expected the king to order Alasdair Macleod's execution there and then. But King James had something else in mind.

'Well, well,' said the king. 'That is quite a claim, Macleod. If such a hall exists then I will have no rest until I see it.'

'Then you had better do just that,' said Alasdair. 'Honour me by visiting Skye, a year to this day, along with any other man here who wishes to dine at my table.'

'I shall,' said King James.

So it was agreed. Alasdair left Edinburgh for Skye a few days later. The year rolled by and the nobles of Scotland awaited the day when Alasdair Macleod must make good on his boast, or pay the price.

FINALLY IT WAS TIME. King James and his retinue left Edinburgh and made their way west. They crossed the sea at Mallaig, landed on Skye and were met by Macleod's men who awaited them with mounts. They rode north then west around the Cuillin Mountains, passing a night at Broadford then another at Sligachan before arriving at Castle Dunvegan in the late afternoon.

Alasdair Macleod stood before his doors, ready to welcome the king.

'Do not keep me waiting a moment longer, Chief Macleod,' said King James as his host approached him. 'Guide me straight to this feasting hall of yours!'

'Tonight, Your Majesty,' said the stooped clan chief with a bow. 'Rest now. You shall see my hall tonight.'

Evening arrived. King James and the other guests were ushered from their rooms and out of the castle by Alasdair's men. The chief himself was nowhere to be seen.

The horses they had ridden across the island were waiting for them. Once mounted, they retraced their route for a short while before taking a smaller road that led southwest. After an hour or two of riding, in the day's dying light, they turned off the road and took a path that led them up the summit of the hill known in Gaelic as *Healaval Beg*.

They reached the summit and saw that it was entirely flat. The hill had a sister on the far side of the road; her summit was equally flat.

Alasdair Macleod was waiting for them.

The king and the other guests dismounted. Alasdair led them to the centre of the summit where a supper of bread, cheese, meat and wine had been laid out on thick woollen rugs. As each of the party took a seat, a Macleod man came to stand behind him, bearing a burning torch.

Once the guests were all seated and surrounded by a great ring of torchbearers, Alasdair Macleod addressed them.

'Your Majesty. My esteemed guests. You will recall that one year ago, at the king's table in Holyrood House, I told our king that in Skye I dined at a table far wider than his.' He extended his arms. 'This hilltop is my table.

'And you will recall my claim that I dined surrounded by candlesticks worth more than the king's own. Those men standing guard behind you are my candlesticks. For in my mind, the loyalty of brave men is worth much more than gold.'

Finally, he gestured upwards towards the starlit sky. 'And lastly, you will recall my claim that I dined beneath a ceiling infinitely more magnificent than that of Holyrood. And so I ask you, Your Majesty. Is there any ceiling in the world more magnificent than this one?'

Everyone looked to King James.

The king laughed and shook his head.

'None,' he said. 'There is none in all creation.'

So it was that Alasdair Macleod made good on his boast. Ever since then, the two flat, tabletop mountains in the west of Skye have been known as Macleod's Tables.*

---

* This is a well-known legend, and one of two that explains the shape of *Healabhal Bheag* and *Healabhal Mor*. The other has it that Columba was refused hospitality by the local chief when doing missionary work on Skye, causing a storm to darken the sky and level the mountains, one of which would serve as his bed and the other his table.

Alasdair Macleod is thought of as one of the greatest chiefs of the Macleod Clan. He was indeed a fierce warlord, and was responsible for the infamous massacre on Eigg among others. He is also said to have been a great lover of poetry and music, and to have founded the famous piping college of Skye. He spent his final years living as a monk on the Isle of Harris.

FENIA & MENIA

Long ago in Denmark, there lived a king called Frodi. He ruled over Denmark from a castle on the coast, and his name is still known to every Dane today. Let me tell you why.

Frodi was a good king but not a great one. There was nothing extraordinary about him or his achievements. But there was something extraordinary lurking in the cellars of his castle. Down in those dank depths was a chamber which housed an enormous set of millstones. No one knew how they had got there, how long they had been there or how they could possibly be of use, for they were far too big for anyone to turn. This puzzle had pecked at Frodi's mind ever since he became king, and he often descended the cellar stairs late at night to sit and ponder the millstones.

FRODI HAD an alliance with the King of Sweden. As part of this alliance, the two kings would make time to visit one another regularly, feasting and hunting and discussing the many challenges they faced. Each found the other to be a source of sound advice, someone who knew the weight of the crown and dealt with it well. So they both looked forward to these visits.

One spring day, a messenger arrived at Frodi's castle, bearing an invitation to visit Sweden once more. Frodi accepted, and later that month he set sail. He arrived at the King of Sweden's castle and his friend met him at the gates. They embraced, entered the courtyard and were making their way towards the keep when Frodi stopped.

Stared.

Over in a far corner of the courtyard, heaving huge rocks from one place to another, were two giants.

'So of course I said to him...'

The King of Sweden noticed that Frodi had fallen behind. 'Ah, I see you've spotted my new labourers. Fenia and Menia, their names are. Giants, yes, both females. I was gifted them by one of my northern nobles. Excellent workers.'

'I'm sure they are,' said Frodi, stroking his chin thoughtfully.

That night, over supper, Frodi turned the conversation towards Fenia and Menia.

'I've been thinking about those giants of yours,' he said. 'They certainly seem strong. Are they obedient?'

'Absolutely,' said the King of Sweden. 'I can't speak for the rest of their kind, but those two follow orders to the letter. They would cut their own throats if you asked it of them. Beat them, work them half to death; they won't complain. But if I value something, be it a gemstone or a giant, I look after it.'

'Wise words,' said Frodi. He swished the ale around in his cup. 'I don't suppose you'd be interested in selling them?'

THE KING of Sweden was reluctant to consider selling his slaves. But Frodi pressed him over the days that followed, raising and raising his bid until his friend relented. When Frodi left for Denmark, he sailed with Fenia and Menia sitting on the deck of his ship. The wind and rain pummelled them yet they seemed indifferent to their fate.

Frodi arrived at his castle. All activity ceased as hunters and grooms, farriers and fighters gaped at the giants. Frodi led Fenia and Menia through the courtyard, into the castle and into the cellars. He led them down underground stairways and cold, damp corridors, all of which had thankfully been built with high ceilings, until he reached the lowermost chamber.

There sat the millstones.

'I bought you and I brought you here with one purpose,' said Frodi. 'Never have I known a man or woman who can turn these stones. I thought it could not be done. But then why were they created, I asked myself? Why do they lurk here in the darkest corner of my keep? These questions have occupied me for too long. Now, perhaps, they shall be answered. Please, if you can, turn the stones.'

Fenia and Menia gave each other a blank and bored stare.

Then they walked over to the stones, bent over and put their hands to them.

They pushed against the stones. They squared their shoulders; their biceps bulged.

Slowly the stones began to turn.

Frodi whooped with joy as Fenia and Menia turned the grinding and groaning stones round and round. At last the mystery was solved; the stones could be turned!

'This is marvellous!' he said. 'Marvellous! I couldn't be happier if the stones ground out gold.'

That very moment, a stream of golden coins poured out of the hole at the centre of the upper stone.

'What? Stop!'

Fenia and Menia fell still.

Frodi climbed over the stones and picked up a gold piece to examine. Being a king, he knew the look and feel of gold well. This was the real thing. He stuffed his pockets, climbed down and then gave Fenia and Menia a new command.

'Start turning the stones again,' he said. 'Only this time, I would like you to grind out some... erm... cheese.'

Fenia and Menia set shoulder to stone. The stones turned and lumps of blue cheese poured from their centre.

'And now silver...

...rubies...

..fine cloth...

...honeyed ham...'

So it went on. Frodi found that his theory was correct: whatever he wished for, the stones could produce. He had fun producing one thing or another for a little while, but he soon returned to grinding out gold.

And more gold.

And more gold.

He filled his cellars. He filled his storerooms, his kitchens and his guest rooms with gold; soon there was no space left in the castle for it all. So Frodi simply gave it away.

He gave sacks of gold to every worker in the castle. Then he gave a sack of gold to every person in the nearest village. Word soon spread that everyone in Denmark was welcome to visit Frodi and collect as much of the yellow metal as they could carry. Many did just that, and Denmark became fabulously wealthy. Nobody stole from anybody else, because everybody had their own gold.

Meanwhile, in Frodi's cellar, Fenia and Menia laboured day and night, without rest.

THE DAYS of endless gold went on until Frodi began to feel strangely dissatisfied.

'Something needs to change,' he said to his queen one day as they walked the castle walls.

'Why?' said the queen. 'We are the wealthiest kingdom in the world. How could things be any better?'

'It's the gold,' said Frodi. 'It made me happy at first. Yet now it is as common as iron. Far more common, in fact. Does it still give you joy?'

'Yes.'

'Well, not me. And not the people of Denmark. They were overjoyed when I first gave them gold, but now, when they drop a piece, they leave it lying there in the mud. Gold was once special, and now it is just...' he sighed. 'I could be doing more for the kingdom. More to make my people happy. I don't just want to make them wealthy. I want them to be fulfilled. Contented. But what could I summon from the stones to make people happy?'

'Well... perhaps... happiness?'

Frodi laughed, but then his laughter trailed away. 'Excuse me,' he said.

He left his wife and rushed into the castle. He vaulted the steps three at a time, all the way down to Fenia and Menia's cellar.

'Stop! I have a new task for you,' he panted.

Fenia and Menia ceased turning the stones and fixed their empty gazes upon Frodi.

'I have no more need of gold. Instead, I want you to grind out happiness.'

The two giants looked at one another, then set to work again.

Nothing appeared to come from the stones. Was it working? Frodi wasn't sure. Yet he found himself thinking that it didn't matter if it worked or not. Everything would be fine either way. Whatever happened, life was precious and wonderful.

He left the chamber, hands in his pockets and whistling a merry tune.

THERE FOLLOWED a time now known as Frodi's Peace. It is remembered in Denmark as the happiest time in their history. Nobody argued or made war; travellers and strangers were treated like the closest of kin. Old rivalries were put to rest while singing, dancing and celebration reigned.

Frodi watched over it all, his heart content.

One day, he descended to the lowermost cellar to check on the stones. They looked unchanged, as did Fenia and Menia.

'Things are well with these stones, and well with my kingdom,' said Frodi. 'How about you two? Is there anything you need, anything you want?'

'Yes, ' said Fenia. 'There is. We've been turning these stones for years now, summer and winter, night and day. We wouldn't mind a break.'

'Oh! Well, yes, that certainly seems reasonable. Though I can't have the stones sitting idle for too long. So... I know. You can rest for as long as it takes to sing a song. How about that? Yes, singing a merry little song will galvanise you, I'm sure.'

The giants shared another look.

'Alright then,' said Menia. 'Off you go, and we'll sing a merry little song.'

'Excellent.' Frodi smiled at them and left.

Once Frodi was gone, Fenia and Menia did indeed sing a song. But it was neither little nor merry.

They sang what is now called the Lay of Grotti.

The Lay of Grotti, or Grottisongr, is a dark and terrible invocation of warfare and pestilence, starvation and misery. It was composed and first sung by Fenia and Menia in that very place, at that very moment. And as they sang it, they turned the stones.

They sang of disease.

Disease spread across Denmark.

They sang of hatred.

Hatred spread across Denmark.

They sang of a pirate army, a fleet of savage corsairs, and that fleet came into being off Denmark's coast. It was led by a pirate king named Mysing, and Mysing was thirsty for blood.

Frodi's Peace ended that night. A dark chapter in Danish history began. Wedding parties turned into massacres; mothers strangled their infant children. Within days every field and house was burning, every road haunted by bands of killers.

In the midst of the chaos, Mysing's pirates came ashore. They found Denmark weak and ripe for ravaging. They raped and burned, looted and slaughtered their way up the coast until they reached Frodi's castle.

Frodi had already seen off several attacks, but only barely. His castle quickly fell to the pirate horde. Mysing's battering ram breached the gates and soon savage pirates were loose in the castle. They opened the throats of everyone they met, including Frodi.

When there was no more killing to be done, Mysing held a celebratory feast in Frodi's hall. His men drank wine from the skulls of their victims, waited on by shackled captives whom they would later sell as slaves.

Late in the night, one of Mysing's captains came to speak with him.

'My king, we've found something you'll want to see.'

The captain led Mysing to Fenia and Menia's chamber.

'Giants! What are you two doing down here?' he asked.

Fenia told him their story.

'You can stop work for now,' he said once she had spoken. 'Bring those stones to my ship at sunrise. You're my slaves now, and you're going to make me rich.'

THE SUN ROSE over the smoking ruins of Frodi's castle. From it walked the pirates, their slaves trudging behind them, everyone's hands full of plunder. The pirates returned to their ships and prepared to set sail.

Mysing found Fenia and Menia awaiting him on the deck of his ship. They had set the stones down amidship, and thankfully it bore their weight. Soon the fleet was back at sea with orders to sail west.

The pirate king didn't make use of the stones straightaway. This was an opportunity he wanted to savour, and besides, killing and feasting was a tiring business. So he took himself off to his cabin for a rest and didn't emerge until the following morning.

Standing on deck that morning, he saw that they had made good speed and reached the Pentland Firth. Scotland was visible to the south and Orkney to the north. His fleet would round the coast of Scotland, turn for Ireland and sell their slaves and plunder at Dublin's markets. But before that, it was time to play with his new toy.

He went to where Fenia and Menia sat by the stones.

'My good women,' he said. 'It's time you earned your keep.'

Everyone stopped what they were doing and gathered round to watch.

'What do you want us to grind out?' said Menia.

'Gold!' cried the pirates. 'Gold! Gold! Gold!'

'My friends!' cried Mysing, addressing his men. 'You are the most bestial and bloodthirsty crew on the high seas. I love you for it. That said, you do lack imagination. Gold, you say? Yes, of course, we could always have more gold. But there are things worth more than gold.'

'Like what?'

Mysing grinned. 'Salt.'

The pirates looked confused.

'You do not listen to merchants, do you, friends? Of course not; you are only concerned with robbing them. Me, I like to talk to a man before I murder him.

'I happen to know that in this day and age, salt is worth more than gold. We can sell salt, and with it we can buy more ships, more swords, more slaves. We will become the greatest fleet that ever sailed, and the world's mightiest emperors will dread the day they see our sails.

'So I ask you. Do you want gold, or do you want salt?'

'Salt!' roared the pirates. 'Salt! Salt! Salt!'

The king grinned at Fenia and Menia. 'You heard them.'

The two giants set to work again.

The roars of the pirates became deafening as the first grains of salt fell.

'More! More!'

Fenia and Menia circled around and around the stones.

Salt streamed forth, covering the deck.

King Mysing ordered his men to fill sacks with the precious salt and take them below deck for storage. They couldn't keep up, though, for salt was pouring and pouring from the stones as Fenia and Menia laboured. Soon the entire deck was covered. Some of the pirates climbed atop the heaped salt and threw handfuls in the air, giddy with their greed.

'More! More!'

A few of the more level-minded pirates suggested they stop. They had noticed that the ship was sitting lower in the water. But nobody would listen.

'More! More!'

At this point King Mysing saw what was happening. He opened his mouth to order Fenia and Menia to cease turning the millstones. But it was too late.

Mysing's ship sank into the ocean.

It sank down, down, all the way to the seabed, where the ship disintegrated. Some of the pirates had managed to swim to nearby ships, where their companions hauled them out of the water. But most of them were pulled under and drowned.

Fenia and Menia did not drown. Air and water mattered little to them. They had been ordered to turn the stones, so they turned the stones down there on the seabed. They are still down there, grinding out salt day and night, in the darkest depths of the Pentland Firth. If you wish to see the spot where this happened, take a ship from Orkney or Sutherland and seek out the Swelkie Whirlpool. But don't get too close, of course.

Fenia and Menia have been grinding out salt on the seabed for hundreds of years. And that is why the sea is salty. *

---

* The song known as *Gróttasǫngr* is included in some versions of the Poetic Edda, one of the key texts of Nordic myth. The story recounted here is a more light-hearted folkloric descendant of that song. In *Gróttasǫngr*, Fenja and Menja are fierce fighters who have been enslaved and are chained to the millstones they turn, while Frodi is a descendant of Odin.

You can read a very different but related story called *Why the Sea is Salty* in *Norwegian Folk Tales* by Peter Christen Asbjornsen and Jorgen Moe.

THE SMITH & THE FAIRIES

On the island of Islay there once lived a blacksmith named Alasdair MacEachern. His forge lay among the fields of Caonis Gall, close to the wild Atlantic Ocean, and his tale is well-known there to this day.

Alasdair's wife had died soon after childbirth, leaving Alasdair to raise their son alone. The boy's name was Neil. Ever since Neil was a baby, Alasdair had dreamed of the day his son would join him in the forge as a fully-fledged smith. They would sweat in the heat of the forge each day and drink ale together in the evenings, spending hours discussing the intricacies of their craft. So Alasdair started his boy young, having him fetch and carry things when he was small and then teaching him to pump the bellows once he grew older.

Neil loved helping his father. The forge was a kind of temple to him, a place of shapeshifting magic where things could become other things according to his father's will. He saw that other men respected his father, who knew things they would never know and whose arms were thicker than their chests.

By the time he was thirteen, Neil was wielding the hammer himself. When he was fourteen, Alasdair entrusted Neil with his first commission, and insisted that Neil keep the coins he earned. He didn't say so, but handing that money over was the happiest moment of Alasdair's life since his wedding day.

'You'll be a better smith than me, son,' said Alasdair. 'Far better. You only need a few years to build your strength, and there'll be no stopping you.'

That was how things were for Alasdair and Neil, until the day when their fortunes turned.

ALASDAIR WOKE up in the hour before dawn. He dressed and went through to the front room of the house, expecting to find Neil building up the fire or stirring a pot of porridge. Neil was always up before him. Today, though, the house was silent and his son was nowhere to be seen.

'He must be tired,' said Alasdair to himself. 'Maybe I work him too hard. The boy needs rest as well as labour if he's to grow strong.' So Alasdair awoke the sleeping fire and made the porridge himself.

'That's the porridge ready, son,' called Alasdair eventually. It was alright to lie in a little but he couldn't let the boy sleep all day.

'Come on now, it's getting cold,' he added.

There was no response.

Alasdair put down his bowl of porridge, went to Neil's bedroom door and let himself in.

Neil's room was as dark as a grave. It smelt terrible, but that wasn't unusual. Neil was in bed, facing away from his father.

'You don't want to lie in bed all day like an old man,' said Alasdair. 'Up you get, son.'

Silence.

'Are you sick, Neil?'

Now Alasdair was worried. He went to the window, opened the shutters to better see his son, and gasped.

Neil's once sleek, dark hair had turned a fetid yellow. His ruddy skin had overnight turned brown and wrinkled like old leather, and it hung loose from his cheekbones. Worst of all, his fine smith's muscles had wasted away to nothing.

'What... what's happened to you, son?' Alasdair shook Neil, frightened by how frail the boy felt. 'What's happened?' he asked again, louder this time.

Neil grunted. 'Nothing. Go away. I'm sleepy,' he said, his voice a dry rasp.

'Do you need a doctor—'

'No! Leave me alone.'

Alasdair wasn't going to drag Neil out of bed; he was scared that he would break him. He went through to the forge, hoping his son would eventually appear at his side, looking and acting as he always did. But Neil never appeared. Alasdair worked alone that day, falling behind on a commission.

Neil looked no better when Alasdair checked on him at lunchtime and again in the evening. The next morning, after a sleepless night, Alasdair visited his son again. The room smelt like a rotting corpse.

'This has gone on long enough,' said the smith. 'I'm getting a doctor in to see you today and that's the end of it.'

Neil had been lying inert. At these words, his head whipped round and he fixed his father with a look that could have melted iron.

'No. Doctor.'

'If... if that's what you wish,' said Alasdair, backing away, his voice trembling.

Alasdair worked alone again that day. He pounded the steel with such fury that the ringing of his hammer echoed across the island. He stopped only to put down his hammer, bend his shoulders and weep.

ALASDAIR'S FORTUNES turned again when Cormac MacEachern came to visit.

Cormac was a distant relative and an old friend. While most people on the island had never travelled further than Jura or perhaps Campbeltown, Cormac had wandered as far north as Orkney and as far south as Newcastle. He loved to stop in with strangers wherever he went, listening to their stories and telling his own, gathering knowledge of new things each day.

'How's that fine son of yours?' said Cormac as he accepted a mug of ale from Alasdair, who had been mending rope by the fire when Cormac knocked.

Alasdair drank deep from his own mug. It wasn't his first that day.

'He's not well, Cormac. He's not well at all.'

So Alasdair told Cormac everything that had happened. Cormac looked increasingly concerned as he listened.

When Alasdair had finished, he said, 'I have a suspicion as to what might be wrong with your Neil. But I'll need you to do something before I say any more.'

'What's that?'

'It will sound strange to your ears.'

'Just tell me.'

'Very well,' said Cormac. 'Listen carefully. This must be done right.'

THAT EVENING, Alasdair MacEachern entered his son's bedroom carrying a basket full of eggshells in one hand and a bucket of water in the other.

Shuddering at the smell, he set down his basket and bucket on either side of the fireplace, then kindled a fire. That done, he carefully placed each eggshell on the floor before the fire.

As he worked, Alasdair heard Neil stir. He felt his son's eyes on him.

Once all the eggshells were out of the basket, Alasdair bent down, picked up two of them, carried them over to the bucket and dipped them in the water, scooping up water as if they were tiny bowls. He then turned and carried the eggshells back to their places before the fire. As he did so, he stooped and grimaced, acting as if each speckled vessel were as heavy as an anvil.

Alasdair returned to the bucket with two more eggshells and then staggered back to the fireplace. He took great care to set them down in just the right place.

Over and over Alasdair did this until a laugh rang out through the room.

He turned to face Neil.

His leather-skinned son was sitting up in bed. Neil's eyes were gleaming in the firelight, his leering mouth revealing broken brown teeth as he cackled hysterically, slapping his knees.

'Eight hundred years,' he said, struggling to speak through his laughter. 'Eight hundred years I've lived, and eight thousand strange things I've seen, but I've never seen anyone do that before!'

CORMAC RETURNED THE NEXT DAY.

'I see from the look in your eyes that you did what I asked of you,' he said to Alasdair.

'Aye,' said the ashen-faced smith, who had passed another sleepless night.

'And I see that you got a fright when you did so.'

'Aye,' said Alasdair. 'Aye, you could say that.'

Cormac nodded. 'Well, then. Don't you look so worried.'

He gestured for Alasdair to sit down at the table and took a seat himself.

'Tell me what happened.'

Alasdair told his tale. Cormac nodded throughout.

'You'll understand now,' said Cormac when Alasdair had finished, 'that the creature through there is not your son. It's a fairy changeling. They swap their youngsters with ours sometimes, and on this occasion they've taken your Neil.'

'What have they done with him?' asked Alasdair.

'Likely they took him to their hall beneath the hill and put him to work. So all you need to do, Alasdair MacEachern, is get into the hall and get him out. And I'm going to tell you how.'

'That's all?'

'Well, no,' said Cormac with a grimace. 'There is something else you have to do first.'

ALASDAIR RETURNED to Neil's bedroom that evening, this time with a basket of logs.

Once more, he kindled and built up his son's fire. He went on adding wood until the fire was blazing and sweat poured from his brow.

Behind him, the changeling stirred.

'Too hot,' it moaned as if half-asleep. 'It's too hot in here.'

Alasdair went on feeding logs into the fire.

'I said it's too hot!' said the changeling, sounding more awake now.

Alasdair fed his final log into the fire.

He stood up and turned to face the changeling.

'Why are you looking at me like that, Father?'

Alasdair approached the bed.

'Father,' said the fairy, it's voice suddenly sounding like Neil's. 'You're scaring me.'

'I'm sorry,' said Alasdair. 'Whoever, whatever you are. I want my son back.'

Alasdair lunged forward and grabbed the creature. He lifted it out of the bed. As it thrashed and tried to break free, he hauled it across the room to the fireplace.

'No! Please, Father, no! I'm your son! I'm your Neil!'

The changeling sounded just like Neil, but Alasdair wasn't fooled. With a mighty roar, he threw it into the fire.

The fairy hit the flames. As it did so, it became a cloud of glittering smoke, which whirled around the room before shooting up the chimney.

Alasdair stood, shaking, before the raging fire.

He had done what had to be done. On the next full moon night, he would get his son back.

A WEEK LATER, Alasdair MacEachern left his house by the light of the full moon.

It was a warm, clear evening. The sea was calm, the moon and stars shining. Alasdair closed his front door and went to his henhouse, stooping to enter. The birds were all asleep. He picked up his cockerel and stowed it under his cloak without awakening it.

Next, Alasdair left his house behind him and crossed the island, heading southeast until he spied, a little way off the road, the fairy hill. Everyone knew that the fairies of Islay lived there. Nobody would be foolish enough to approach it on a full moon night when the fairies were feasting. But that was the way Alasdair went.

Drawing closer, Alasdair heard faint sounds of music and revelry. He saw a doorway outlined in firelight on the hillside. Alasdair approached and saw that it was a door leading into the hill itself. The door was open wide enough for him to slip inside, and beyond was a tunnel leading to the fairy hall.

'I'm coming for you, son,' he whispered.

Alasdair drew his dirk knife from his belt and plunged it into the doorframe, just as Cormac had instructed him. He pulled his hood down over his face and entered the fairy hill.

The hollow hill was full to bursting. Alasdair did his best to keep his head down and avoid staring, but it was hard. Though the changeling child had been an ugly thing, most of the fairies here were beautiful. Their hair was long and shimmering; they wore exquisite clothing and danced with elegant abandon. The music was unlike anything Alasdair had ever heard: subtle and sensual yet wild and galloping. Surely he could allow himself one dance?

No, he told himself. Cormac had warned him of such temptations. *Neil. Find Neil.*

Alasdair skirted the room, passing tables where older fairy folk ate and argued and told tales. He avoided eye contact and soon heard the ringing of a hammer.

At the far side of the hall Alasdair spotted an antechamber leading off the main hall. He made his way there and stepped inside.

It was the fairy forge. Metalwork and tools lined the walls, all of such fine craftsmanship that Alasdair could have spent weeks admiring them. But he paid them no mind, for at the far end of the chamber, sitting before the forge with hammer in hand, was Neil.

Alasdair choked down a sob. He approached his son and put a hand on his shoulder.

Neil looked up at his father. He frowned, looking at Alasdair as if he had met him once but couldn't quite remember where.

'Son,' said Alasdair, 'it's me. It's your father. I've come to get you out of here.'

Neil just stared at his father.

'Working,' he said eventually. He went back to inspecting the sword on the anvil before him.

Alasdair glanced at his son's work. It was breathtaking. Pride and pain warred in his heart.

'There's plenty of work back home, I promise you that. Come on, son.'

Alasdair went on cajoling Neil until he reluctantly set down his hammer. The smith half-led, half-dragged his son away from the forge as Neil looked back longingly.

They left the forge and re-entered the main hall. The revelry seemed to be at its peak and nobody paid them any attention. Alasdair led Neil at a quick pace around the hall until they neared the tunnel leading to the way out.

They had just reached the tunnel's entrance when the music jerked to a halt. A caterwauling cry went up among the fairies.

Alasdair and Neil slowly turned around. Every single one of

the fairies was staring at them, anger and horror writ large on their faces.

A fairy man came forward. Tall and sharp-eyed, he had the look of a leader.

'You have entered our home unbidden,' he said to Alasdair, 'and are attempting to steal our smith.'

'He's not your smith,' said Alasdair. 'He's my son, my apprentice, and I'm taking him home.'

'I do not allow it.'

'In that case,' said Alasdair, rolling up his sleeves, 'I'll fight you for him.'

The fairy man laughed wildly at that. All the fairies joined him, pounding their fists on their knees and the tables. The noise was near-deafening.

Just as Cormac had predicted.

Beneath Alasdair's cloak, the cockerel awoke. As he always did upon waking, he crowed his greeting to the sun.

The fairies stopped laughing.

They began screaming.

Fairies love the night better than the day, Cormac had said to Alasdair. *The cry of a cockerel is agony to them.*

Cormac's words proved true. The fairies fell to the floor, wailing and cursing and covering their ears as the cockerel crowed and crowed. Alasdair held it high above his head, laughing himself now.

'Get out!' screamed the fairy man. 'Take your son, take that vile creature and never come back!'

Alasdair was happy to oblige. He stuffed the cockerel back under his cloak, grabbed Neil's hand and dashed for the door.

On their way out, he pulled his dagger from the doorframe, causing the door to swing shut behind him.

They were safe.

ALASDAIR AND NEIL RETURNED HOME. Neil went straight to bed and slept right through to the following morning. When he finally woke up, he came through to the front room and accepted a bowl of porridge. He ate it all up and took a second helping. Alasdair wore a radiant grin as he watched his son eat. This was no fairy changeling. This was Neil.

'Will you come through to the forge today?' asked Alasdair. 'I don't mean to push you. You've been through a lot. But I could do with a hand and... well... best not to dwell on things, see? You'll feel better with a hammer in your hand and work on your mind.'

Neil nodded. 'Aye. I will do. Later.'

'...Alright then.'

But Neil didn't come through to the forge that day.

He didn't come the next day either, or the next week, or even the next month.

Alasdair despaired. He tried gentle coaxing; he tried shouting and swearing. Nothing worked.

'Give him time,' said Cormac when Alasdair went to visit him. 'The days your son spent with the sidhe would have seemed like years to him.'

So Alasdair did just that. Yet as the seasons passed with no change in Neil, he began to believe he would never truly have his son back.

Then, one day, he was working in the forge when a voice said, 'Let me see that.'

Alasdair turned around.

It was Neil. He hadn't set foot in the forge since coming home.

Alasdair got up to make room for his son. Neil put on a leather apron, sat down and carefully studied the sword his father had been working on.

'It's for the clan chief,' said Alasdair.

Neil nodded distractedly. Alasdair recognised the look in his son's eyes. It was the look a smith gets when they see a hidden shape waiting inside a length of steel.

'Hammer,' said Neil.

Alasdair handed his son a hammer.

Neither father nor son left the forge that night. Alasdair assisted Neil, pumping the bellows and bringing his son everything he needed without having to be asked. He watched in wonder as his son forged the finest sword he had ever seen.

That sword is still famous in the Western Isles. It is known as the *Claidheamh Ceann-Ileach*, the Islay Hilt. It went to Lord MacDonald, Chief of Islay, who was overjoyed with it. His descendants carried copies of it for generations.

Alasdair and Neil worked together for many years. Their fame spread far and wide and soon rich folk were offering extravagant sums for their work. Yet they had no interest in money, for all they cared about was smithing. They worked together in the forge each day and drank ale together each night, rarely taking a day off. It was the life Alasdair had dreamed of, and it was better than he could ever have imagined. *

---

* Scotland has many changeling stories. What makes this one stand out for me is that it doesn't end with 'They came home and lived happily ever after' but instead explores the slow and challenging process Alasdair and Neil go through as Neil readjusts to his old life. I imagine many readers who have undergone intense experiences and then tried to return home will relate to this.

The mythologist Martin Shaw writes about myths as following a progression through severance, threshold and return. The hero is severed from their ordinary reality; they spend a testing period of time in a crucible of transformation; then they return to their community as a renewed person with gifts to share. Shaw suggests that the return stage of this process is the most difficult in the modern world, as our communities do not understand initiatory processes and are therefore unequipped to help the changed person re-integrate into society.

THE KING OF THE CATS

On the outskirts of the village of Roslin lies one of Scotland's most mysterious buildings. Rosslyn Chapel (the chapel retains the older spelling of 'Roslin') is a medieval chapel whose walls are lined with esoteric carvings and arcane imagery. Long associated with the Knights Templar, the chapel attracts over a million visitors every year. Yet the strangest thing to ever happen in Roslin has nothing to do with the chapel.

Beyond the chapel lies Roslin Glen, a deep river gorge which some call the most beautiful glen in Scotland. Down there you'll find caves, waterfalls, ancient trees and, right by the river, a castle that seems to grow right out of the rock.

That's where it happened: the strangest thing you ever heard of.

~

ONE SATURDAY NIGHT IN DECEMBER, many years ago, the Rosslyn Arms was packed. Only men went into pubs in those days, and these men were happily drinking, smoking and gossiping while outside the full moon shone down, making the frost-mantled village sparkle. Though it was cold outside, the pub was warmed by a roaring fire. Baskets of logs sat on either side of the fire, and in front of the fire lay a cat.

It was no ordinary cat.

This cat was bigger than a house cat. It was bigger than a dog, bigger than a seal; it was the size of a lioness. Its fur was jet black and its gleaming claws were the length of kitchen knives. The cat was asleep that evening, but if it had opened its eyes, you would have seen that they were a deep ruby red.

You might be thinking that the enormous cat's presence was a remarkable thing, and that surely all the patrons should be discussing it. Yet nobody was talking about the cat. Nobody gave it so much as a glance. For the cat had always been there. It had lived in the Rosslyn Arms and lazed in front of the fire for as long as anyone could remember, including the landlord. And no matter how strange something is, time will make it ordinary to human eyes. Thus the pub's patrons ignored the cat, and leaned over it to throw a log on the fire.

The evening proceeded like any other evening until without warning the door slammed against the wall. A gust of freezing air blew in as a man named Tam strode into the pub, his face as white as the snow outside.

'I need a drink!' he declared.

He marched over to the bar.

'Whisky!'

The barman hastily poured Tam a whisky. Tam downed it in one gulp.

'Another!'

He knocked back his second dram and ordered a third.

By this time, the pub's patrons were gathering around Tam.

'Steady on, Tam,' said a man named Willie as Tam ordered a fourth whisky. 'You won't make it home at this rate. What's the matter? Have you had another row with your missus?'

Tam shook his head. 'No! Nothing like that.'

'Well, what's wrong then?'

By now the whisky was doing its work. Tam took a few deep breaths and said, 'I'd like to tell you. I would. But you wouldn't believe me.'

There was a murmur of disapproval at that. 'Come on now, Tam,' said Willie. 'Everyone here knows you for an honest man. Whatever's happened, you can tell us about it. We'll believe you.'

Tam looked around, meeting the eyes of every man.

'You all promise you'll believe me?'

The men nodded and said, 'Aye. We promise.'

'Alright then,' said Tam. 'Here's what happened.'

'YOU ALL KNOW I live on the far side of the glen,' began Tam.

'Aye,' said the men.

'So you know that when I come here on a Saturday, I walk through the glen.'

'Aye.'

The pub was silent now but for the crackling of the fire.

'Well. I left home earlier this evening. I was wrapped up warm as it's bitter cold outside. I kissed my wife goodbye, walked out the door and made my way down into the glen.

'I took the same path as always down to the river. I know it well enough that I could walk it with my eyes closed, but tonight I could see my way by the moon's light.

'I reached the river. You all know the bridge? And how you cross the bridge then walk up the steps, underneath the big stone archway by the castle, which takes you out of the glen on this side?'

'Aye,' the men chorused.

'Right. Well. I had just crossed the bridge when... when... ach, no! It's no good, you'll never believe me!'

'We will, Tam!' said the men. 'We will!'

By this point, all of the patrons and both of the barmen were thoroughly engrossed in Tam's story.

None of them noticed that the cat had opened its eyes.

It was watching Tam intently.

Tam took another gulp of whisky. 'Alright then. Alright. So. As I was saying, I reached the river and crossed the bridge. I was about to take the steps that take you under the archway and out of the glen when I... I saw firelight up ahead, and I heard a chorus of voices singing a strange song.'

'What was the song?' asked Willie.

'It went like this,' said Tam. Raising the pitch of his voice, he sang, 'Miii-aoow, miii-aoow.'

At this, some of the assembly looked away, covering their mouths as they sniggered.

'Is that so, Tam?' asked Willie, fighting to suppress a smirk. 'What happened next?'

The enormous cat got to its feet and stretched out. Its ruby eyes were fixed on Tam.

'Well, I thought this was all very odd,' continued Tam, 'and I was frightened, you understand? So I dived into some bushes to hide, and I watched what happened next.

'The firelight and the singing drew closer. Then there came down the steps, beneath the arch, a procession... of cats! And I don't mean wee cats like you have at home. I mean big cats, man-sized and woman-sized cats! They were walking on their hind legs, and carrying blazing torches, and they were walking in a slow, sombre, stately kind of way, as if something important was happening. And all the time they were singing, "Miii-aoow, miii-aoow".'

By now everyone was sure Tam had gone daft. They were thoroughly enjoying his story, though, so they encouraged him to continue.

Meanwhile, the great black cat had left the fireplace. It joined the rear of the gathering, unnoticed.

'That's incredible, Tam. Absolutely incredible,' said Willie. 'So what happened next?'

'I stayed hidden in the bushes. I watched as the cats reached the bottom of the path and gathered in a big circle. They then turned and looked back the way they had come.

'I followed their gaze and saw these six big, burly male cats walking down the steps. They were carrying a coffin on their shoulders. Huge, it was!

'They reached the circle of cats and stood in the middle.

The other cats gathered in close, and then sang a new song. It went like this:

> Tommy Tildrum is dead,
> Tommy Tildrum is dead,
> Yes, Tommy Tildrum is dead,
> Miii-aoow, miii-aoow

By now half the men had collapsed into fits of giggles. Tam was so caught up in his story that he didn't notice.

'Once that was done, the coffin-bearing cats took the coffin to the river and heaved it into the water. It landed with a great splash and drifted out towards the middle of the river. The current caught it and carried it away…'

Tam stopped mid-sentence. He stared past the men, horror on his face.

The great black cat was making its way towards him, striding through the assembly as they leapt back from it.

The cat reached the front of the gathering and faced Tam.

It gazed up at him, grinning, revealing rows of huge, sharp teeth. Then, as everybody leapt back in horror, it rose up to its full height, balancing on its back feet, towering over them.

The cat 's eyes were fixed on Tam. Its teeth were shining swords.

As Tam shuddered and whimpered, the cat spoke.

'If Tommy Tildrum is dead,' it said, 'then I'm the King of the Cats!'

The cat turned and ran towards the fire. It leapt into the fire and disappeared up the chimney in an explosion of multi-coloured flames, and has never been seen in Roslin since. And that's a true story.*

---

* Well, maybe it isn't a true story. It's a classic that crops up all over Scotland, Ireland, England and I would imagine other places too. I first heard it from the author and storyteller Peter Snow, and my version owes a lot to his. I like to set the story in Roslin as the nearby glen makes a perfect backdrop. It's a place I've wandered through many times as I used to live in the village.

A related legend is that of the Cait Sith, sometimes described as a great black cat with a white spot on its chest, which may derive from the Scottish Wildcat, a (now very rare) Scottish feline descended from the European Wildcat.

This story has inspired many writers including China Mieville. I think it speaks to the sense many of us have that our cats live double lives. We have no idea what happens when they leave the house at night. What other worlds might they inhabit?

THE TROWIE WEDDING

Unst is the most northerly of the Shetland Islands, and there once lived on Unst a fiddler named Ranald. He made his living by playing at weddings, parties, funerals and other occasions, and he was always in demand up and down the islands due to his remarkable skills. Folk said he was the finest fiddler Shetland had seen in generations.

Ranald was newly married. One day in June, not long after the wedding, he sat down to breakfast with his wife. She dished out a bowl of porridge for him and said, 'So, Ranald, what are you doing today?'

'I am playing at a wedding today,' said Ranald.

'Is the wedding taking place here on Unst?'

'Yes, it is.'

'And will you be home for your supper?'

'Well,' said Ranald, 'it depends. What are you making?'

Ranald would usually be offered a meal wherever he played, but he thought he might save his appetite if something special was on offer.

'Oh, nothing much,' said his wife. 'Just leek and tattie soup.'

Ranald's head jerked up. He dropped his spoon.

'Did you say... leek and tattie soup?'

'Yes.'

'Oh!' said Ranald. 'Leek and tattie soup is my favourite! In that case I will certainly be home for my supper. Oh yes.'

His wife set her hands on her hips. 'Now, Ranald,' she said. She had already begun to learn his ways. 'Think this through. You are going to be playing at a wedding today. There will be dancing. There will be drinking. There will be music, and merriment, and catching up with old friends and distant relations. Are you sure you will want to come home for your supper?'

'Yes, wife,' said Ranald. 'If you are making leek and tattie soup, I will be back in time to eat it, and no more needs to be said.'

'Well, alright then,' said his wife.

Ranald finished his breakfast. He donned his coat, put his fiddle under his arm, kissed his wife and set off.

RANALD STROLLED DOWN THE ROAD, whistling tunes as he considered what he might play that day. A cloak of unmoving, iron-dark clouds covered the sky, which counts as fine weather in Shetland.

After an hour or two, Ranald reached the wedding house. The company cheered when they saw him enter. Ranald was the one who brought the music and dancing, and besides that, he was well-liked for his kind heart and easy way.

Ranald had time to greet a few folk before the ceremony got underway. He played for the ceremony, and then after the ceremony came lunch and speeches. After that, it was time for music and dancing.

Ranald needed no direction. He set bow to string and struck up a bright and breezy tune. Even those who had eaten too much and sworn they wouldn't dance found themselves on their feet and twirling. Ranald slipped from tune to tune with effortless ease, always seeming to know exactly what his audience needed to hear next. He delighted them with old favourites, giving each one a new twist; he surprised them with tunes he'd composed himself or that came to him in the moment.

Ever so subtly, Ranald upped the tempo. He had the wedding guests dancing faster and faster until everyone from the youngest child to the oldest grandparent was red-faced and whooping and cheering. This was as good as life could get, and everyone knew it.

The day became the night. Ranald was no straw-armed apprentice but even he had his limits. Eventually he put down his fiddle with an air of finality. A whisky was thrust into his hand.

'Wonderful playing, Ranald,' said the bride's father as one after another guest came to thank Ranald. 'Just wonderful. You're a treasure, you really are.'

'Oh, thank you, thank you. It's a joy to play for you, indeed it is.'

'It's late now. Can we give you some supper before you set off?'

Ranald's stomach rumbled. 'Oh yes,' he said, 'that would be just the thing...' He paused. 'Ah. No, actually. I won't stay for supper. It's my wife, you see. She's making leek and tattie soup! So I'll be going home for my supper.'

'Very well,' said the man. He paid Ranald and saw him to the door.

RANALD WALKED HOME. Shetland is so far north that there are no dark hours at all at midsummer, while in winter there are only a few hours of light each day. It was June, so although Ranald had left the wedding late at night, he had plenty of light to see by. The wind had picked up, setting Ranald's coat flapping.

He was following the road along a stretch of clifftop when a wall of fog blew in off the sea. It enveloped him with the speed of a hunting hawk.

Ranald halted.

Shetland's sea-mist, known as the 'haar', can be as thick as sheep-wool. This one was as dense as Ranald had ever known. He couldn't see a foot before him or in any direction, and if he went on walking, there was every chance he would tumble off the cliff.

Ranald stood in that spot, shivering. What was he to do?

Stay there all night? His soup would get cold! He'd never seen the haar come in quite as fast as this. It was odd...

Voices interrupted his thoughts.

The voices drew closer. There were many of them, all around him.

Tiny people appeared out of the mist.

Their heads reached no higher than Ranald's waist. They were thick-set and ruddy-cheeked, the men full-bearded. Their lined faces spoke of harsh winters and harsh lives.

Ranald had never seen these people before, or seen anyone quite like them. But he knew exactly who they were. They were trowies.

Trowies, or trows, are the hidden people of Orkney and Shetland. They are somewhat like fairies, though stockier and swarthier in appearance. They are said to live in the old burial mounds that dot the landscape of the islands, and it is well known that any Shetlander who encounters a trowie must be on their absolute best behaviour.

'Good evening,' said a trowie man who had an air of authority about him.

'Good evening,' said Ranald.

'Your name is Ranald.'

'Yes, it is.'

'You are a fiddler.'

'I am.'

'You've been playing at a wedding.'

'Yes. You seem to know more about me than I do!'

'Ranald. I want you to listen to me carefully. Tonight is an important night for us trowies. Tonight we are having a trowie wedding.'

'Really? Well, congratulations, that's marvellous.'

'No, Ranald. It's not marvellous at all. For you see, we don't have a fiddler for our wedding.'

'...Oh.'

'And you'll know, Ranald, you'll know better than anyone, that a wedding with no fiddler is no wedding at all.'

'Yes, that's absolutely right. No wedding at all,' said Ranald.

'Well then, Ranald. I know it's late. I know you've had a long day. But do you think you could see your way to playing a wee tune for us at our wedding? Just one peedie, tiny little tune?'

'Oh dear. Oh dear. I'd love to, you see, but it's my wife. I'm married now, see, and I said to her I'd be home for my supper. She's making leek and tattie soup...'

Ranald got no further. As one, the trowies burst into tears.

They wailed and moaned, their eyes and noses pouring. Ranald had never heard such an outpouring of grief. It was too much for his gentle heart to take.

'Oh my... well, I suppose I could come and play one tune...'

The crying stopped at once. Every trowie grinned as their leader clapped his hands. At once a little white pony trotted out of the mist.

Ranald climbed onto the pony's back. The trowie man slapped her rump and she set off at a gallop through the mist. Ranald clutched at the nape of her neck, his fiddle tucked under his arm. He couldn't see where he was going, he didn't know where he was going. He could only hold on. In time, the sounds of the pony's hooves striking the road changed, and Ranald discerned they were crossing a stretch of sand.

The sound changed again as the mist-laden air darkened. The pony's hooves clattered against stone; the sound echoed around Ranald. They had entered a cave.

Ranald spied lights up ahead. They turned a corner and the pony slowed to a trot, then halted as they entered a vast cavern.

Ranald was in a trowie cave. Torches hung in brackets on the walls; bright tapestries stretched between them. Flowers nestled among the rocks and the cave was full of gaily dressed trowies.

Nobody had marked Ranald's entrance. The entire company was facing the far end of the cave, where a trowie man and woman stood before a tiny druid.

'I now pronounce you trowie man and trowie wife,' said the druid, his voice soaring through the cave. 'You may kiss the bride.'

The newlyweds kissed; the crowd cheered. The trowie chief, who had suddenly appeared at Ranald's side, gave him a nod. It was time.

Ranald dismounted and readied his fiddle.

He struck a tune. The trowies cheered and set to dancing. Despite Ranald's intentions, his first tune flowed into a second, and his second into a third, and so it went.

Ranald played, and the trowies danced, and Ranald realised that something was happening to him. He was playing in a way that he had never played before. Tunes unknown to him sprang from his fiddle, one after another, often in styles absolutely foreign to him. He felt as if some unseen force was playing his fiddle through him. His playing grew faster and wilder, and the dancing grew wilder and faster, and that made Ranald play more fiercely in turn. Thus the dance grew ever more frenzied until finally Ranald admitted defeat.

He played a final note and put down his fiddle. Gasping for breath, he accepted a proffered cog of ale and gulped it down as the trowie chief came over to him.

'That was fine playing, Ranald. Very fine playing! I've rarely heard the like of it. It's been a splendid wedding, and we've you to thank for it.'

'Oh, it's no trouble at all,' said red-faced Ranald, still catching his breath. 'It was my pleasure.'

'Listen, Ranald. I'm afraid we have no money to pay you with. We have no gold nor silver, no yellow nor white.'

'That's alright. I've been paid already today. Your joy and your dancing are payment enough for me.'

The man nodded. 'Very well. In that case, let me give you something else as payment.' The trowie chief lowered his voice. 'You see, I have a gift, Ranald. The gift of prophecy. I can see into your future. Would you like to know your future, Ranald?'

'Er... well, yes, I suppose so.'

'Kneel down then.'

Ranald knelt. The trowie man squinted at him, gazing deep into Ranald's eyes. He nodded slowly.

'You and your wife will know good health, Ranald. You will have many years together, and you will have eight children.'

'Eight bairnas? Oh my! That's wonderful!'

The trowie man shook his head. 'No, Ranald. I'm sorry, but it's not wonderful.'

'But—'

'Your first bairn will be a little boy.'

Ranald gasped. 'A son! My own wee lad! How marvellous—'

'No, Ranald, it's not marvellous! For you see, the moment that lad comes into the world, he will start squealing and wailing, bawling and howling, and it shall be torturous to hear, Ranald! Torturous! He'll cry louder and louder, every day and every night! You won't sleep, you'll go gibbering mad with it... and then along will come another child.' The chief paused. 'This one... this one will be a little girl.'

Ranald covered his mouth. 'A little girl,' he whispered. 'How perfect—'

'Not perfect, Ranald, not perfect! For if that boy's cries were terrible, this girl shall howl and shriek like a demon! A demon from the utmost darkness, Ranald! The utmost darkness!

'Louder and louder she will cry, day and night. And at the sounds of her terrible song, the sea shall succumb to an endless storm. Great terrors will arise from the abyss; the sky itself will be fire. You'll roll and howl on the floor as she wails, you'll lose your mind, you'll put knives in your ears to stop the screaming, but it won't stop, Ranald, it will never stop!'

The trowie smiled.

'But don't worry, my friend, don't you worry. For I'm going to give you a tune. A trowie tune. Play this peedie tune on your fiddle, or have your wife sing it to the bairnas, and the minute they hear it, they will stop their crying, and fall asleep as peaceful as a perfect sunrise. Now listen carefully.'

Ranald listened as the man hummed a soft, simple tune. It was beautiful.

'Will you remember that?' the trowie asked when he had finished.

'Of course. I hear a tune once and I never forget it.'

'Well, then. It's time you were off.'

So Ranald was set upon the pony's back again. The trowies called a last round of thanks, the chief slapped the pony's rump and it set off.

The mist was still thick when Ranald left the cave, yet the pony knew its way. They crossed the island and arrived outside Ranald's house just as the mist was clearing.

Ranald climbed down and thanked the pony. He saw there was a light in the window; he knew it must be very late by now but hopefully his soup was still warm.

Ranald opened the door and entered his kitchen.

His wife was sitting at the table.

'Good evening,' Ranald said.

'Good evening.'

He grinned as he spied a bowl of soup on the table.

'Is that my leek and tattie soup?'

'Yes, Ranald. That's your soup.'

Ranald shivered with anticipation. He sat down, picked up his spoon and put a spoonful of soup in his mouth.

He spat it out all over the table.

It was the foulest thing Ranald had ever tasted. He heaved and retched, then gulped some ale and sloshed it around his mouth before spitting that out too.

'It's... it's awful!' he said, getting to his feet. 'It's disgusting! That... that is no leek and tattie soup!'

Ranald's wife's eyes narrowed. 'Oh, but it was, Ranald. It

was.' She slammed her fist on the table. 'Fourteen days ago, when you were supposed to be home!'

Ranald saw tears spring to his wife's eyes. 'I thought you were dead, Ranald. I thought you'd been press-ganged, I thought you'd been murdered or fallen from a cliff... tell me, Ranald, tell me right now, where have you been?'

'Nowhere! I went to the wedding, I played a few tunes and I came back... oh. Now, hang on. I did play at the trowie wedding.'

Ranald's wife narrowed her eyes. 'Trowie wedding, Ranald?'

'Yes. The trowie wedding.'

Silence.

Ranald's wife stood up.

She circled the table to stand face to face with Ranald.

Then she leapt at Ranald and threw her arms around him. 'Oh, my darling. My dear, darling husband. I thought I'd lost you forever. I'm so glad you came back to me.'

She kissed him deeply, then set to making a fresh pot of soup while an exhausted Ranald dozed in front of the fire.

THE TROWIE MAN'S prophecy came true. Ranald and his wife did indeed have eight children, and the first two were indeed a boy and a girl. They each bawled and howled frightfully. Yet all Ranald and his wife had to do was to play that tune, or sing it or even hum it, and the bairnas would fall asleep with smiles on their peedie faces. The following six had more peaceful natures.

That tune is still known and played in Shetland. It's called the Trowie Lullaby, and parents in Shetland sing it to their children to send them to sleep. I'm told that sometimes it works and sometimes it doesn't. *

---

* I heard this story from the legendary Scottish storyteller, David Campbell, who told it to me at his kitchen table in Edinburgh one afternoon. The term 'trow' or 'trowie' is likely derived from the Scandinavian word 'troll'; Shetland is as close to Norway as it is to the Scottish mainland and cultural ties run deep.

THE BLACK DINNER

The Stewart Dynasty ruled Scotland for hundreds of years. Mary Queen of Scots was of this line, as was James Douglas Stewart, better known as Bonnie Prince Charlie. It was a Stewart king who took the throne of England and brought about the union of the crowns, making him James VI & I. Of all the stories told about the Stewarts, one of the most famous concerns King James II, and a fateful dinner party which may seem strangely familiar.

The first Stewart king, James I, was nicknamed 'the wisest fool in Christendom'. He had grown up as a well-treated hostage of the English court, during which time he became an accomplished poet and musician. At court he fell in love with an English lady, Joan Beaufort, whom he married after he was eventually freed. They returned to Scotland and James was crowned king. Determined to make the country a better, more just place, he set out to limit the powers of his nobles.

The nobles didn't think this made things better. They thought the best way to improve Scotland would be to get rid of King James. So on a cold winter night in 1437, the Earl of Atholl led a group of assassins into James's Palace at Perth. James made it as far as a storm drain before the assassins found him. He was murdered right there in the damp and the dark, yet Queen Joan escaped.

The crown now passed to their six-year-old son. He became James II of Scotland, and he may have wondered whether a fate like that of his father awaited him. There was every reason to believe so, for the Stewarts had powerful rivals in the form of the Douglas clan. The Douglases had vast lands, vast wealth and a bloodline that was entangled with that of the Stewarts.

Yet young James was not alone. He had enemies but he had allies too. Lord Crichton, the Lord Chancellor of Scotland, and the powerful Lord Livingston of Callander, were loyal to the Stewarts. They guided the boy king and did everything they could to keep the Douglases at bay.

Then, in 1439, opportunity struck for James and his allies.

The fifth Earl of Douglas, who was next in line to the throne and James' most dangerous rival, died suddenly. His sixteen-year-old nephew, William, was now head of Clan Douglas.

He was young. He was untested.

He was vulnerable.

A YEAR after his father's death, William Douglas, Sixth Earl of Clan Douglas, received a curious invitation.

The invitation was to dine at Edinburgh Castle. It came from the young King James himself.

William was unsure what to make of this. He himself was second in line to the throne; James was king. Their clans had a long-established rivalry and the two of them were natural enemies. Why would James invite him to dinner? Surely it would be unwise for him to walk into the wolf's jaws, into Edinburgh Castle, the seat of Stewart power?

'I shall not accept the invitation,' William said to his younger brother David. 'James' advisors may wish for peace between our families. But they might equally have foul intentions.'

'I would be inclined to agree,' said David. 'But for one thing. The invitation is to dinner. The guest right, the law of hospitality, applies to kings and commoners alike. No man would break it by mistreating his dinner guest, for he would be damned in the eyes of God forevermore.'

'True,' said William. 'The Boy King must surely be frightened of me. He might think to win my friendship by showing me round his grand castle.'

'Of course he fears Clan Douglas,' said David. 'He knows what happened to his father. He probably cries himself to sleep imagining we will hunt him down with daggers and leave him rotting in a sewer.'

'I would never do such a thing,' said William, looking shocked.

David froze. Then a smile broke William's face. 'When the time comes, I will think of something far more original. And far more public.'

David laughed. 'So we accept the invitation?'

'We accept it,' said William. 'Let the runt think he has a friend in me.'

TWO WEEKS LATER, William and David Douglas rode through Edinburgh's Netherbow Gate.

They rode up the Royal Mile, gagging at the stench of the city streets. The night was cold and dark and the wind hurled sheets of rain at the two travellers. They passed the church of St Giles, its walls lined with heads on spikes. They passed the Mercat Cross where a forlorn figure crouched, his bloody hand nailed to the cross as punishment for theft.

Further up the Mile they rode. Finally, Edinburgh Castle loomed out of the darkness before them. They rode up to the gates, shouted to the guards and soon the gates opened.

William and David rode into the castle courtyard and dismounted. Servants and liverymen saw to their horses before escorting them into the high tower known as David's Tower. They strode up spiralling stairs until they reached the feasting hall.

King James II awaited them there.

The hall was warm and brightly lit. Servants lined the walls and a band of musicians played in one corner. At the glittering table sat the Queen Regent, Lord Crichton, Lord Livingston and King James himself, along with a handful of favoured nobles. The company rose to welcome their guests and soon the

Douglases were sitting comfortably, wine in their cups and meat on their forks.

William was given the seat of honour next to James. At first, William was polite yet reserved. He allowed himself time to study the ten-year-old king. To see how he spoke to those around him, and to see if his own presence made the boy nervous. As he had hoped, James appeared to be afraid of him. He looked often to Crichton and Livingston, as if expecting them to tell him what to say. Inwardly, William grinned. Things were just as he had hoped.

And as for Crichton and Livingstone? They were well-practised men of the court. Impeccably polite, warm yet restrained, relaxed yet dignified. Whatever intentions they might have harboured in bringing William there, they let nothing slip.

William played his part, speaking and behaving exactly as was proper. He made sure to keep all contempt from his eyes. When the day came for the Boy King to die, Crichton and Livingston would not be far behind him.

Midway through the meal, William set to work on James. He asked the boy questions and listened to his answers with great attentiveness. He told amusing stories, making James laugh and relax his guard. Crichton and Livingston watched carefully, all the time assessing William and his intentions. Well, what could they say? There was nothing untoward in flattering the king, and certainly nothing unusual in it.

By the time the final dish was served, William practically had James eating out of his hand. He relaxed a little himself as he reclined in his chair, throwing back his head to laugh at some pathetic joke the king had made. The evening was a success. Crichton and Livingston were watching him with satisfied smiles. They thought that he wished to be their ally. That he would seek to wield power by manipulating the king rather than fighting him.

They would be far less wary of him now. It was perfect.

The final dish was cleared away.

'Well,' said William, 'it has been an enchanting evening. I thank the king for his most entertaining company.'

King James smiled at William and got to his feet. William and the other guests began to rise but as they did so, Crichton spoke.

'A moment please, my king, my lords and ladies,' he said. 'We have one final dish still to serve.'

James sat down, seeming confused. The rest of the company followed him.

The musicians ceased to play.

A strained silence fell on the feasting hall. It was broken a few moments later by the drummer, who struck up a slow, sonorous rhythm, almost like the beating of a heart.

The door to the kitchens opened.

Two serving men walked in, straining at the weight of the cloth-covered platter which they carried between them.

They placed it on the table before William Douglas.

Lord Crichton smiled and whipped back the cloth.

On the platter sat a black bull's head.

In those days, this was a symbol of death.

Before William could open his mouth, he and David were seized from behind. They were dragged from the hall, frantically struggling, calling to the king for help. The king was weeping, demanding to know what was going on, but nobody paid him any attention.

William and David were dragged out to the courtyard. Crichton and Livingston ordered the serving men, who were really castle guards, to beat them. The guards happily obliged while King James wailed at them to stop.

Finally Crichton raised a hand. The guards withdrew, leaving William and David groaning on the flagstones, spitting blood.

'William and David Douglas,' said Crichton. 'You stand accused of conspiring to seize the throne from your lawful king. How do you plead?'

'You will pay for this, Crichton,' said William. He stopped to cough up a stream of blood and bile. 'The Douglases will see you dead.'

'You all heard it!' said Livingstone to the other guests, who were milling around nearby. 'A threat to the king's advisor is a threat to the king himself.'

'Indeed,' said Crichton with a smile. 'I have no choice but to declare William and David Douglas guilty of treason, and to sentence them both to death. On your knees.'

Guards came forward and roughly dragged the Douglas brothers to their knees. The king's executioner stepped forward from the shadows, his face hidden beneath his black hood, his well-used blade drawn and ready.

The Douglases had the will to resist but not the strength. The executioner's blade flashed down once, twice, and their heads rolled. Noble blood and rainwater sluiced away down the castle drains.

That was how the Lords Crichton and Livingston dealt with the Douglas threat. The Douglas clan remained a powerful force yet they never dared move on the Scottish throne, which the Stewarts held for another two hundred years. Anyone who plotted treason in Scotland after that night must have thought hard on the Black Dinner, when the sacred law of hospitality was broken and dinner guests were murdered. *

---

* Many people reading this story will be immediately reminded of a certain episode of *Game of Thrones* (skip this paragraph if you're planning to watch it/read the books and want to avoid spoilers). George R.R. Martin is a huge fan of Scottish history, and he took inspiration for the Red Wedding from the Black Dinner as well as from the Massacre of Glencoe.

    The exact manner in which events unfolded on the night is cloaked in legend, and will never be known. There may well not have been a bull's head. I can't offer the facts, only the story.

AN ENDLESS VOYAGE

If you drive to the end of the Uig road on the Isle of Lewis, through Carishader, past Mangersta and on down the coast, you will come to a white sand beach. Standing on that shore and looking out to sea, you will see a scattering of islands. One of those is *Eilean Mhealasta*, Mealista Island. It has a fine beach on its east coast; its west coast is nothing but rocks. Mealista Island used to have a living, working population, but they were cleared in 1823 to make room for sheep. It's a sad story, but perhaps not as sad as another tale from that island.

The story begins with trees, or rather, with the lack of them on Lewis. Most of the land is peat bog. Peat will do you fine for a fire but is no good for roofing or boat-building. Thus there was always a shortage of timber on Lewis, and the islanders usually obtained it by scavenging the storm-scalded beaches, where driftwood washes up from as far away as America. But Mealista's rocky western shore rarely received such gifts. So while the residents of nearby Uig managed for timber, the people of Mealista did not.

So what to do? It was an ongoing problem. The men of Mealista would sail north and south searching for driftwood, or else buy timber or barter for it. One autumn day, a group of Mealista men were sitting together when one mentioned he had a cousin working on an estate in Gairloch, over on the mainland.

'I reckon he could arrange for us to buy some timber there,' he said. 'The estate manager is a fair man, he says, so we should get a good price for it.'

This sounded like a sound plan to everyone. So the trip to the mainland was arranged and, one grey day soon afterwards, the inhabitants of Mealista gathered at the beach on the eastern shore. All the adult men would sail together to make the purchase and bring back their cargo. The women, children and elderly folk said goodbye to their men and watched the boat depart. Though they would miss their men, and would surely worry for their safety on the high seas, they smiled and laughed as the boat sailed south and out of sight.

But not Annie.

She could not stop herself from crying. She hated that boat for bearing her beloved away from her. She and Fraser had been sweethearts ever since they were bairns scampering on the sand. He had asked for her hand only a month before the boat set sail; they were due to marry in the spring. Annie loved Fraser in a way that made her whole body ache every time she thought of him, and now he was gone. As the boat departed, she turned and ran home, unable to bear the sight of Fraser sailing away.

Time passed. There was nothing for Annie or any of them to do but simply to get on with life. There was always plenty of work going, which was doubly true now that so many hands were missing. And keeping busy kept worry at bay. Though nobody said it, every islander feared for the boat's safe passage. The Minch, the sea between Lewis and Scotland, was fierce and treacherous. Wrecks and drownings were far from uncommon. And that was without accounting for the Blue Men, who roved the Minch preying on slow-tongued sailors and raising supernatural storms.

Days and days went by with no word. Annie watched the weather obsessively. The sea around Mealista was restless on many days, which did nothing to ease her worries.

Then, one wet, windy day, a boat pulled into Mealista's eastern beach. Its crew were fishermen from Stornoway. Their captain strode up the beach to greet the islanders who were already gathering there.

'I know your men are away to Sutherland and that you'll be wanting news of them,' he said, stuffing tobacco into his pipe. 'I heard talk of them in Stornoway. Apparently they landed safely in Badachro, bought their wood and were last seen leaving the harbour there.'

There were deep sighs of relief at that, but not from everyone.

'So why aren't they back yet?' asked Annie.

'The Minch has been rough lately, I won't lie. But I've seen it a lot worse. I expect they crossed safely, made a landing and are now waiting out the weather.'

The captain shared some more talk then went on his way. Annie and the rest of the folk on Mealista felt a little better, but they would not know true peace until their men were home. They continued to wait.

A week later, the boat still hadn't returned.

Everyone on the island was deeply fearful now. Whenever a boat passed by, they waved it down and begged for news, but nobody had fresh news of the boat from Mealista.

'I think something has happened to them,' said Annie to her mother.

'That's enough of that talk,' her mother replied.

'But Fraser—'

'Do you think you're the only woman on Mealista who loves a man on that boat? Everyone is fretting. Yet we keep our heads up for each other's sake, and I expect you to do the same.'

Annie knew her mother was right. She kept herself together after that, except when she was alone. That wasn't often; the islanders now came together more than ever to share their work and keep their spirits up. The men were fine, they would say over and over. They were probably holed up somewhere east, enjoying good hospitality and too much ale. Yet a foreboding hung over the island that no laughter could dispel.

AT LAST, a message arrived, yet not from a passing boat.

It arrived in a dream.

In Annie's dream, she was sitting atop a rocky knoll on Mealista's west coast. It was a place where she and Fraser used to sit watching clouds, boats and birds pass by. Yet Annie sat alone in her dream, until a figure rose out of the sea before her.

It was a man, or rather the remains of one. His skin was blue and blotched, his face bruised. He bled from many cuts. Seawater dripped from his clothes as he clambered onto the rocks.

The man resembled a corpse fished from the sea. Yet it was a corpse she knew.

It was Fraser.

Annie leapt up and climbed down the seaweed-strewn rocks to meet him. She threw herself at him and he wrapped his cold arms around her.

'My Fraser,' she said. 'You came back to me.'

'No, Annie,' he said. 'I can never come back to you.'

She drew back. 'What do you mean?'

'We made it to Sutherland safely,' said Fraser. 'We docked at Badachro, went to the estate and bought our timber. We returned to the boat and recrossed the Minch.

'The sea was wild, Annie. We only just made it back to Lewis, and in bad shape at that. We made port and steered into a sea loch where the water was calmer.

'There was a village on the loch shore. We cheered when we saw it. Everyone thought the folk would come out and assist us, give us food and shelter until we went on our way again. But when they came out of their houses, it was not to welcome us, Annie. They came with weapons. Axes, knives, sticks. They pulled us from the boat, beat us and murdered us. Every last man, and all for the cargo we carried.'

'No,' said Annie, sinking her hands into his cold flesh. 'It's not true. I don't believe you...'

Annie woke up.

Her heart knew the truth.

Fraser and all the men of Mealista were dead.

Annie's pain was terrible. Yet in a strange way, she found peace that night. Knowing that Fraser was truly gone, she could begin to grieve.

The question was: should she keep her dream to herself or share it? If she shared it, doubtless some would believe her and others wouldn't. Arguments and fights would break out. It could make things even worse than they already were, and Annie didn't think the island could take that. So she kept quiet.

Time passed. The atmosphere on Mealista changed as, one by one, the islanders accepted that their men were never coming back. News of the tragedy spread, and soon friends and relatives from other parts of Lewis arrived to offer comfort and helping hands.

That winter was as hard a time as anyone on Mealista had known. Yet they came through, as they always did. A string of weddings took place the following spring as lonely women remarried.

Annie was not one of them.

She knew that there might come a day when she found

someone else to love. It was the way of things. But she knew that day was far away.

Late in summer, a party came over from Hushinish to visit Mealista. One of them was Annie's cousin. He said that he and his friends were planning a trip to Stornoway to visit the Bennadrove Market. Besides the bidding on livestock there would be games, contests, music and stories. It would be a fine few days, and wouldn't Annie come along?

'Yes, she will,' said Annie's mother before Annie could refuse. 'You're going, lass, you'll have a good time, and I won't hear another word on the matter.'

Annie realised it was no good arguing. The next day, she left with her cousin, his friends and a few other girls from Mealista. They sailed around the coast to Stornoway, docked in the harbour and made their way to the market.

It was a fine day, the sun scorching hot. The market was packed and Annie ran into plenty of folk she knew. The collective good spirits were infectious and Annie found herself smiling and laughing. She hadn't done those things in a long time.

Realising that she was feeling happiness at last, a wave of shame washed over Annie. How could she laugh and joke when Fraser's bones lay on the seabed? But she quickly pushed the feeling away. No one could ever doubt how much she had loved Fraser, and he would want her to be happy. It was almost as if he were there with her in that moment, his hand on her shoulder, smiling and telling her it was alright. That he was happy to see her happy.

'There's a seanchai telling stories in the pub,' Annie's cousin said to her, jolting her out of her reverie. 'She's worth hearing, apparently. Shall we go and get an ale?'

'Aye,' said Annie, who was feeling thirsty, though not for ale on a hot day like this. She spotted a lemonade stand. 'You go on ahead. I'll catch up.'

The cousin went on ahead as Annie joined the queue for lemonade, standing behind a man wearing a gantsy, a fisherman's jumper. The heat of the day, and the strange sensation of Fraser watching over her, had put her in a dreamy frame of mind. She stared at the man in front of her, her thoughts far away. Her mind was with Fraser. The way it had felt when he stole up and wrapped his arms around her. She could feel those thick arms around her now. Annie smiled a bittersweet smile.

'Oh, my Fraser,' she said softly.

The man in front of her turned around. He gave her a quizzical look.

'Sorry!' said Annie, blushing. 'My mind was somewhere else.'

The man gave her an awkward half-smile and turned around again.

That was when Annie noticed something about his gantsy.

She knew it.

In those days, every town and village and small island had its own pattern which they wove into their gantsies. Annie stared. There was no mistaking it; that was a Mealista gantsy, with a tiny break in the pattern about halfway down the back.

It was the gantsy which Annie had knitted for Fraser. That break in the pattern was her own error.

Annie's heart hammered in her chest, so loudly that she

feared the man would turn around, realise that she knew his secret, drag her away and murder her. Just like he and his friends had murdered Fraser.

But he didn't turn around. He shuffled forward in the queue, his hands in his pockets. He had curly blonde hair that was greying ever so slightly. How could a killer look so ordinary?

The queue was shortening. The man would get his lemonade soon, wander off and disappear. Annie had to act.

She left the queue and ran to the nearby pub. Her cousin was sitting with a group from Hushinish, listening to the seanchai.

Annie motioned at the group to come outside. There must have been something in her expression, for they got up as one and followed her.

Outside, Annie told them what she had seen.

Their faces turned grim.

Soon after that, the man at the lemonade stand took his drink in hand, turned around and found a silent host awaiting him.

WHAT DID THEY DO? The recorded story doesn't say. Perhaps this was to protect the islanders who meted out justice that day. Perhaps that part of the story is lost, or perhaps it was considered too ugly to speak, and obvious enough.

Whatever happened on the day, the people of Mealista went on living. Widows remarried and children were born; they died young or grew up and had children of their own. Life on Meal-ista went on in all its beauty and hardship.

That is, it went on until the laird ordered everyone off the island to make way for sheep.

That's all there is on Mealista now. Silent, lifeless ruins. And sheep. *

---

* This is another story I learnt from Ian Stephen and which you can find in his *Western Isles Folk Tales*. Another version can be found in *Tales and Traditions of The Lews* by Donald MacDonald. Though the details are hazy, this is believed to be a true story.

The Scottish Clearances by T. M. Devine is a good source for anyone looking to learn more about the Highland Clearances. The story of the Clearances isn't over; Scottish land reformer Andy Wightman, author of *The Poor Had No Lawyers,* has calculated that just 440 people own half of Scotland's private rural land.

THE MAN WITH NO STORY

I t was a dark winter's night in Argyll, and Colla was looking for a place to sleep.

Colla had been born to a farming family in Ayrshire. His father had sent him away to find work, for times were tough and food was scarce. Colla had an uncle up in Mallaig and his father had suggested he head up there. So Colla made his way north on foot, stopping each night in strangers' houses.

Scottish people saw it as their duty in those days to welcome travellers and share what they had with them, so the going had been easy enough for Colla, despite blisters and rainy days. But then, one night, Colla's luck ran out.

He had arrived at a strangely quiet stretch of road. The cloud cover was thick, only the occasional sliver of moonlight seeping through. Colla hadn't seen a house since late morning, and now night had fallen without a habitation in sight. The road wound between the coast and a range of hills, and Colla would have expected both farmers and fishers to dwell there-abouts. Yet there was no sign of life. So Colla carried on down the road, shivering under his cloak, hoping to spy a light that promised warmth and welcome.

In time, his prayers were answered. Colla saw a pinprick of light up ahead. He quickened his pace and, by a shard of moon-light, saw that the light came from a house standing on a river-bank beside a ford. Light shone through every window and, as he drew closer, Colla heard the sounds of laughter and conver-sation coming from inside. He let out a deep sigh of relief.

Colla approached the house and knocked on the door. Silence fell and a moment later, an old man opened the door. He had sparkling blue eyes and long, white hair tied back in a horse tail.

'Good evening,' said Colla.

'If it's good out there, it's better in here,' said the old man. 'You look half-frozen. Come inside and we'll get some food in you.'

Colla followed the old man into the main room of the house. A long, narrow fire pit burned in its centre and folk of all ages sat around the fire on benches strewn with rushes. Chil-dren dozed in their parents' arms.

'Everybody,' said the old man, 'this is...?'

'...Colla.'

'...Colla,' resumed the old man. 'He's here to stay the night and to join our ceilidh.'

The company greeted Colla warmly and made room for him to sit. He squeezed onto a bench and gratefully accepted a bowl of broth and cup of ale.

'Now, where were we?' said the old man. 'Ah, yes. Ruaraidh was going to sing us a song.'

A young man sitting opposite Colla cleared his throat and began to sing. It was a saucy ballad which had Colla near choking with laughter as he tried to eat his broth. After that, the woman beside Ruaraidh embarked on an epic tale about a prince whose shirt turned into a snake. Colla's broth turned cold in his hands as he listened, each story unfurling before his eyes as if he were asleep and dreaming. There had never been any ceilidhs at home; his father insisted that old ballads and stories were naught but pagan nonsense. Finally Colla was experiencing his first ceilidh, and it was the most wondrous night of his life.

Deeper and deeper into the night they travelled. Colla's cup was filled again and again without him noticing; he was too busy slaying stoor worms, dancing with wolf women and wandering dark forests with the Fianna. He hoped it would never end.

'And true to tell, that's where music comes from,' said the woman sitting next to Colla, concluding her story. There was some conversation, some refilling of drinks, then the old man said, 'Well, Colla, it's time you gave us a story.'

Colla laughed. 'Oh, no, I don't know any stories.'

The company gave a playful jeer, as if this was all part of a game.

'Ach, come on now, give us a story,' said the old man with a smile.

'No, I can't,' said Colla, shaking his head. 'I honestly don't know any stories.'

Nobody was smiling now. They looked at Colla with confusion on their faces.

'Alright, I can see you enjoy your dramatics,' said their host with an uneasy laugh. 'You like to tease your audience, eh? Good man. But the night's getting on, so let's have it. Let's have your story.'

'I'm sorry,' said Colla, 'but I really mean it. I don't know any stories, so I can't tell you one.'

A long silence followed this. It seemed to Colla that the room had suddenly grown cold.

The company shuffled in their seats. Nobody would meet his eye. He looked imploringly at the old man, who was regarding Colla as if he had turned into a giant beetle.

The old man shook himself. 'Well,' he said loudly, clapping his hands together. 'Not to worry, not to worry. Heather will tell us a tale, and we all love a tale from Heather, don't we? Something warm and bright, eh?'

The company recovered themselves. They cheered for Heather, who was the woman sitting on Colla's left. As she took a long gulp of ale, the old man leaned over to Colla and said, 'We're short of water, Colla. Take that bucket there and fill it from the stream. You can do that, can't you, lad?'

Colla nodded and gave the old man a thin smile. He picked up the bucket and went out into the night, his face glowing like a hot coal.

The dark clouds of evening had passed. A pelt of stars blazed in the sky. Colla walked by their light to the river, grieving that such a wondrous night had gone so sour. It wasn't his fault he didn't know any stories! Well, perhaps he remembered a couple of wee ones that his mother had told him. But the other ceilidh-goers had told their tales so masterfully; how could he compare to them? And what if he had forgotten a bit? What if folk found him boring?

Anyway. It was done now. He could fetch water, at least.

Colla reached the river. A little rowing boat was tied up there beside a tiny pier. He stepped out onto the pier, which creaked under his weight. It was slippery; he would have to watch his footing...

Too late.

Colla slipped. The bucket fell from his hands as he came crashing down... but not onto the pier. He fell into the little boat, his head hitting the hard wood of its frame.

The force of his weight carried the craft forward. Colla could have sworn it had been tied fast, but evidently not. It drifted out into the river, caught the current and was now bearing Colla downstream.

Colla felt all this but could not see it; he was lying prone on the keel of the boat. He came from a fishing family, so wasn't too worried.

'I'll give my head a few minutes to clear,' he said to himself as the stars danced above, 'then I'll row myself to shore.'

Eventually his head cleared enough for him to sit up. When he did so, he got a shock.

Colla had been carried out to sea. He couldn't see in which direction the land lay, and there were no oars in the boat.

This wasn't good.

What to do? It seemed all he could do was to sit tight,

praying for morning to come or for the current to carry him ashore.

Hours passed before Colla's second prayer was answered. Having fallen asleep, he was jolted awake by the grinding of keel against stone.

Colla had come ashore on a pebble beach. He whooped for joy as he hopped out onto the pebbles, dragging his boat behind him. He dragged it as far ashore as he could then left it, climbing atop a high bank of sand dunes.

From the top of the dunes, in the dim light before dawn, Colla looked out onto a land he had never seen before.

A range of mountains lay in the distance. Between the shore and the mountains lay a landscape of rolling, low hills dotted with patches of forest. The sea must have carried him north. Perhaps Mallaig was not so far away now?

Wherever he was, Colla knew one thing: he needed to get warm. He was shivering hard, dripping wet, his teeth knocking together. The only thing to do was to head inland and hope he came to a house soon.

Colla climbed down the far side of the dunes. He made his way inland through narrow, marshy glens studded with gnarled hawthorns. He passed a fox on its way home from the hunt and disturbed a heron at its fishing.

Not so far inland, Colla spied a house ahead of him.

It sat beside a woodland at the bottom of a glen. A few little fields and a vegetable patch were laid out before it, and a light shone in the window.

Colla ran down the hill. He slipped and fell, picked himself up and stumbled onwards until he arrived at the door. He knocked hard.

The door was opened by a young man, perhaps four or five years older than Colla, with long, dark curls and hazel eyes.

'I'm l-l-lost,' said Colla, struggling to speak through his chattering teeth. His voice sounded strangely high-pitched; perhaps an effect of the cold. 'Please, help me, I'm soaking wet and I've been at sea all night...'

'It's okay, dear, it's okay,' said the man. His accent was strange. 'Come away in, you must be frozen. Let's get you warm and dry.'

The man spoke to Colla as if he were soothing a little lamb. That was odd. But there was true kindness in his voice and eyes. Colla let the man guide him inside and into a cosy chair by the fire. Oh, the room felt so warm!

'Now, we'll get the kettle on for you, eh? I'm just after getting my fishing gear together, but I'll give the fishing a miss today, I think. We'll stay here and fill you with hot food and drink until you're warm to your bones.'

'Aye,' said Colla. 'Thank you. Thank you so much. I can't think of anything I want more than to be warm and dry. I'd better start by getting these wet clothes off.' He stood up and began to pull off his jersey.

The man's eyes bulged. 'Erm... I... maybe I could give you some privacy?' he said, turning away.

'Ach, it's no bother, I don't want to soak more of your house than I already have. Could I borrow some clothes from you, if it's not too much bother?'

The man still had his back turned. 'Well... of course, but... I'm not sure I have anything appropriate.'

Colla began unbuttoning his shirt. 'What do you mean? I'm not fussy...'

His fingers froze.

Colla looked down.

His chest had taken a curvaceous new shape.

Colla reached for his chin. He was as beardless as a bairn.

No. By all the gods, no.

With a trembling hand, he poked at his trousers.

'No!' screamed Colla.

His host's head whipped round. His jaw fell open and he turned away again.

'Sorry! I didn't mean to look, you just startled me...'

'It's not you! It's... it's me. I'm... I don't think I'm feeling quite right. I must have hit my head harder than I thought. Maybe I need a wee sleep, and I'll feel better afterwards.'

'Right. Well, you take my bed. I'll get on with a few things. Sleep as long as you like.'

With lots of apologies and looking the other way, they managed to get Colla into some new clothes. The man showed Colla to his bed. 'Sleep well... what should I call you?'

My name's Co... Col...' Colla sighed. 'My name's... Kirsty.'

'Goodnight then, Kirsty. Or good day. I'm Padraig. I'll see you when you wake up.'

'If that ever happens,' said Kirsty as her eyes closed.

It was evening when Kirsty awoke. Padraig was singing softly as he cooked a stew for their supper.

They sat down to eat. Kirsty ate ravenously, Padraig giving her a second and third helping. 'I made plenty,' he said.

'Thank you,' said Kirsty after they had finished.

'You can thank me by telling me how you ended up here.'

So they moved from the table to the fireplace. Padraig filled two small cups with whisky and Kirsty told her tale. When she got to the part where she went from being Colla to Kirsty, she hesitated. Padraig might think her mad. But she couldn't bring herself to lie to him, and somehow she sensed that he would believe her. So she told the truth.

'Well, I never heard a story like that,' said Padraig after she'd finished. 'And folk tell many a strange story round here.'

'Where is here?'

'Ireland, Kirsty. You're on the east coast of Ireland, beneath the Mountains of Mourne. It's a long way from Scotland, but at the same time it's not so far.' He shifted and poured some more whisky into their cups. 'And I suppose that now you're rested, you'll want to go back?'

'I suppose so,' said Kirsty.

'That's a shame. I'm on my own here, and there's far more needing done each day than I can manage.'

Kirsty looked up from her food. Padraig looked away as she did so, studying the contents of his cup, and she noticed his face had turned red. Surely he wasn't thinking...

'It's a lovely home you have,' said Kirsty. 'I'd be happy to stay. But I need to get back to Scotland. Not that I have a home there. But still. I mean, my family will want to see me again... at some point...'

'Of course, of course,' said Padraig. 'I was just thinking out loud. Sorry. Anyway...' He swallowed his whisky and got to his feet, '...I'll get this cleared away.'

Padraig saw to their dishes, then banked up the fire. He sat down again, but the conversation didn't come so easily after that. Soon Kirsty excused herself, pleading exhaustion. Padraig insisted she take his bed again, and he slept by the fire.

In the morning, he brought her some nettle tea and asked, 'Will you be leaving today then?'

Kirsty hesitated. 'Maybe I'll just stay one more night? Help you out with a few things, as thanks?'

Padraig grinned. 'I'd like that.'

So that day Kirsty tended the crops while Padraig went fishing. He came home to find she'd cooked a delicious supper for them both. The talk was easy that evening, and Kirsty found herself enrapt as Padraig told her tales of an Irish warrior so fierce that he fought an entire army single-handedly.

In the morning, Padraig said, 'Will you be going today then?'

'Well... I suppose I should.'

'It's just that I went and had a look at your boat yesterday. She's seen a bit of damage. Might be worth doing a bit of work on her before taking her out to sea again. I like working on boats, I'd be happy to do it.'

'Oh, well, if you think so.'

That meant another week at Padraig's house for Kirsty.

When the work on the boat was done, Padraig took Kirsty down the shore to look at it.

'I'd say she's seaworthy again. I can round up a few lads to row you over. You could leave today.'

'Thank you, Padraig.'

'So will you be going today?'

'No,' said Kirsty. 'I won't.'

She took Padraig in her arms and kissed him.

KIRSTY REMAINED in Ireland with Padraig. They married as soon as they could and for the first time in her life, Kirsty felt like she belonged somewhere. She'd never been the hardest of workers in the house where she grew up, but having her own home and her own husband changed her outlook. She took delight in seeing that her fields, her house and everything in them were well-tended. Padraig was kind, sweet and a tireless worker, so neither her belly nor heart ever went empty.

A few months after marrying, Kirsty began to feel sick in the mornings. A herb-wife came to look at her and told her she was with child.

Kirsty had never seen a childbirth, but she'd heard stories. They frightened her. What if she wasn't wholly a woman? What if her mind wasn't up to it? She'd heard women back in Scotland laugh at men when they complained of pain, saying that no man would ever know real pain; that was only found on the birthing bed. What would she learn about herself come that hour?

There were no answers to those questions. She simply had to bear them.

The day itself came in early winter. Kirsty's water broke; Padraig dashed away to fetch the midwife. Soon Kirsty was surrounded by women who held her down, mopped her brow and sang secret songs which somehow soothed her pain. But only for a while. At other times she was pulled into a pit of torment; the walls themselves were made of her screams. But at the end of it all, a blood-wet baby was put in her hands.

They called the boy Angus. After Angus came a girl, then two more boys. By this time, ten years had passed. Kirsty had almost forgotten that she had once been Colla. That life was a dream to her, and one she recalled only rarely.

Though things were peaceful in Padraig and Kirsty's house, a shadow had fallen over Ireland in those days. Raiders from over the sea harried the coast: savage Northmen who worshipped strange gods, fought like demons and thirsted for blood and plunder. Tales of their travesties circulated, at first a trickle but soon a flood. Few people living by the coast in those days failed to search the horizon, dreading the sight of dragon-prowed ships.

Years passed by. No raiders came to their stretch of coast-line. Padraig and Kirsty trusted in their gods to keep them safe.

But at last, the Vikings came.

Padraig was out hunting. Kirsty had been glad to see the back of him. They'd taken on a maid a few weeks back, a handsome young girl. Kirsty had seen the way Padraig looked at her and the way she looked back at him. Harsh words had passed between them the previous night, and he'd gone out in silence that morning. Kirsty worked outside all morning, avoiding the girl. She wanted to get rid of her, but wasn't ready to do it yet.

Could she blame him for looking? A voice in her mind said it was only natural he should look. She was not the woman she once was; seven births and two lost children had made sure of that. But she was his wife! And he was not some dog in heat. Could she not expect more of him than...

The ringing of horns shattered her thoughts.

The children. She had sent them to the market. That was good; the market lay inland.

Heart hammering, she ran up the hill beside the house and looked out towards the sea.

Longships had docked in the harbour a few miles south. Smoke rose from a nearby village.

Kirsty found she could not move; she could only stare at the dreaded sight. Then the sound of footsteps brought her to her senses. Footsteps and shouting coming towards her from behind, fast.

It was Padraig. He sprinted up the hill until he reached her, then took in the scene. 'Northmen,' he gasped. 'Where are the children?'

'I sent them to the market,' she stammered. The nearest market lay three miles inland; the children were safe for now, at least.

But Kirsty and Padraig weren't.

Savage cries broke the quiet. Kirsty turned and saw that a band of men had crested the nearest hill. Armed to the teeth with axes and swords, they had seen Kirsty and Padraig, and were coming for them.

'Run! Run!' Padraig shouted.

Kirsty ran. She was at the bottom of the hill before she realised that Padraig hadn't followed her.

He stood alone on the brow of the hill, arrow notched, aiming at the Northmen.

'No! Padraig!'

Kirsty turned and began climbing back up the hill. She was out of breath, and went slowly.

The Northmen reached Padraig. He dropped his bow and reached for his belt knife. Before he could unsheathe it, an axe cleaved his chest and brought him down.

Kirsty collapsed. She had to get up. She had to run. But her legs would not obey her. Padraig must have shot some of the Northmen down; there were only three left.

They saw her, cheered and ran down the hill towards her.

Kirsty scrambled to her feet. Into the woods? They would follow her. Better to fight. Better to die fighting her husband's murderers than flee like a coward. She needed a weapon.

Kirsty ran inside. A pot of water was boiling over the fire. She lifted it from the hook and went to wait behind the door.

The Northmen entered the house. Kirsty roared and hurled the pot, soaking them in scalding water. Two of them fell screaming to the ground, but one remained; the others had stood between him and the water and only a little had touched him. He growled and came for her.

She backed away, falling to the ground. The Viking man laughed. His clothing was already stained with blood. 'They skin you alive for that,' he said in broken Gaelic. 'I have my fun now, before you are spoiled.'

The man got to his knees, pushing Kirsty's frantically kicking legs aside, and reached for her throat. Her hands scrambled for a weapon and alighted on the poker.

As her attacker bent down close, she swung it at his head. His skull cracked and he fell on top of her, unconscious.

The other Northmen were coming to their senses. Kirsty wriggled free and made for the door, avoiding hands that reached out to grab her. She ran, not looking back, and made it to the beach.

There was her boat.

She dragged it to the water's edge, pushed out and climbed in, grabbing the oars. It was years since there had been rowing strength in her arms, but she somehow made it out onto the open sea before collapsing in the keel.

Grief took her, pulling her into a pit where she could see no way out. From there she slipped into sleep.

WHEN KIRSTY AWOKE, it was to find that her boat had run aground. She climbed out, hoping that she had come far enough to be safe from the Vikings. Memories of the attack assailed her, but she pushed them away as best she could. The children. She had to find out where she was, and then find her children.

She climbed out the boat and heaved it ashore. It was night time, but there was light enough to see.

'Best to head inland,' she said to herself. 'They never go too far inshore, people say.' So she headed inland, up the bank of a river that looked strangely familiar.

Very soon she came to a house. Light shone through the windows and the sound of laughter came from within.

Kirsty stopped and stared.

She knew that house.

Very slowly she cast her eyes downwards.

She patted her chest with hairy hands.

She patted her skirts.

She was a man again.

Kirsty, or Colla, walked up to the house and opened the door.

Inside sat the snowy-haired old man and his guests. There was Ruaraidh who had sung the bawdy song; there was the woman who had told the snake-shirt story. Heather looked up at Colla and nodded. There was an empty space next to her; the space where Colla had sat before he went out to fetch water.

The old man grinned at Colla, a mischievous glint sparking in his eyes. 'Well, Colla,' he said, 'you have a story to tell now!'*

---

* This is a story which historian Dr Michael Newton claims is unique to Gaelic culture, with variants existing across Scotland and Ireland. In some versions of this story, the man with no story goes through a series of bizarre adventures after leaving the ceilidh house. In others, he accidentally sails to a strange land where he lives a more ordinary life, but as a woman. I found the gender swap variant more exciting to retell.

You can listen to a very interesting discussion of this story with Dr Newton on the Knotwork Storytelling Podcast.

THE BLUE MEN OF THE MINCH

On the island of Skye, in the glen of Sligachan, there once lived a young man named Finlay. His family were farmers but he cared nothing for farming; his heart belonged to the sea. As a boy Finlay had played at being a fisherman casting his lines, a captain navigating a storm or a whale gliding through the ocean's deepest depths. As he grew older, he took to spending all his spare time sitting or walking by the shore. He watched the fishermen go by on their boats and yearned to be one of them.

When he reached the age of fourteen, Finlay said to his parents, 'I don't want to be a farmer. Now that I'm old enough, I'd like to look for work on a boat.'

'That's for the best, son,' said Finlay's father. 'It's time you made your own way in the world. Take yourself to Portree and find work there.'

Finlay's mother baked him a bannock and gave him the few

coins she could spare. She hugged him fiercely, knowing it would likely be a long time before she saw him again.

After saying his goodbyes, Finlay set off. It was mid-morning and the spring sun soared through a perfect blue sky. Finlay couldn't stop smiling. At last, his dreams were coming true!

Finlay took the coast road along Loch Sligachan. He passed Achnahanaid then took the overland road through Camastianavaig. The road wound its way back to a point on the shore where Finlay could stand and look out over Portree Harbour.

Finlay had visited Portree just a few precious times. He knew of nowhere else so wondrous. Brightly painted buildings covered the steep slopes leading down to the harbour where scores of ships lined the docks, sailors scurrying between them.

One of those ships would be Finlay's ship. It would carry him away from Skye and into a life of adventure.

Finlay kept on walking until he reached Portree. He made his way to the harbour and looked around. Thick-muscled men hauled nets full of fish or strode by bearing heavy wooden crates. Further down the pier, an army of fishwives sang songs as they gutted fish and packed them into barrels.

How exactly was he going to find work?

Finlay spotted a person who didn't look busy. A brown-bearded man was leaning against a stack of crates while filling his pipe with tobacco. He had the wind-scoured skin and far-seeing gaze of one long wedded to the sea.

Finlay approached him and said, 'Good morning. My name's Finlay and I'm looking for work on a boat. Do you know of any captains who're hiring?'

'I might do,' said the man, putting away his tobacco pouch and striking a match. He lit his pipe and said, 'But you've never been to sea before, have you?'

'I haven't. But I'm hardworking and I'll do any job that's asked of me.'

'I hope so, because if not you'll be booted off board, whether there's land in sight or not. Come with me.'

The man turned away and walked north along the harbour. Finlay eagerly followed.

'What's the name of your ship?' Finlay asked.

'*The Crescent Wind*, based out of Stornoway on Lewis.'

'What's the captain's name?'

'Anndra Morrison.'

'What's your name?'

'Innes Robertson. There she is.'

Innes pointed towards a ship that outshone every other; she nearly outshone the sun itself. Her sails were as white as a gannet's wing and the wood of her hull could have been cut that morning. On her deck stood a white-bearded man wearing a black captain's hat. Captain Anndra Morrison.

Innes led Finlay onboard and introduced him to the captain.

'Finlay here is looking for work,' said Innes. 'First time at sea and willing to work hard.'

'If that's true, you're welcome aboard. We're in need of a new hand. Take an oar with Innes and do as he tells you. We sail on the hour.'

They took a bench. Men returned to the ship in twos and threes until the ship was full. On the noon bell, they set sail.

'Are you nervous, lad?' asked Innes as they rowed out of the harbour, the fishermen calling greetings to men on other boats.

'No. Well, a little.'

'You'd be daft if you weren't. There's nothing in this world that can compare to the open ocean, but that's not to say you can trust her. She's a harsh mistress, and I've lost many a friend to her. But you've less to fear than most, for Captain Morrison is no fool. He knows the sea better than most men know their wives, and composes verses quicker than any captain I've known.'

'Why would a captain need to compose verse?' asked Finlay.

Innes gave Finlay a strange look. 'Hopefully you'll never find out. But that's enough talk for now.'

They continued rowing until the clamour of Portree faded behind them and was replaced by the sounds of the sea. The fishermen joked and the captain called orders as waves splashed against the hull. Gulls and cormorants swooped by while brown-eyed seals surfaced to peer at the men before disappearing again.

Captain Morrison ordered his men to stow the oars as wind filled the sails. They followed the Skye coastline north up to Rubha Hunish and past it, then turned northwest. Soon Finlay spotted the outline of Harris on the northwestern horizon.

'Those are the Harris hills there,' said Innes. 'An Cliseam is the highest. And see those smaller islands between here and Harris? Those are the Shiants.'

'I've never heard of the Shiants.'

'There's not much to hear of. Just a few teeth of rock amid the Minch. Normally we'd take the shortest route across the

Minch, over to Scalpay, then catch the tide north to Stornoway. But the way the winds are blowing today, we'll have to take a longer passage past the Shiants. Many ships won't go near those islands, whatever way the wind is blowing, but there's nothing to fear with Captain Morrison onboard.'

'Why do ships avoid the Shiants?'

Innes pursed his lips. 'Never mind that,' he said. Finlay pressed him, but the older man fell silent and wouldn't be drawn out.

The Crescent Wind drew closer to the Shiants. Gannets, gulls, guillemots and razorbills circled their craggy peaks. The ship passed the islands before turning northwest and entering the Minch. The Shiants disappeared behind them and Lewis loomed near. Finlay eagerly scanned the horizon, trying to make out every detail he could. The captain had said that *The Crescent Wind* was based out of Stornoway on Lewis, meaning this would be his new home. Perhaps he would explore these cliffs and beaches when *The Crescent Wind* was in harbour.

'I feel like my life began when I got on this ship,' said Finlay.

Innes smiled. 'Savour that feeling, son.'

The afternoon passed peacefully. Finlay continued to stare towards Lewis, his mind roaming this way and that until, sometime towards evening, he spotted movement on the water.

Something was surging through the sea, cresting a wave then disappearing below the surface. He'd seen creatures move that way before.

'Look there, a dolphin!' he said to Innes. 'Or maybe a porpoise.'

He didn't expect a great show of interest from Innes; the

fisherman probably saw dolphins all the time. Yet he turned his head sharply and stared out to sea. So did the men on the oar in front.

'I'm not sure of the difference,' said Finlay. 'I think porpoises are smaller...'

Word passed quickly across the deck. All the men were silent now, craning their necks, shielding their eyes from the sun as they stared in the direction Finlay had pointed. They looked scared.

'Sorry,' said Finlay. 'Is it bad luck to talk about... erm... silver swimmers?'

A man two rows ahead cursed loudly. 'It's them,' he said.

'Stay calm!' called Captain Morrison as the men began to shout their own curses. 'Oars in hands. We stay our course.'

Finlay took up his oar as he searched again for the dolphin, or whatever it was. He spotted it again; it was closer now.

But it wasn't a dolphin. Or a porpoise.

It was a man. A blue-skinned man, slipping in and out of the water as if he were a creature born of the sea. Another followed him, and another.

'More out starboard!' someone shouted. Finlay craned his neck and saw it to be true. More and more appeared until *The Crescent Wind* was surrounded by a great circle of blue men. They swam against the sun, spiralling inwards, and as they drew closer they began to sing. Their deep, throaty voices bellowed out far over the water.

The sea answered. Waves leapt up high; black storm clouds appeared on the horizon and hurtled towards the ship. Thunder rattled Finlay's bones and soon *The Crescent Wind* was at the centre of a tempest. The men rowed furiously as the day turned dark, rain fell in sheets and seawater sloshed over the deck.

Finlay rowed as best he could, grateful for Innes' iron grip on the oar. The blue men went on singing, their song darkening and deepening. Lightning crashed down all around.

'Stay steady!' shouted Anndra Morrison. 'I've sailed through worse than this and so will you. We'll be drinking in Stornoway tonight, and I'm paying.'

Finlay wasn't so sure. He fought not to empty his stomach as the ship lurched from wave to wave. The blue men were very close now, so close that Finlay could look each one in the eye as he passed. Their skin was a deathly blue-grey; their hair was long and thin, their faces aged.

'What are they?' Finlay shouted to Innes over the storm. 'Where do they come from?'

'They're the Blue Men of the Minch, lad. They live in caves at the seabed around the Shiants, and make wrecks of half the ships passing this way. But you just hold steady. Our fate's in the captain's hands now.'

At that moment, a figure emerged from the water before *The Crescent Wind*'s prow. It was another blue man, one larger than the others. He was aged yet broad-backed and muscular, with a proud, regal bearing. The other blue men fell silent and still, watching him. This must be their chief.

The chief held out his hands, turning his palm downwards. The sea immediately around the ship calmed. Rain continued to fall.

'Who is the captain of this ship?' called the chief.

'I am. Captain Anndra Morrison of Lewis,' said the captain, moving forward to stand on the prow.

The chief of the blue men grinned. When next he spoke, he addressed the captain, and he spoke in the rhythms of a bard.

> Man of the black cap, what do you say,
> As your proud ship cleaves the brine?

CAPTAIN MORRISON IMMEDIATELY ANSWERED,

> My speedy ship takes the shortest way,
> And I'll follow you line by line.

SAID THE CHIEF,

> My men are eager, my men are ready,
> To drag you below the waves

SAID THE CAPTAIN,

My ship is strong, my ship is steady,
If it sank it would wreck your caves.

FROWNING, the chief said,

Your wives shall weep and wail tonight,
Knowing you will never return

SAID THE CAPTAIN,

I'll hold my wife in my arms tonight
And kiss her as the hearth fire burns.

SAID THE CHIEF,

Fat fisherman, you stink of fear,
There is no strength in your arms

SAID THE CAPTAIN,

> Climb aboard and test those words,
> I think you'll come to harm.

SAID THE CHIEF,

> You shall pay the price, old man,
> For trespassing on my waters

SAID THE CAPTAIN,

> We've already passed here many times,
> Visiting your daughters.

THE CHIEF'S EYES WIDENED. Finlay feared that the captain had gone too far; the blue men would wreck their boat for sure. Today would be his first and last day as a fisherman.

Then the chief of the blue men broke into a hearty laugh.

He bowed low to Captain Morrison before disappearing below the water, as did all his men.

The clouds dispersed and the sun came out again. The crew of *The Crescent Wind* stowed their oars and unfurled the sail, correcting their course as they continued on their way.

They reached Stornoway soon after that. Captain Morrison bought drinks for all his men, as he had promised.

Finlay was shaken by his encounter with the Blue Men of the Minch. Another man in his position might have decided against a life as a fisherman. Yet Finlay loved the sea too much for that. He knew he had no reason to fear the Minch, thanks to the seamanship and nimble tongue of Captain Anndra Morrison.*

---

* This story is endlessly adaptable. You can make up your own verses for the chief and the captain to recite, or make a game of it with your listeners. Another variation of this story has all of the crew and all of the blue men exchanging riddles rather than rhymes.

The verses which the chief and the captain exchange here are taken from Donald A. Mackenzie's *Wonder Tales from Scottish Myth & Legend*, up to and including the line 'If it sank it would wreck your caves'. The lines that follow are my own compositions. Have fun coming up with a few more yourself.

It is thought that the origin of the legend could lie in blue-robed Moorish traders, who may have passed through the Minch on their way to sell slaves at the Viking slave markets in Dublin.

You can read another tale of the blue men in Ian Stephen's excellent *Western Isles Folk Tales*, which also provides some interesting background information. You can hear Ian Stephen on House of Legends Podcast.

HERDING HARES

Among the rolling hills of the Scottish Borders flows the Happertutie River. A poor widow and her two sons once lived in a cottage on the riverbank, a few miles south of the village of Yarrow, and this is their story.

One day the older brother noticed a beard sprouting from his chin. He went straight to his mother and said, 'I'm a man now, Mother, so it's time I went out into the world.'

'That's true enough, son,' said his mother. 'But don't be on your way just yet. Fetch some water from the burn and I'll make you a bannock for the road.' She handed him a sieve and a cracked bowl. 'Just you mind, more water means a bigger bannock, and there's no telling when and where you'll get another one.'

The boy left the house. It was high summer, the sun bright enough to make him dizzy. The sky was cloudless and the air full of birdsong. He took the path leading to the river and, as he walked, a little brown bird flew down and landed on a nearby branch. Rather than singing the kind of song that little birds usually sing, it sang these words:

> Stop it with fog, and flag it with clay,
> And that'll carry the water away

'AWAY WITH YOU!' said the boy. 'I'm not doing something just because a wee bird tells me to do it. What do wee birds know about anything?'

He reached the river and knelt down to scoop up some water in the sieve and the cracked pot. Of course, the sieve collected no water at all, and the pot collected only a little.

Returning home, he handed the sieve and pot to his mother. She raised her eyebrows and set to work on baking his bannock. A while later, she handed it to him. It was tiny.

'There you are, son. Good luck,' she said with a sad smile.

'Aye, Mum.'

He stuffed the bannock into his pocket and walked out the door.

THE OLDER BROTHER set out into the world, taking one path then another with no destination in mind. He had never been more than a few miles from home.

The sun climbed higher and the day grew hotter. The older brother wandered up into the high hills where nothing stood between him and the sun. His head spinning, he searched for shade and spotted a lone hawthorn. He made his way to it and sat down beneath it, stretching out his weary limbs. A soft breeze tussled the long grass.

'I think I'll have a bite of that bannock,' the older brother said to himself, 'though there's not much to it.'

He took the bannock from his pocket and bit into it. As he did so, the little brown bird he'd met that morning flew down and landed at his feet.

'If you give me a bite of that bannock, I'll give you a feather which you can use to make a whistle,' it said.

'Not you again! It's only a wee bannock and I'm not sharing it with you.'

The bird cocked its head and flew away.

Eventually the older brother got to his feet and continued onwards. Where exactly he went, I don't know, but I can tell you that he found his way to a glen where a castle stood on the bank of a river, surrounded by fields which were in turn surrounded by forest. As castles go, it wasn't a big one, but it was bigger than any castle he had ever seen.

'A castle! Where there's a castle, there's a king, and kings are rich. If I can wangle some work here then I'm sure to be paid handsomely.'

The boy crossed the bridge over the river that led to the castle gates. He rapped on the wood and a few moments later a servant opened the gates.

'Good afternoon. I'm here looking for work, and I'm a hard

worker,' he said, though that wasn't entirely true. 'Do you have any jobs going?'

'You'll need to see the king about that,' said the servant, a bent-backed old man. 'He likes to make every appointment himself. Come inside.'

The serving man led the boy to the throne room where the king was sitting on his throne. Beneath his crown were a pair of piercing eyes which burrowed into the boy as the king looked him over.

'I hear you're looking for work, boy,' said the king. 'What is it you can do?'

'I can sweep floors and scrub dishes. I can mind sheep, goats and cows.'

'Hmmm. And can you herd hares?'

'Erm...'

"I have a flock – or a husk, I should say – of hares. They are of great value to me. I need someone to take them out to their meadow each day, mind them and bring them back in the evening. Can you do that?'

'Well... yes. Yes, Your Majesty. I can herd your hares for you.'

'Very good. You'll start tomorrow. My serving man here will show you to your room.'

'Thank you, Your Majesty,' the boy said with a brief bow.

'Perform your duties well,' said the king, 'and you will marry my daughter and become king one day yourself.'

The older brother's mouth fell open.

'Perform your duties poorly and you'll be hanged.'

The boy's mouth snapped shut. The serving man ushered him out of the throne room and upstairs to a narrow attic room.

'I'm hungry. Is there nothing for my supper?' he asked.

'You've missed supper, and Cook is in bed already. You'll be fed tomorrow,' said the servant before closing the door.

'My mother should have baked me a bigger bannock,' said the boy as he climbed into bed. 'But one thing is certain: I won't go hungry when I'm king.'

MORNING CAME. The older brother climbed out of bed and went downstairs to the dining room.

'There you are!' said the king. He was seated at a wide table, eating a breakfast of eggs and sausages. The sight made the boy's mouth water; he had dreamed of nothing but food all night. 'Your breakfast is over there.'

The boy looked over to where a place had been set for him. He had been given nothing to eat and only a cup of water to drink.

'Drink your water quickly,' said the king as the boy sat down. 'The day is fine and it's time for you to start work. Listen carefully.'

The boy drank his water as the king told him where to find the hares' stable and which path would lead him to their meadow. Then he went outside and found the stable. He opened the door and watched as the husk of hares hopped out, one after another. Once the stable was empty, he led them to a little meadow surrounded by soaring ash trees.

The boy opened the gate and the hares filed in. Once they

were all inside and the gate closed, he lay down on the grass, resting his head on his hand.

The meadow was full of long grass dotted with daisies and buttercups. Dewdrops shone in the morning sunlight.

'I suppose this is me for the day,' said the older brother. The warm sun felt good on his face, and he was glad of the easy work. But it was hard to relax when he was so hungry.

A few hours passed. The boy dozed off for a while and woke up again. He half-watched the hares hopping around the field and nibbling the grass. His stomach felt like a clenched fist. He had to eat something. Could he eat grass? Animals ate it, and it didn't seem to do them any harm...

Then he noticed something he hadn't noticed before.

One of the hares was much smaller than the others. It was scrawny and weak-looking, with a bandy leg which made it hop awkwardly across the meadow.

A dark thought entered the boy's mind.

'They're a fine bunch of hares, this lot,' he said to himself. 'Sleek and bright-furred, as you'd expect of a king's hares. Not that one, though.'

As he said this, the bandy-legged hare turned and looked at him.

'It's weak,' he went on. 'A runt. Small and skinny and scrawny. It's an embarrassment to the rest of them. It's an embarrassment to the king himself.'

The hare's eyes widened. Its ears stood on end.

'The king told me to look after his hares. But that creature is hardly a hare at all.'

He made up his mind.

The boy got to his feet. He casually ambled over to the hare as it stared up at him, its nose twitching. As he drew close, it turned to run, but it couldn't move quickly enough. The older brother dashed forward and easily caught it.

He held the bandy-legged hare up high. It wriggled frantically but couldn't escape. The other hares looked on, their noses twitching, their feet stamping.

He snapped its neck.

THE OLDER BROTHER tossed the bandy-legged hare's body aside. If he was going to eat it, he would need to cook it, which meant making a fire. There were a few sticks scattered across the meadow and plenty underneath the hedge that bordered it. He set to collecting them and soon had enough for a fire.

Once he had built a fire and lit it with his flint and steel, he made a skewer from a twig, then turned to the carcass itself. With his pocket knife he cut it open from neck to navel. Afterwards, he peeled off its skin and removed the offal, discarding both in a stinking pile at the edge of the field.

The remaining hares watched it all.

The bandy-legged hare was now ready for cooking. The boy skewered it and set the skewer over the fire. He was hungrier than ever now, but it was a good feeling because he knew his hunger would soon be satisfied. He savoured the smell of the hare's flesh as it cooked, the meat turning dark and crisp.

Finally, it was ready. The older brother lifted his skewer to his mouth and ate. He savoured every bite, chewing each morsel over and over. He had never enjoyed a meal so much in his life.

Still, the other hares looked on.

After eating, the older brother lay down and fell asleep. When he woke up, it was evening.

'Time to get these hares home,' he said, 'and then see about marrying the princess! Come along, you lot.'

There was a problem, though. The hares refused to go home with him. Every time he came near a hare, it would dart away to the far side of the meadow. He went around and around the meadow like this, his frustration mounting, until finally he gave up.

'There's... no herding this lot,' he panted. 'Maybe the king meant a different husk of hares. Maybe it was a joke. Maybe...'

He looked at his smouldering fire and the bones scattered beside it. The summer evening suddenly felt cold.

Perhaps he shouldn't have eaten the king's hare.

'It'll be fine,' he said to himself. 'I only ate the wee runt, and they never gave me anything else to eat. It's not my fault.'

He left the field and returned to the castle. The servant let him in and escorted him to the throne room.

'Ah, there you are,' said the king with a warm smile. 'Did you find my hares in their stable this morning?'

'Yes, Your Majesty.'

'And did you let them out and lead them to the meadow?'

'Yes, Your Majesty.'

'And you watched them all day?'

'Yes, Your Majesty.'

'Splendid, splendid. And when evening came, you brought them back to the stable and shut them in?'

'I... well... I tried. I had a bit of bother rounding them up, Your Majesty.'

'Ah.'

'I'm sorry.'

The king sighed. He waved his serving man forward.

'Take him outside and stretch his neck,' said the king.

The serving man grabbed the older brother and dragged him outside. He kicked, punched and spat, so the serving man called for help and two guardsmen came running. The three of them pulled him out to a courtyard where a wizened old gallows stood.

They dragged him up the steps and forced his head into a noose. The guards pushed him off then stood back to watch as his skin turned purple, his eyes rolled back and his life ended. Crows ate his eyeballs within the hour.

A YEAR to the day after the older brother left home, the younger brother said to his mother, 'It's time I saw what the world looks like.'

'You'll leave a broken-hearted old woman behind you,' said his mother. 'But that's the way of things. I'm sure you'll do well for yourself, son.' She handed him the sieve and cracked pot. 'Fetch some water and I'll bake you a bannock for the road.'

The boy went down to the river as asked. The sun shone

through the treetops and birds sang among the branches. As he neared the river, a little brown bird flew down and sang to him,

Stop it with fog, and flag it with clay,
And that'll carry the water away

'THANKS,' he said. 'That's good advice, and I'll take good advice from anyone.'

When he reached the burn, he scooped up some mud and used it to seal the pot, and tore handfuls of moss from rocks to seal the sieve. He collected plenty of water, which he brought back to his mother. She made him the biggest bannock he had ever seen.

'Goodbye, Mother,' he said. 'I'll miss you.' He kissed her on the cheek and set off.

The younger brother put one foot before the other without thinking about where he went. Midway through the afternoon, he stopped to take a rest. Amid a grove of twisting beech trees he sat down to eat a bite or two of his bannock. Their swaying leaves made a shimmering curtain of dappled light, and the boy thought it was a fine thing to be out adventuring in the world.

'I've only this one bannock,' he said to himself, 'and I don't know where my next meal will come from. I'll go easy on it.' So he ate only a quarter and contented himself with that.

As he lay there, a little brown bird, which he recognised as the one that had advised him earlier, flew down and landed on the grass beside him.

'Share a bit of your bannock with me,' said the bird, 'and I'll give you a feather which you can use to make a whistle.'

The boy was reluctant to share his bannock given his limited supplies, but he didn't want to be unkind.

'I'll share my meal with you,' he said. 'But I don't know how to play a whistle, and I wouldn't want to hurt you by pulling out one of your feathers.'

'It's not a bother. Go on, pull out a feather.'

The younger brother refused again, but the bird insisted until he eventually took hold of a feather and pulled it out.

'There you go. Now, you'll need to split the shaft in half, cut off the strands at the root then notch holes in the shaft with your knife. Do that and you'll have a whistle to play. Give me that bite and I'll be off.'

The younger brother broke off a chunk of the bannock and tossed it to the bird, which seized the morsel in its beak and flew away. The boy followed the bird's instructions and soon had a whistle in his hands. He played a few notes and thought it didn't sound so bad.

'I'll get better if I keep practising,' he said. 'But I can't sit here all afternoon. Time to be off.'

He pocketed his whistle and set off again. The evening saw him standing outside the castle where his brother had met his end, though of course he didn't know that.

'I shouldn't have any trouble finding work and a bed here,' he said.

He knocked at the gate and soon found himself in front of the king.

'I might have some work for you,' said the king, who was sitting on his throne and sipping a cup of mead. 'What can you do?'

'I'm no great craftsman, or soldier, or man of letters,' said the boy. 'But I can sweep floors, I can mind sheep, goats and hens, and whatever I do, I'll put my back into it.'

'I see.' The king sipped his mead. 'And have you ever herded hares?'

'No, Your Majesty, but I don't see how herding hares can be much different from herding sheep.'

'You might be surprised. Very well. From tomorrow onwards you shall take my hares out to their meadow each day and bring them back safely. You'll be given a bed to sleep in, and, if you do well, you'll marry my daughter.'

'I... I'm sorry, Your Majesty, I think I may have misheard you.'

'If you do well, you'll marry my daughter. The princess.'

'...I see.'

'Good. Disappoint me and you'll swing from a gibbet.'

The king's serving man led the boy out of the throne room and up to his bedroom. It was the same room his brother had stayed in. Like his brother, he wasn't given any supper, but thankfully he had saved most of his bannock. He ate another quarter and went to bed, wondering what the morning would bring.

MORNING CAME. The younger brother went downstairs to find the king awaiting him in the dining room.

'There you are! Your breakfast is ready. Drink up and be about your work.'

The younger brother sat down and drank his cup of water. He rose, bowed to the king and left the castle.

It was another bright and sunny day. The boy followed the instructions the serving man had given him the previous evening. He found the hares' stable, let them out and led them to their meadow. Once they were inside, he closed the gate and leaned against it for a while as he watched them. He noticed that one of the hares had a bandy leg and was smaller than the others.

'I'll need to keep an eye on that one, in case it gets into trouble,' he said.

He sat down amid the buttercups. Since his cup of water hadn't quite filled him up, he ate what was left of his bannock. The hares all kept half an eye on him as he ate. After he was finished, the younger brother lay back to watch the hares and to watch the day pass by.

'This doesn't look to be a hard job,' he said, 'though it might get a little dull. It's honest work, though, so I can't complain. And did the king mean that about marrying his daughter? He was probably sporting with me. Still, I'll do the job as well as I can. You never know.'

He fell quiet and settled into watching the hares. They hopped here and there and nibbled the grass. The bandy-legged one seemed to be getting on fine. The younger brother got the impression that the other hares looked out for it.

The sun rose and the day grew hotter. The few clouds burned away, leaving nothing but a curtain of blue above him.

'I'm getting tired in this heat,' said the younger brother eventually. 'I mustn't fall asleep on the job. How can I keep myself awake?' He remembered the whistle in his pocket. 'That's what I'll do; I'll play my whistle. Hopefully the hares won't mind.'

He sat up, took his whistle from his pocket and began to play. The hares gave him some startled looks, but they soon got used to the whistle. The boy practised playing every note in turn until he could move smoothly between them, then had an idea.

'I could try to play the tune the wee bird sang. Aye, I'll try that.'

It took him a while to figure out the tune, but eventually he had it. And as soon as he played it correctly, something very strange happened.

The hares stopped eating. They stopped hopping about.

As one, the hares turned to look at him.

Then they gathered in around him and began to dance.

Solemn and stately, elegant and graceful, the hares danced in perfect unison. They leaped in great arcs; they wiggled their long ears. As they danced, all the other living beings in the field fell still: the bees, the buzzing insects, the ants and spiders and songbirds.

The boy played the tune again and again. He watched the hares, entranced by their dance. They inspired him to extend and elaborate upon the melody, so that the boy and the hares soon played and danced together in perfect harmony. The bandy-legged hare couldn't manage all the moves, but it never stopped dancing all the same.

Eventually, and with great reluctance, the younger brother put his whistle away. The sun was setting and the shadows lengthening.

'That was incredible. I didn't know hares could dance like that. But it's time you were away to your beds. Come on now.'

He rounded up the hares, who seemed happy to head home. They gave him no trouble. When he approached the bandy-legged hare, he said, 'The walk home might be tiring for you after all that dancing. I'll put you in my coat pocket and carry you home.' Which he did.

The younger brother herded the hares home and into the barn. He took the bandy-legged hare out of his pocket and was about to set it down when he hesitated.

'You're such a wee thing. I'm worried you'll get cold here in the barn tonight.' Making his mind up, he put the hare back in his pocket and returned to the castle. He went upstairs to his room and put the hare in his bed.

There was a knock at the door.

'You're wanted downstairs,' said the serving man. 'The king would like a report on his hares.'

The younger brother followed the serving man to the throne room.

'Did you go to the field, as I asked?' asked the king.

'Yes, Your Majesty.'

'And did you keep a close eye on my hares, all day long?'

'Yes, Your Majesty.'

'And you brought them all back safely?'

'I did, Your Majesty.'

'I would like to take your word for it but I've been disappointed before. Go to the barn and bring the hares here, so I may inspect them myself.'

The boy did as the king ordered and soon the king's hares were hopping all over the throne room. The king gazed at them fondly, then frowned.

'There is one hare missing.'

'Missing? No, Your Majesty, I brought them all back... oh. Yes. Sorry, Your Majesty. There was another hare, a wee bandy-legged one. I was worried it would be cold in the barn so I put it in my bed to keep warm.'

The king gave him a decidedly strange look.

'You put the small, bandy-legged hare in your bed?'

'Er... yes. Sorry.'

'Bring it down here.'

The boy bowed and left. He ran up the stairs to his attic room and opened the door.

A beautiful girl lay sleeping in his bed.

She sighed, turned over and opened her eyes.

'Who... who are you?' asked the boy. 'Where is the wee hare?'

'Do you really need me to explain it to you?'

'Yes.'

'I am the king's daughter,' she said. 'And I am the wee bandy-legged hare.' She yawned and climbed out of bed. 'You certainly did a better job than your brother. He killed and ate my sister. Come along now, it's best not to keep Father waiting.'

THE YOUNGER BROTHER and the princess stood before the king.

'I told you that if you discharged your duties well, you would marry my daughter,' said the king. 'You've got a little ahead of yourself there, but all the same. The work was done well. If my daughter wills it, the two of you will marry. What do you say, daughter?'

The princess ran her eyes over the younger brother, inspecting him like a pig at market. The younger brother realised that he was very much hoping she would say yes.

'I'll think about it,' she said eventually, and turned away from him.

'If I may,' said the younger brother, thinking quickly. He took his whistle from his pocket. 'Perhaps I could play a tune or two while you think.'

Without waiting, he put his whistle to his lips and played the little bird's tune.

At once the hares began to dance.

The doors to the throne room opened. Everyone who lived and worked in the castle crowded in: serving men and women, the farrier and the smith, swineherds and soldiers, cooks and cleaners.

The melody gathered pace and soon they were all dancing.

The hares danced. The people danced. The king got down from his throne and danced. The princess danced with the swineherd; the king danced with the cook's boy; the hares danced with the housekeepers. They danced all through the night to the little brown bird's song.

Morning sunlight streamed in through the windows. The boy set down his whistle and wiped his brow.

Everyone turned to look at the princess.

'He'll do,' she said.

The people clapped and cheered as the hares stamped their feet.

The king was overjoyed. He wanted the wedding to take place there and then, but the younger brother protested. He wouldn't get married without his mother present. So the king let him go to the cottage by the Happertutie River and fetch his mother. When they returned, she was treated with every honour and the ceremony went ahead. It was a splendid affair, with the whole husk of hares and even the little brown bird in attendance. It went on for a month.

The boy's mother was given a cottage close to the castle, where she lived out her days close to her remaining son. In time he became king, and the princess became queen, though some days she would spend as a hare. The new king inherited the old king's hares, and he went to the meadow and played music for them whenever he had time. *

---

* I first heard this story told by Scottish storyteller Dougie Mackay, and later heard it from James Spence, who includes it in his wonderful *Borders Folk Tales*. Somehow it captures for me the atmosphere of hot summer days in the endless green of the Scottish Borders. Some well-known stories from this region are Tam Lin and Thomas the Rhymer.

The story is of a very common tale type in which two siblings, one virtuous and one not-so-virtuous, undertake the same quest, with wildly differing results according to their nature. It may remind you of The Well at World's End from *Scottish Myths & Legends: Volume One*.

SARAH, DAUGHTER OF JOHN, SON OF FINLAY

Sarah was alone in her house. Her father, John, had gone out for a dram, which she didn't mind at all. It was nice to have the house to herself for an evening.

Autumn rain had soaked Sarah as she walked home from market that day, her shadow lengthening before her. After seeing to the cows, she had come inside just as her father was heading out. She banked up the fire and sat before it for a long time, sighing as the cold seeped from her body and steam rose from her clothing.

Sarah's stomach whined as evening turned to night. It was time to start cooking her supper, yet she didn't feel like moving. She loved the peace that rode the dark hours, the tunes the raindrops played on the tiny windows of the blackhouse. Her father was a talker, always blathering about something or nothing, and after falling asleep his talk invariably turned to snoring. Sarah wanted to sit and enjoy her peace for as long as she could. So she did.

Finally, her stomach said enough was enough. So Sarah got up, filled a big two-handled pot with water from the rain barrel and hung it over the fire to boil.

She stood by the fire, watching the pot.

Behind her, she heard the door to the house open.

Sarah turned and saw that a young man had let himself in. He was tall, slim and muscular, with pale skin and sleek, dark curls. Rainwater dripped from his hair and clothes onto the floor.

He closed the door behind him, then turned to stare at her.

'It is time to begin courting, Sarah, Daughter of John, Son of Finlay,' he said.

Sarah didn't like the way he looked at her. She thought for a moment and replied, 'It is time, it is time, when this water boils.'

The young man took a step towards her, past the spinning wheel.

'It is time to begin courting, Sarah, Daughter of John, Son of Finlay,' he said again.

'It is time, it is time, when this water boils,' repeated Sarah.

The young man took another few steps, passing the workbench and the dresser lined with plates and jars.

'It is time to begin courting, Sarah, Daughter of John, Son of Finlay.'

'It is time, it is time, when this water boils.'

Sarah glanced towards the pot. Steam had started to rise from the water's surface.

'It is time to begin courting, Sarah, Daughter of John, Son of Finlay,' said the young man.

He drew closer. She could smell him now. He smelt of salt-water and seaweed. Looking closer, she could see strands of kelp half hidden in his hair. That told her for certain what she already suspected: that this was a kelpie come to her in human form.

'It is time, it is time, when this water boils,' said Sarah. She smiled at him, ever so slightly, holding his gaze. He didn't look away.

The water in the pot bubbled over.

'It is time to begin courting, Sarah, Daughter of John, Son of Finlay,' said the kelpie.

Sarah turned and seized the handles of the pot. With a roar she flung the boiling water over the kelpie's groin.

He ran away screaming and never returned.*

---

* This is one of those extremely short stories I mentioned in the introduction. They tend to be recorded dispassionately, more as events that actually occurred than as entertaining stories, somewhat like news articles today.

I find this one striking, partly because of how it relates to the schoolyard game, What's the Time Mr Wolf, a variant of Blind Man's Buff, which was popular when I was a child. The story was recorded by John Gregorson Campbell in *Superstitions of the Highlands & Islands of Scotland*, which is a great source of kelpie stories. Campbell doesn't say where this story was sourced.

FIONN & THE SEVEN MEN

One glorious evening, Fionn and the Fianna were camped on a hillside on Scotland's west coast. The day's hunt was done. Venison was roasting over fires and the men were lounging in the long grass, talking and laughing or just enjoying the peace of the evening.

Fionn himself was restless, for hunger had its claws in him. He had led the hunt since dawn and hadn't eaten a single morsel all day. The smell of roasting meat was maddening. As their meat roasted, Fionn's son, Ossian, said, 'A ship comes our way at speed.'

Fionn looked, and saw a little boat sailing into the bay beneath them. It was rowed by one man alone. He brought it into the bay, hopped out and ran the boat ashore. Without pausing for breath, he sprinted up the hill and did not stop until he stood, panting, before Fionn and his warriors.

Fionn took his measure. The man was young and strong,

with fiery eyes and broad shoulders. There was a subtle breath of the sidhe about him; clearly he walked the shadowlands between day and dreaming.

'You are Fionn Mac Cumhaill, captain of the warrior band which protects these shores,' he said to Fionn.

'I am,' replied Fionn.

'I have travelled far to find you. Now that I have done so, I lay upon you bonds, bindings and seven fairy fetters that you shall not eat, drink or sleep until you give me aid.'

Without waiting for a reply, he turned and ran back the way he had come. He pushed out his boat and rowed out to sea.

Everyone looked at Fionn.

'I suppose supper will have to wait then,' he said with a sigh.

Fionn stood, wished his men farewell and walked wearily down to the shore. He really was hungry now, and parched too. Yet the man's words had woven themselves about him; he could feel them like an invisible cloak. He would have to help the young man before assuaging his appetite. But how?

He walked north up the shore as dusk scattered its feathers. He walked a mile then another, crossing a headland before arriving at a narrow bay. Here, he saw a group of seven young men crossing the sands towards him. They were well-dressed and well-armed.

Fionn called out a greeting. The men did the same, and stopped before Fionn.

'Well met,' said Fionn. 'I am Fionn Mac Cumhaill, and you have the look of men seeking adventure.'

'That is exactly what we are,' said one.

'You are in luck, for I can provide adventure, but I only take on capable men. What skills do you have?'

We are all capable men,' said the first man. 'I am a carpenter. I could carve a ship from that branch over there with two strokes of my axe.'

'And I am a tracker,' said the second. 'I could track a wildcat through a hundred miles of forest, a hundred years after it passed that way.'

'I am a gripper,' said the third. 'I could hold lightning in my hands and it would not escape.'

'I am a climber,' said the fourth. 'I could climb to the top of an oil-slicked cliff with my hands and feet tied behind my back.'

'I am a thief,' said the fifth. 'I could steal grief from a lover betrayed.'

'I am a listener,' said the sixth. 'If a fish whispers at the bottom of the sea, I hear it.'

'And I am a marksman,' said the last. 'I could shoot the speckles off an egg.'

Fionn was convinced. 'I would be honoured to adventure with you,' he said. 'And perhaps I will get my supper tonight after all.'

He ordered the carpenter to craft them a ship. He did so with two strokes of his axe, just as he had promised. Fionn and the seven men pushed out their ship and soon they sailed towards the sun's last light. The tracker found the young man's trail, and thus their adventure began.

Fɪᴏɴɴ ᴅɪᴅ ɴᴏᴛ ɢᴇᴛ his supper that night. They sailed all through the night and through the next day, heading further and further out to sea. The wind whipped their sails, salt-spray lashed their beards and Fionn grew increasingly irritable.

Finally, they spotted land ahead. They turned towards it, still following the young man's trail, and made out the shape of a tiny, low-lying island. A solitary house stood there, surrounded by storm-scarred pines.

They guided their ship onto the shore and saw the young man awaiting them. He greeted them as they stepped onto the sand.

'You did well to find me,' said the young man.

'You gave me little choice,' said Fionn, whose stomach was growling louder than a bear with a toothache.

'Did I not send seven helpful men your way? Come, food and drink await us inside.'

They followed him up the track to the house. Inside, a fire blazed in the hearth and the table was laden with food and drink. Fionn finally had his supper with the seven men and their host, and he ate and drank more than the rest of them put together.

With Fionn's good mood restored, the talk turned to serious matters.

'Six years ago,' said the young man, 'my wife birthed a boy. She gave birth in our bedroom, and the very moment the child was born, an enormous hand reached out of the fireplace and snatched him from her arms. The same thing happened when she birthed another boy three years later.

'My wife recently grew pregnant for a third time. She is in

our bedroom with the midwife right now, for tonight we expect her to give birth again. I ask for your help, all of you, in saving our child.'

'I am sorry for your suffering,' said Fionn. 'Your sorrows end here. These seven heroes and I shall see your child safe.'

It was time to take rest. Fionn bid the seven men sleep while he took a seat by the fire. Their host went to be with his wife.

Fionn was tired, but he had no intention of sleeping. He lay an iron at his feet, putting one end in the hearth fire. Whenever he felt himself growing drowsy, he gripped the hot iron in his hands.

The night rolled by. Fionn gazed into the flames, listening to the mingled sounds of the surf and the seven men's snores.

In the bedroom, the labour hours began. The young man's wife would cry out for a while, then grow quiet again.

Deepest night arrived like an army of silent ravens. Fionn readied himself.

In the next room, the young man's wife screamed. She screamed louder and louder and then a new voice, an infant's voice, joined her. Yet her screaming only grew louder.

This was no cry of pain; it was a cry of terror.

'Gripper, with me!' shouted Fionn. He leapt up from his chair and ran across the room, leaping over sleeping men as the gripper arose. Fionn burst into the bedroom, the gripper behind him.

The young man and the midwife stood beside the bed. The young man's wife lay in the bed, her sheets bloodied. All three of them were frozen in fear, watching as an enormous hand withdrew towards the fireplace. It clutched a wailing, bloody, baby boy.

The gripper pushed past Fionn. He ran towards the fireplace as the hand retreated into the chimney. Leaping forward, he grabbed hold of the thumb and forefinger, pressing his feet upon either side of the fireplace.

Outside, the giant who had come to steal the child pulled and pulled but could not break free of the gripper's grip. Roaring his frustration, he pulled even harder, using all his strength, thinking nobody able to fit inside such a small house could possibly win a tug of war with him. But he was wrong.

The giant pulled so hard that his hand broke off and crashed down upon the hearth, scattering ash and still clutching the baby.

The gripper fell backwards, the severed hand still in his grasp. The others were about to cheer when the giant reached in with his remaining hand, prised the boy from his severed hand and snatched him away.

A BLACK SPIDER of sorrow settled on the house. Fionn and the seven grim-jawed men set sail by torchlight and moonlight, the tracker following the giant's trail which only he could perceive.

They sailed for a night and a day, rowing with all their strength, not a single song escaping their lips. Evening had come around again when they spied an island ahead. Sheer cliffs of black stone led to a high, narrow peak. Upon that peak sat a high-walled house.

Fionn and the seven men found a tiny harbour and tied up their ship. They climbed narrow, rocky paths to the island's highest point.

The house atop the peak was less a house and more a fortress. It was as tall as a hill and had no doors or windows.

'How are we going to enter this house?' asked Fionn.

'Leave that to me,' said the climber. He shimmied up the smooth walls all the way to the roof, then climbed back down.

'This is what I have seen,' he reported. 'The roof is covered in eel skins. It has but one window. Through that window, I saw the giant sleeping in a bed in an attic room. He sleeps with the baby in his one remaining hand.

'Nearby, two boys are playing shinty with a gold ball and silver sticks. By the fireplace lies an enormous wolfhound, and she is suckling her two pups.'

'Carry me to the roof,' said the thief, 'and I shall steal back the boys.'

'Steal the pups too,' said Fionn.

The thief hopped onto the climber's back. The climber scurried up the wall again and disappeared into the darkness. It wasn't long before they returned with the two boys, whom they handed to their companions before returning for the baby and then finally the two pups.

'Our work here is done,' said Fionn. 'Let's return to the ship and hope we can escape without notice.'

They returned to the ship and set sail. Fionn kept the boys entertained, telling them tales of the Fianna's adventures while holding the baby tightly to his chest. The pups huddled at his feet, shivering as sea spray assailed them. The seven men rowed with all speed as silent stars shone above them.

Morning came. Still the seven men strained at the oars. Suddenly the listener turned his head and frowned.

'The giant has awoken,' he said. 'He has seen that the children are missing. Now he is telling the wolfhound to come after us and get them back.'

'Row faster,' said Fionn.

The men obeyed, but they did so in vain. Soon they spotted the wolfhound racing towards them, fire blazing from her feet as she ran across the surface of the sea.

In moments she was almost upon them. She howled for her pups and the pups howled to her. The seven men looked at Fionn with imploring eyes.

'We will throw one of the pups into the sea,' said Fionn. Grabbing a pup by the scruff of the neck with his free hand, he tossed it overboard. The mother hound darted forward, seized it in her jaws, then turned and raced away. The seven men cheered.

'This isn't over,' said Fionn. 'She'll be back.'

He was right. Very soon the wolfhound was upon them again, having deposited her pup safely at home. Her breath was warm upon them when Fionn seized the other pup and threw it overboard. The mother caught it in her jaws before growling at Fionn and turning for home.

Again, the men cheered. Fionn said, 'It is not yet time to cheer.'

'You're right,' said the listener. 'She has reached home, and the giant is angry with her, and he is coming after us himself now.'

There was nothing for it but to row. Thankfully, the giant was not as fast as his hound. The island where the young man lived was already in sight when they spotted the giant on their trail, striding through the sea. He roared as he spotted them and doubled his pace.

'Fire at him!' called Fionn.

The marksman dropped his oar, set an arrow to his bow, aimed and fired. He struck the giant in the throat but his arrow bounced off.

He fired again and again. He hit the giant on his forehead, his breast, even his eye, yet each arrow bounced off as if it struck iron.

The giant's shadow fell over the ship. He reached out to seize the mast. There was nothing that the carpenter, the tracker, the gripper, the climber, the thief, the listener or the marksman could do.

But Fionn had his Tooth of Wisdom.

Ever since he had tasted the Salmon of Wisdom as a young man, Fionn only had to touch his thumb to his tooth for all knowledge to be revealed to him. He didn't use it too often, for it could take the fun out of adventures. But now he did so, and he knew at once that the giant had a mole on his right palm. It was his only weakness.

'Shoot the mole on his right palm!'

The giant reached for the mast, his palm exposed.

The marksman loosed his arrow and struck the mole.

The giant's eyes rolled back and his body went limp. He fell into the sea and disappeared below the waves.

The seven men cheered. Once their cheering had subsided, Fionn ordered them to turn the ship around and return to the giant's island.

He wanted those pups.

The climber and thief stole the pups from their sleeping mother once more. When that was done, Fionn announced that it was finally time to return to the young man's house. They made their way there without pursuit, and feasted for three days and three nights. Fionn ate and drank his fill but did not talk much; he was busy playing with the pups.

Fionn gave one of the pups to the young man. That pup was the Grey Dog, whom you might meet in other tales. The other pup Fionn kept for himself, and he called her Bran. She ran at his side ever after, and was always his favourite hound.

There are many accounts of how Fionn acquired Bran. In this tale, he took her from the giant's house with the help of the seven men. If you have a hound, may you love them as deeply as Fionn loved Bran.*

---

* The stories of Fionn Mac Cumhaill and the Fianna originated in Ireland and later spread to Scotland, changing as they travelled. They tell of the deeds of Fionn Mac Cumhaill and his warriors, notably his son Ossian and his friend and sometime-enemy, Diarmuid. In Ancient Ireland, groups of young men are thought to have spent summers living wild in the forests as an initiatory practice. These groups were known as Fianna.

This particular story is believed to have originated in Scotland. I sourced it from Norah Montgomery's *The Fantastical Feats of Fionn Mac Cumhaill*, an often-overlooked compilation of Scottish Fianna tales. I like how the characters in this story combine their powers in a way that is reminiscent of modern superhero films.

My book *Finn & The Fianna* brings the Fianna stories together as a continuous cycle. You can hear me read from the opening chapters on episodes 53-57 of House of Legends Podcast.

KEEPING OUT THE SEA MAN

There once lived in Orkney, on the island of South Ronaldsay, an old widower and his daughter. The widower went out fishing every day while his daughter saw to their animals and crops. In the evening they would sit by the fire, mending things that needed mending and making things that needed made. Sometimes they gossiped and told stories as they worked; at other times they sat in companionable silence.

One winter evening, they were working by the fire as usual. The widower rose and went to bed earlier than his daughter, leaving her to her sewing. In the morning, he came through to find her still sitting in her chair, her sewing in her lap. She looked as if she hadn't moved from there all night. Her face was as grey as the ash in the fireplace.

'Is something wrong?' asked the widower.

His daughter nodded. 'Yes,' she said. 'Something's very wrong.'

'What is it?'

'After you went to bed,' she said, 'I sat up a while longer. I finished my sewing and set to work on mending that net you tore last week.'

'And?'

'And... I was sitting there, not really thinking about one thing or another, when a man came in the door and sat in your chair.'

'A man? Who?' asked the widower, for of course he knew everybody on South Ronaldsay and the neighbouring islands.

'I didn't recognise him. He was... strange. I mean, he didn't look unusual; he was just an old man, with a grey beard and a weathered face. But he came in and sat down right there, not moving from your chair and not saying anything, all night long.'

'Had you not barred the door?' asked her father, for they always barred the door against the wind in the evening, and he thought he'd seen her do so last night.

'Aye, I'd barred it. But he came in all the same.'

'And he didn't say a word all night?'

'Not a word. He just sat and stared into the fire, even after it went out.'

'But why didn't you speak to him, ask him who he was?'

'I was frightened! It was so strange, the way he came in despite the door being barred. And there was... there was just something about him. I can't describe it. I wanted to move, I made up my mind to move so many times but I couldn't. It was as if a great weight was pressing down on me. All I could do was sit here, as silent as he was. He only left a short while ago, just before you got up and came through from your bedroom.'

The widower stroked his beard. He'd heard a few stories about men like this. The old stories said that these men came from the sea, just like finfolk and water bulls, and had magical powers. Yet he wasn't one for jumping to fanciful conclusions when there was a perfectly ordinary explanation available.

'You must not have barred the door properly,' he said. 'The man must have been a wanderer. Down on his luck, perhaps. The worse for drink. Get yourself to bed early tonight. I'll stay up, and I'll make sure the door is properly barred.'

AFTER SAYING goodnight to his daughter that evening, the widower walked over to the door. He barred it tightly, giving it a few firm shoves until he was sure it wouldn't budge. That done, he sat down in his usual chair to wait.

Winter nights are long in Orkney. The sun only rises above the horizon for six hours or so at midwinter. The widower knew he might be in for a long vigil. He fed a peat brick to the fire, filled his pipe, struck a match and sat back to wait.

Outside, the wind howled. The night creaked by.

The old widower fell into the trance of the flames.

He heard footsteps behind him.

His head whipped round as an old, grey-bearded man stepped into the firelight and sat down in his daughter's chair.

The widower's heart skittered in his chest as the greybeard

reached into his coat and pulled out a pipe. The door had been firmly barred, yet the man had come in anyway. He was surely a sea man.

'Good evening,' said the widower.

'Good evening,' said the visitor. 'I don't suppose you have a pinch of tobacco to spare?'

'Of course. Let me get you a cog of ale too.'

The widower handed the sea man his pouch and went to fetch two cogs. Soon the pair of them were smoking and drinking together.

'Sounds like a fierce wind outside,' said the widower.

'That it is,' said the sea man.

They talked for a while, their talk roving here and there, until eventually the widower said, 'I've been having a problem with one of my cows.'

'What's the problem?'

'It's a sea bull. He's been coming into the byre at night and having his way with her. It's happened so many times now, she'll be ruined if it goes on much longer.'

'Ach, that's nothing at all to fix,' said the sea man. 'Here's what you need to do. Cut your cow's tail and keep hold of the hair. Pare back her hooves. Take the parings from her hooves and the hair from her tail, put them in a pouch and hang the pouch over the byre door. The sea bull won't trouble you again.'

'Thank you. That's very helpful.'

They havered on through the night until finally the sea man took his leave. Not long afterwards, the widower's daughter awoke and emerged from her bedroom.

'Was he here?'

'Yes.'

Her lip began to tremble. 'What are we going to do then?'

'Exactly what he told us.'

THAT EVENING, the widower took scissors to his daughter's hair. After he had cut off a lock, she cut her toenails and fingernails and gave him the clippings.

He put the lock of hair and the clippings in a pouch, then hung the pouch over the door.

They sat down to wait.

Soon enough, they heard a creak as someone pushed on the door from outside. Yet the bar held, and the door didn't open.

'Well, how about that,' they heard the sea man say. 'There's many a man done himself in with his tongue, and I'm one of them.'

That was the last they heard from the sea man. *

---

* This is another snapshot story, which I first heard from my storytelling student Eileen Balfour. It's a fantastic example of how folk magic which has been mostly forgotten can survive, hiding in plain sight, in stories.

SAWNEY BEAN

Scottish legends are not for the squeamish. Especially this one.

In the market town of Haddington, in East Lothian, there once lived a man named John Bean. His son was Alexander Bean, or, as folk tended to call him, Sawney Bean.

Sawney's mother had died in childbirth, leaving John to raise their son alone. You might imagine that John tried to honour his late wife by raising Sawney as best as he could. But you'd be wrong.

John gave his life and his love to whisky. He spent every spare coin and every spare minute in the tavern. He was a ditch-digger, with few coins to spare, so he took to begging his fellow patrons to buy him drinks, and was soon barred from every tavern in the town. He drank in the street instead, or at home. Filling his cup at the kitchen table, John Bean would harangue his son.

'It's your fault we've come to this,' he would say. 'Your mother would be alive if it weren't for you. Some deal I got, your mother for you. The Devil was in Haddington the day you were born.'

The one thing John liked about his son was putting him to work. John ordered his son out each day to earn money however he could, and had him cook every meal the two of them ate. This wasn't so unusual. Like other boys, Sawney could earn a handful of pennies each day by running messages, minding animals or tending fields. Only he didn't.

If Sawney was paid to mind animals, he would wander off and leave them untended. If a shopkeeper gave him a penny to deliver a message, he would buy a pie and forget the message. He simply had no inclination for work. If that meant going hungry, he went hungry. If it led to a beating, he would take the beating. Rather than work to improve his lot, Sawney did his best to forget the world and everyone in it.

Sawney grew older. By the time he was fifteen, he was past the age of carrying messages; he should have been learning the foundations of a trade or else digging ditches alongside his father. Yet Sawney still would not work. He inherited his father's height but was lean and scrawny, with a pale complexion and empty gaze.

No work meant no food. John Bean rarely came home now; he would sleep in the street or wherever he passed out. Sawney had to feed himself. He found he could fight hunger for a while, but it always beat him in the end. So he took to thieving.

Sawney had always had light fingers. As a boy he had stolen from market stalls and farmers' fields. Now he took to thievery as his sole occupation. The problem was, he was no good at it, and too big to disappear into a crowd as he once could. There eventually came a day when Sawney could not steal or scavenge a thing to eat in his home town. The moment he set foot in the market, word went out among the traders, who threatened him with violence should he stay.

So Sawney left town.

SAWNEY TOOK the western road out of Haddington. He had no real plan, other than to go somewhere he was not known and start afresh.

It was easy enough to steal from farmers' fields. But where would he sleep? How would he cook what he lifted? Out here in the open countryside there were no alleys to shelter or hide in. Would he starve or would he freeze to death first? It was summer, heading towards autumn. That meant harvest time was approaching, but after that would come winter.

Sawney kept on walking as the day darkened. He followed the road as it turned south towards Gifford and the Lammermuir Hills beyond. His belly was aching, yet food was everywhere; the landscape was a patchwork quilt of fields. Uncooked potatoes wouldn't keep him alive but maybe he could find some cabbages or carrots. He had no way to start a fire, but maybe he could eat them raw...

The road passed by a woodland. Mighty elms and oaks cast long evening shadows. Maybe Sawney could sleep among the trees tonight. He could choose a camping spot, gather wood then use the last of the light to go out and find something to cook.

Sawney climbed the fence and entered the woodland. He made his way beneath the trees, wondering if he would be caught and accused of poaching. He would happily be a poacher, if only he knew how.

Sawney moved deeper into the dusky green. It filled him with a strange feeling; a sense of safety. Nobody could find him here. He might be cold tonight, he might go hungry, but nobody would beat him.

Sawney walked and walked until he spied firelight up ahead.

He halted. Who could this be? A poacher? Or perhaps a traveller, some vagabond who couldn't afford an inn? Poachers were tough nuts, folk said. Canny. But they surely slept like everyone else. If anyone was sure to have meat, it was a poacher... and if it was a traveller, well, maybe they would be willing to share what they had. If not, well... he would see. Sawney had never been one for direct confrontation. But maybe times had to change.

For Sawney could sense that today was a new beginning in his life. Wherever he went tomorrow, he'd never go back to Haddington. He wouldn't see John Bean again. Today was a day of possibilities. A new life. A new Sawney.

He crept forward. Or he tried to, anyway. There was a dry twig everywhere he stepped, and every snap was as loud as a church bell ringing.

'I hope you're better at fighting than you are at sneaking,' said a voice from up ahead.

It was a female voice.

Sawney sighed with relief. He had nothing to fear from a woman... did he?

He stepped into the firelight, hands in the air.

Sitting by her fire, roasting meat on a skewer, was a woman perhaps ten years older than he was. Her face bore the lines of hard living, and her weasel-like eyes were fierce as they sized him up.

'I wasn't sneaking,' said Sawney. 'Just coming to say hello. And maybe to share the warmth of your fire.' What kind of woman, he wondered, camped out in the forest?

'You don't look like a poacher,' she said. 'And you certainly don't move like one. Heard you coming a mile off. And I can see you don't live on the road. Too soft. So what brings you out here?'

'Got caught stealing too many times.'

'Why don't you get a job then?'

Sawney shrugged his shoulders.

The woman was quiet for a time as she looked him over.

'Sit down,' she said eventually.

Sawney sat. She picked up a water skin and tossed it to him. 'Drink,' she said. 'The woods are cold at night, even on a summer evening.'

Sawney uncorked the skin, which was full of cheap-tasting whisky. He drank gratefully.

'Meat'll be ready soon. You're welcome to some.'

'Thank you.'

'I'm Agnes. Agnes Douglas.'

'Sawney Bean.'

They sat quietly for a while. When the meat was cooked, Agnes tore off a chunk and passed it to Sawney, who gulped it down.

'No home,' she said. 'No work. No coin either, I'm guessing. So let me ask you, Sawney, how do you plan to survive?'

'Don't know.'

'Stealing?'

'...Maybe. I've got to eat, haven't I?'

'Course you do. And nothing wrong with stealing, the way I see it.'

'How's that?'

'Is it wrong for the fox to hunt the rabbit? Should cats go to jail for catching mice? The strong prey on the weak. It's the way of nature.

'Me, I could earn a pittance as a scullery maid or a tavern wench. Groped by drunkards, sleeping in some stinking little room, one afternoon off each fortnight if I'm lucky. That's how I would live if I was weak. But I'm not. I go where I want, I take what I want and I answer to no one.'

'Well... I suppose that makes sense.' It truly did. Sawney felt as if Agnes had placed a second sun in the sky, so that for the first time he could see the world as it really was.

'Only problem is,' Agnes continued, 'I'm a woman. Most men forget that when I wave a knife under their eyes, but not all of them. If I was a man, or I had a man with me, I could put the fear on folk easier. Less chance of violence; better for every-one. Do you see where I'm going with this, Sawney?'

'Aye,' said Sawney with a grin. 'I see where you're going. I like where you're going.'

Sawney and Agnes drank late into the night. They talked, they laughed, and when it was time to go to sleep, Sawney lay down close beside Agnes.

'For warmth,' he said under her hard stare.

'You warm yourself, Sawney Bean,' she said, and kicked him away.

THE VERY NEXT DAY, WITH AGNES' guidance, Sawney committed his first robbery. They stopped an old man who was walking from Gifford to Haddington. A dark patch spread across the man's trousers as Sawney waved Agnes' knife under his nose. He gave them everything he had.

They rushed off into the forest. Sawney was elated. 'It was so easy. Did you see how frightened he was?'

'Aye,' said Agnes. 'How do you feel now, Sawney? Did it make you feel strong? Powerful?'

'Aye,' said Sawney with a grin. 'Maybe we should celebrate.' He stepped towards Agnes.

'You'll celebrate by buying your own knife,' said Agnes, taking hers from Sawney. 'That's the last time you use mine.' She put it in the sheath and patted it absent-mindedly, as if she had missed it while it was gone.

'So what do we do now?'

'We're getting away from here. Up towards the hills, the opposite way that mark was heading. Never linger after a robbery; a mark will tell the first person he meets what happened, and they will tell the next person they meet, until everyone for miles knows what happened, and what the robbers looked like. We can stop in the next village to spend his coin, then on we go.'

That was how it went. They bought food, drink and an unremarkable kitchen knife in Gifford before heading on, making camp that night in a high, cold glen in the Lammermuirs. They made their fire and, after they had eaten, Agnes showed Sawney how to sharpen a knife on a whetstone.

'I should have left home years ago,' said Sawney as he ran his blade across the stone, savouring the rasping sound it made. 'I feel as rich as a king, and as free as a bird in the sky.'

'You are,' said Agnes. 'I saw the look in your eyes when that mark wet his breeks. You were born for this life, Sawney Bean. Now you've got a taste for it, you'll never go back. You were a sheep; now you're a wolf.' She took his knife from him and set it down on the ground, then grinned at him. 'Wolves lie down with wolves.'

So SAWNEY and Agnes began their life together. At first, all went well. Sawney followed Agnes' hard-learnt rules. They were always on the move, staying ahead of the fearful tidings they left in their wake. They sheltered in forests and on riverbanks; they kept each other warm and their bellies stayed full. Most of the marks Agnes chose were quick to give up their purses; she was careful whom she preyed upon.

'A wolf can take any sheep without fear,' she would say. 'But a wolf that hunts another wolf, she's going to have a fight on her hands.'

Sawney's confidence steadily grew. He sometimes disagreed with Agnes as to who was prey and who wasn't, but he accepted she had final say. He was in awe of Agnes, and already falling in love with her. He had never met anyone so hard, so canny.

Yet even she could slip.

SAWNEY AND AGNES had made their way south over the Lammermuirs and into the Borders. Autumn had come and winter awaited them. Sawney and Agnes stacked their fire high each night and looked for marks wearing warm clothes.

After a successful robbery north of Duns, they went into the village to spend their earnings. They bought bread, cheese, ale and a rabbit for the pot. As they paid the butcher, Sawney noticed the man giving Agnes a strange look. The butcher saw Sawney watching and smiled broadly.

'What brings you to Duns, friends?' said the butcher.

'I've a brother in Kelso, we're visiting him,' said Agnes. *Don't give a name, and don't mention a place so close that they'll know everyone,* Agnes had instructed Sawney.

'I grew up in Kelso. What's his name?'

'Tam. Tam Mitchell. But he's not been there long, he's just come to work the harvest. We'll be off now.'

'Well, you be careful. The roads aren't safe these days, so I hear.'

'Thank you. We will.'

They left. Agnes seemed ready to break into a run as they took the road southwest.

'What's wrong?' whispered Sawney.

'He recognised me.'

'What? Where from?'

'I robbed him once. Not here. It was a while ago, maybe up near Glasgow. But I remember him, and he remembered me.'

'So what are we going to do?'

'The only thing we can do. Keep moving.'

THEY WALKED all afternoon without a break. Rainclouds blew in mid-afternoon and soon they were soaked to their under-clothes.

'It'll be dark soon,' said Sawney eventually. 'We should make camp.'

Agnes shook her head. 'I told you. We keep moving. Put as much distance between him and us as possible.'

'But he's only a fat old fool. What's he going to do?'

'You think that fat old fool doesn't have friends? Friends who'd enjoy meting out justice to the woman who robbed him? Keep moving.'

Sawney stopped. So did Agnes. He turned to face her.

'I don't care if he does come after us. I don't care if he brings all his friends; I don't care if he brings along everyone from Duns to Longformacus. We'll take him. They're old. Soft. They're fat, woolly sheep. We're wolves. We can do anything. If we choose to hide, they won't find us. If we choose to fight, we'll kill them.'

Agnes looked angry as she held his gaze; Sawney was expecting her to reprimand him again. But something changed in her eyes. He saw the tension leave her. 'I once had that fire in me. Before hard years and hard lessons robbed me of it. Maybe I learnt my lessons too well. Maybe with my young wolf beside me, I needn't be afraid.'

'You needn't. Come on. Let's make camp in that wood over there. We'll keep our fire low.'

They left the road. An hour later, they were roasting their rabbit over a hissing and crackling pine fire.

An hour after that, they were swigging the last of their ale.

An hour after that, they were in one another's arms.

It was only much later, as they lay entwined in sleep, that visitors crept into their camp.

SAWNEY AWOKE to a boot in his gut.

A kick to the ribs followed, then another. Sawney was pulled to his feet and held against a tree, a thick arm across his throat.

The men carried torches. In the torchlight Sawney saw Agnes hauled to her feet and pressed against another tree.

'You sure it's her?' said one of the men.

'Of course I'm sure,' growled the butcher. 'I told you I was sure; I was sure the moment she came into my shop!'

'That's good enough for me,' said a short, wiry man. He

drew back his fist and punched Agnes across the face, sending blood and teeth flying.

The others laughed. 'Again! Both of them!' said the butcher. 'Teach them what they get for robbing honest folk!'

Sawney lost track of time after that. Punches rained down on his face, his gut. He would fall to his feet, only to be pulled up again. He heard Agnes cry out over and over as they beat her too. Once, far into the beating, he even thought he heard her ask for mercy.

At last the men stopped. They were all heaving for breath.

'If we see either of you again,' said the butcher, who had mostly hung back to watch his friends work, 'we'll kill you.' He came forward to give each of of them one heavy punch to the gut. He spat on them both before leading his friends away.

Sawney groaned. 'Bastards,' he moaned. 'Bastards. I'll get them for this. I'll kill them...'

With a howl, Agnes threw herself at him. He was bigger and stronger but she was a far better fighter. Within seconds she had him pinned and was raining down punches on his bruised and bloodied face. Her own face was a ghastly sight; eyes swollen and bruised, nose broken, bleeding from half a dozen cuts.

'You'll kill them, will you? You? It was your fault this happened! Your fault! I told you we should keep going, but no! Sawney was so big, so brave, he was going to take them all on. He was going to keep Agnes safe.' She drew her knife and held it close to his eyes. 'You're green, Sawney. You don't belong to this life and you never will.'

A look came into her eyes that he had never seen before. It

frightened him more than the butcher and his friends had done.

'I can't punish those bastards for what they did to me. But I could punish you, Sawney. You're in my power now. How does it feel?

'It feels good to me,' she went on. 'I could teach you a lesson. One you'll actually remember.' She brought the knife up close to his right eye, then closer, then closer. His heart hammering in his chest, he felt the blade touch his eye.

'No, no, please no.' His trousers were suddenly warm.

Agnes laughed. She withdrew her knife, climbed off of him and collapsed.

He closed his eyes.

They lay that way through the dregs of the night. Sawney woke after dawn to see Agnes breaking camp.

'We need to go,' she said, not meeting his eyes.

Silently, they broke camp. They headed south over the fields, keeping off the roads.

WINTER on the road was as tough as Sawney feared it would be. He and Agnes roamed the Borders, gradually moving west, until spring saw them in Galloway. They moved north from there, spending a summer in Glasgow before making their way further north and into the mountains.

Three years passed in this way. If Sawney had been green when he met Agnes, he wasn't now. He didn't think of himself as a wolf anymore, at least not often. Watching rats scurry past him in a Glasgow alley one night, their eyes searching everywhere for danger, he recognised himself. That night south of Duns wasn't the last time he got into trouble, but he learnt to fight, to take a beating and to enjoy giving one. Agnes would watch and smile at such times, though there was no joy in her smile.

Taking a beating was hard, but nothing like as hard as winter. Sawney was sure each winter aged him a decade. When the air turned sharp and cold each year, he would find himself wondering how it might be to sit at home in the evening, an honest day's work behind him. But it was like imagining being a fish, or a cormorant, or a king. There was no going back from the life he had chosen. Besides, it had its pleasures. A robbery well-executed. A look of approval from Agnes. The warmth of her fast-ageing body. The taste of hard-won food, cooked over an open fire.

There were things to be said for a life on the road. All the same, it was a hard life.

IT WAS NOVEMBER. An early snow had fallen, carpeting the Ayrshire coast. Sawney and Agnes had travelled that way after a second stint in Glasgow. The sun was setting and neither of them had eaten in two days.

In silence they trudged down the coast, their path leading them beneath a line of cliffs. They didn't waste energy on words; each knew how the other felt. Sawney was dreaming of a driftwood fire in a cosy, hidden cove when he spied an opening in the rocks ahead.

He went to inspect the opening. Sure enough, it was a cave. Sawney called out, and his words echoed for a long time before fading into silence.

'It's deep,' said Agnes.

'We could make a fire. Make torches,' said Sawney.

Agnes smiled wearily, relief on her face. Sawney had learnt that Agnes liked caves; they seemed to be where she felt safest. 'Aye. Let's.'

They left, returning with torches as dusk bit the day.

Into the cave they went. Their torches revealed a narrow passage which split after ten or fifteen feet, each passage leading to a low chamber.

'Enough space to make a fire here,' said Sawney as they stood in the right-hand chamber. 'Enough space to lie down.'

'Aye. There's plenty you could do with this place,' said Agnes. 'I say we pass the night here. Maybe two. Maybe three.'

'Maybe the whole winter,' said Sawney.

'You know we can't,' said Agnes. 'You know the rules—'

'Aye, I know. Always keep moving. All the same, it's a nice thought.'

'It is,' said Agnes, her tone wistful. 'It is.'

They did pass the night there, and the next, and the next. Somehow that cave felt like home. They both felt it that first evening. So they set snares for rabbits instead of snaring travellers, and Agnes used her knife-throwing skills to bring home some squirrels.

It was a better time than they had known in years. They went out walking, just to walk, and made fires on clifftops before sitting to watch the sunset. It reminded Sawney of their first days together. Agnes' voice lost its hard edge; there were times when it softened so much that he thought he caught glimpses of the girl she had once been. Sawney found he could make her laugh a new laugh; not bitter or vengeful but light and lilting.

One night, as the sun made a furnace of the sky, she walked down to the water's edge and sang. Her song emerged ever so quietly, ever so tentatively, as if the slightest breeze might have stolen it away. She seemed to be singing not to Sawney but to the world itself. It had treated her so cruelly and yet, Sawney saw in that moment, there was still love in her heart for it.

THEY WALKED HOME that spring evening along the coastal road, knowing few travellers passed that way so late. Yet as the night's thousand eyes opened above them, they spied a traveller walking their way.

The man had the look of a farmer, thick-limbed and peaceful of mind. Sawney was well-used to the wary looks that lone travellers would give the pair of them. Though thin and haggard, they were predators and only fools failed to see it. Perhaps this man was a fool, or perhaps they wore a different look that evening. For whatever reason, the man smiled at them and wished them a good evening.

Sawney glanced at Agnes. The circumstances were ideal for

a robbery. But to do so would break the spell of those peaceful days. Agnes did not have the look of the hunt about her.

Agnes smiled back at the man. 'Good evening to you, sir,' she said as she passed him.

Sawney smiled with relief.

The man passed them by.

She spun around, drew her knife from her belt and plunged it into the man's neck.

He fell to the ground, limbs jerking, eyes bulging, blood spouting from the wound. Agnes watched the man die as if it were another beautiful sunset.

'Don't just stand there staring,' she said as the man grew still. 'Help me.' She bent down and put his arm around her shoulder.

'Where... where are we taking him?'

'Where do you think? We're taking him home, Sawney. Home.'

THEY DRAGGED THE MAN HOME. He seemed to grow heavier with every step. Finally they reached the cave and heaved him inside, setting him down in the chamber where they had built their fire.

'Get the fire going, Sawney,' said Agnes.

He did as she asked.

'Are you thinking to dump him in the sea?' asked Sawney. 'We'll need to weigh him down or the body could wash up...'

Sawney's words trailed off as Agnes pulled the man's boots

off. *Good thinking,* he thought. They could make a few coins from boots like those, or maybe he could try them on? They looked a bit small...

Agnes took off the man's shirt. That wouldn't be worth much. Then she stripped him of his belt and trousers, so that he was down to his underwear.

Agnes stripped his underwear from him too.

Sawney wrinkled his nose as Agnes tossed it all in a heap in the corner. 'There's nobody will buy them...' he began to say, then fell silent as Agnes drew her knife again.

Calmly, efficiently, Agnes set her knife to the man's thigh and began to flay the skin.

Sawney's mind ceased to function. He knew only a horrible stillness, time stretching out and then disappearing like something pulled and pulled until it snaps. The man's eyes stared up at the ceiling; he seemed strangely disinterested as Agnes skinned one thigh, then the other. Blood trickled across the cave floor, pooling in places and forming intricate patterns.

'Make skewers, Sawney,' said Agnes, jolting him from his reverie.

He looked at her blankly. Her words hadn't quite registered.

'Skewers,' she said again.

Sawney dumbly nodded. He took sticks from the pile and peeled one end of each with his own knife, revealing the soft belly beneath the bark. He handed the two skewers to Agnes, who perforated upon them two hunks of dripping, glistening flesh. She set them on the rack over the fire.

They watched the meat cook in silence, Agnes turning each skewer occasionally. Sawney recognised the set of her face, her turned-in lips. It meant that what she did troubled her but she would not admit it to herself, much less to him.

Meat smells filled the cave. Sawney's mouth watered; he couldn't help it.

All too soon, Agnes was offering him a skewer.

He met her eyes. Searched them.

'However badly you think of me,' she said, 'worse has been done to me.'

Sawney took the skewer.

Holding it in his hands, examining the meat, he thought of his father. What would he say if he could see him now? Or his mother?

No. Such thoughts led nowhere good. His mother had died, leaving him at the mercy of John Bean. And who was John Bean to judge anyone? He hadn't wanted Sawney. Nobody had ever wanted Sawney, save Agnes. He was not welcome in the world, so why play by its rules? Good and bad, right and wrong; they were all traps set to snare him. Well, he was a wolf and he wouldn't be snared.

Sawney bit into the meat.

It was delicious. He moaned with delight, chewed, swallowed and took another bite. His eyes met Agnes' eyes and saw laughter in them. He laughed, and she laughed too, their mouths full of meat and blood dripping down their chins.

Sawney had thought himself free. Wretched, often starving, yet free. But with this meal in his belly, he truly was free. The fetters with which he had chained himself blew away like blossom in the winds of spring. Let the king have his court, his castle, his riches; he was a slave next to Sawney. He

knew it beyond doubt, and saw the same truth in Agnes'
eyes.

Sawney and Agnes gorged themselves that night. They ate
until they could eat no more, then ate some more anyway. They
slept, woke up and ate again, and when they kissed they tasted
hunger and blood. At their side, the traveller stared up at a sky
he could not see.

THEY REMAINED in that cave for many years. It became their way
of life to murder travellers, drag their bodies home and eat
them. After eating their fill they would salt and pickle the rest
of the meat, storing it in scavenged barrels.

Agnes fell pregnant. This had happened before, and she
had always done what was needed to ensure no child would be
born. Yet she stopped doing such things, and for the first time a
son was born to her. Then a daughter, another daughter,
another son. Sawney and Agnes raised their children in the
cave, feeding them human flesh, taking them out hunting once
they grew old enough. When the time came for the eldest children to find wives and husbands, their parents encouraged
them to wed one another. Grandchildren were born, and the
Bean clan grew and grew.

Many travellers disappeared along their stretch of coast in
those days. This did not go unnoticed. Folk gossiped about
demons, devils, witches and wolves, especially when bones
washed up on the shore. Search parties scoured the countryside
from time to time, but the cave was never discovered. More

than one innkeeper was lynched, for innkeepers were often the last to see those who disappeared. Yet travellers still went missing.

ONE AUTUMN, twenty-four years after Sawney and Agnes discovered their cave, a church fair was held in the nearby town of Ballantrae. The day turned out bright and sunny as visitors poured in from the surrounding villages.

A newlywed young couple travelled to the fair from Lendalfoot, where they were staying with relatives. They spent the day at the fair and in the afternoon set off for home.

'You're not taking the path north, are you?' said the boy who had earned a penny by minding their horse.

'Why shouldn't we?' said the husband.

'It's not safe. Everyone knows that. There's a monster that'll come out of the sea, drag you underwater and eat you. You'll never be seen again, except when your bones wash up on the shore.'

The man laughed. 'Thank you for the warning, young sir,' he said as he handed the boy his penny, 'but I have my sword and my pistol. That should be quite enough to fend off your monster.'

The boy looked unconvinced.

Soon the couple were riding home along the shore. It was mid-autumn, close to Samhain, golden leaves falling from the trees and scattering along the path.

'Could there be anything to those stories of monsters?' said the woman. 'I heard a woman at the fair say something similar, only she spoke of wolves.'

'Nonsense,' said her husband. 'I don't hold with that kind of fanciful talk, and neither should you. If there's anything to fear on the road, it will be ruffians. A blast from my pistol will send them scurrying.'

They rode on in silence as the sun sank into the sea. The air turned cold as the night darkened.

'Do we have far to go?' said the wife. 'I don't like this path. It feels strange.'

The husband sighed. 'Yes, yes. Not long now.'

He wouldn't admit it, but he was starting to feel uncomfortable himself. The night was so quiet. He could hear nothing; no birdsong, no hooting owl. Yet he felt as if he were surrounded by watching eyes.

Somewhere nearby, a leaf crunched.

'What was that?' said the wife.

Her husband didn't respond. He searched the shadows around them. Was there something...

Howls broke the night as shadowy figures surrounded them.

The man cursed and dug in his spurs. Before the horse could bolt, the figures on the banks leapt at them, trying to pull them to the ground. The horse lashed out with its hooves while the husband fumbled for his pistol with one hand, the other desperately trying to hold on to the reins as hands pulled at him from both sides.

His fumbling hand finally freed his pistol from its holster. He aimed it at the nearest figure but then stopped.

He stared, his pistol forgotten.

It was a child.

His wife's screams brought him to his senses. She had been pulled to the ground. The horse could not break free; hands held onto the reins and its neck, swamping it and pulling it inexorably down.

His pistol was snatched from his hand. He roared and drew his sword, swinging it wildly at his attackers. He had some skill, but it was not enough to push them back.

The attack paused as his assailants eyed him warily. He could see little of them in the late evening light, yet he spied at least two dozen attackers, at least of half of them children. And standing on the bank, watching rather than partaking, were two more figures. He could see only shadows, yet he somehow knew they were older. They seemed calm while the rest were frenzied. There was even something oddly peaceful about them.

All this he saw in the space of a moment before he heard his wife dragged away.

He looked back. There she was, prone upon the ground. Surrounded by children wearing rags and animal skins. Her limbs jerked as they kneeled over her and...

It couldn't be.

He had to be dreaming.

They were eating her.

His horse lashed out with its hooves, broke free and galloped away. He tried to turn, to go back for his wife, but nothing would make his mount stop until it reached home.

THE YOUNG MAN and his hosts thumped on the local magistrate's door that night. The magistrate wasn't happy to be woken, yet the horrific tale he heard gave him a strange sense of relief.

It all sounded like the ravings of a madman. Yet it explained so much. The disappearances. The bones washed up on shore. The lynching of the innkeepers, one of whom had been his close friend.

'What are you going to do about this?' said the husband after he had finished his report and answered the magistrate's questions.

'What am I going to do?' he answered. 'I'll tell you what I'm going to do. I'm going to take this to the top, son. The very top.'

A WEEK LATER, King James was sitting on his throne, listening to the petitions of his nobles.

'Lord Hamilton,' said James as a grave-faced man stepped forward.

'Your Majesty,' said Lord Hamilton. 'I come to you seeking justice, and the scourging from my lands of an evil so foul that it taints the very name of Scotland.'

'And what evil is that?'

'Over the past twenty years and more, a stretch of my coast-line has grown infamous. Travellers set off down the road and never arrive at their destination. Over the course of those years, many a bone has washed up on the beaches. Tales are told thereabouts of monsters, hell hounds, hags in service of the Devil. And meanwhile, good, innocent men have been lynched by townsfolk seeking someone to blame.

'I know what you must be thinking, Your Majesty. Bandits. Simple bandits. Not your responsibility. I might have thought so too, had I not met this man.'

At a wave from Lord Hamilton, a young fellow with a hunted look in his eyes stepped forward, followed by an older man in a magistrate's uniform.

'Tell the king what you saw,' said the magistrate.

'Your Majesty,' said the man, bowing. 'I was riding – I mean, beg your pardon – that is... my wife and I were travelling from a church fair. We were on the coastal path, and almost home when...' he took a deep breath, his lip quivering. 'They weren't wolves or monsters. They were people. Men, women, children. They dragged my wife down from the horse and began to...'

The magistrate stepped forward. 'The man claims these people practised cannibalism, Your Majesty.'

Uproar followed. King James ignored it; instead he studied the man. He knew the look on his face. James had seen it on the battlefield, on the faces of men who had committed or witnessed unspeakable horror.

The king stood.

The court fell silent.

'There have always been wild beasts in this land,' said King James. 'The answer has always been the same. Hunt them down and kill them. The creatures haunting our coast, whether they walk on four legs or two, will meet that fate.'

He paused.

'If this man's tale is true, then these fiends are an affront not just to the godly people of Ayrshire, but to the nation itself. As such, I shall lead the hunt myself.'

FIVE DAYS LATER, King James led the hunt out of Ballantrae.

Half the county saw them off; the other half took part. Pack after pack of hounds raced out of Ballantrae, followed by an army of huntsmen. They scoured the cliffs and coves, the woods and valleys and heather-clad hills.

The day passed. The sun set.

They had found nothing.

King James led his party along the coast. He urged his men on, trying to keep their spirits up as he saw the high hopes of the morning fade. It would not do for a hunt led by the king himself to fail. Yet not the faintest trail had been found.

That is, nothing was found until King James' party came to the north end of Ballantrae Bay.

The bay ended in a wall of sheer cliffs. James was about to turn the party around when one of his best hounds began to bark furiously, pulling a huntsman towards the cliffs.

The huntsman and the hunting party followed. Over slimy wet rocks they hopped until they stood before a black gap in the cliff face.

A cave.

Looking at that cave, King James found himself shivering.

While most of the hounds were barking furiously now, a few were whining and slinking away.

James' captain of guard approached him. 'Shall I take some men in?'

The king nodded. 'Go carefully.'

The captain bowed and picked out his men. They lit torches and moved into the cave.

James and the rest of the hunters waited.

Soon, the guards emerged. Their faces were deathly white.

'Your Majesty... we have found the culprits.'

'Then bring them out so they may face justice.'

The captain hesitated. 'I... I would rather not go back in there, Your Majesty.'

James searched the man's face. The man was a veteran of countless battles. What could he have seen to strike such fear in him? He glanced at the others; they avoided his eyes.

James made up his mind. He climbed down from his horse.

'I will see for myself.'

'But—'

'I am going in. Will you accompany your king?'

The captain turned and looked at each of his men before turning back to James. He gave a stiff nod. 'Of course we will, Your Majesty.'

James drew his blade and followed the captain inside.

They moved down a narrow tunnel. Somehow, it felt like he were not in a cave but a house. A home.

Moving further, James smelt the scents of human life: sweat, refuse, meat and drink.

Rounding a corner, he stopped and stared.

The cave ended in a chamber. A fire burnt in the centre. Sitting around it were men, women and children. Their features bore such similarity that there could be no doubt this was a family. Their eyes were dull or else bore a fierce, predatory look. Every mouth was a cave full of black, broken stumps.

The king and his men stared; the cave-dwellers stared back. Young children tried to wriggle free of their parents' arms; they reached out at their visitors with grasping hands.

All of them, young and old, wore animal skins.

No.

Human skins.

As James' eyes roved the quiet, staring company, he noticed a pair who were older than the rest. They did not look to be brother and sister, yet they did not have the strange look of some of their offspring. There was something else in their eyes.

Defiance. James had seen that look in the eyes of the condemned. While their offspring looked at him as if he were both predator and prey, these two did not. They knew they had met their end, but they would not show fear. They would not beg for life, or repent. That defiance went as deep as their bones, and only torture would take it from them.

James backed away, turned and left the cave as fast as he could.

Outside, he said to his captain, 'Send men to fetch gunpowder.'

It was late in the evening when the men returned. By this time, fires lined the cliffs up above. Word had spread.

James had his men position barrels of gunpowder outside

the cave mouth. Standing well back, they blew it, destroying the cave mouth and sealing in the family of predators.

He could have hauled them out, taken them to Edinburgh in chains. Made a gruesome, grisly show of punishing them. People would have flocked from across the country to see it, and praised him for keeping the country safe. Yet he didn't. The sight of those people had frightened James in a way he had never been frightened before. He wanted to go to sleep that night knowing they would never be seen by mortal eyes again. It should not be known that man could sink so low, becoming worse than beast.

Or worse, that a person could sink so low, yet still know pride. And love.

The Bean family died in that cave, but their story spread, becoming a legend passed on down the ages. Perhaps they would have been proud of that.*

---

* The legend of Sawney Bean is one that sits apart from Scotland's folklore canon, perhaps because of its disturbing subject matter. It inspired the iconic horror director Wes Craven's *The Hills Have Eyes* and is referenced by many musicians, authors and filmmakers, yet seldom comes up in writings on Scottish folklore.

The story was popularised by its appearance in The Newgate Calendar, an 18-19th century London publication which documented grisly crimes. The details of the story are sparse and vary widely. Sawney is said to have grown up in East Lothian, the son of either a tanner or ditch-digger, somewhere between the 14th and 16th centuries. At some point after realising he didn't fancy a life of hard work, he left home with a woman named Agnes Douglas, or Black Agnes Douglas. They married and found their way to Bennane Cave, close to Ballantrae in Ayrshire. At this point Sawney and Agnes turned to cannibalism, and produced their incestuous clan of over forty children and grandchildren.

There are two well-known endings to the story, both of which begin with a man escaping the Bean clan's attack and reporting what happened to the local magistrate. The matter is then brought before King James (which particular

King James depends on when the story is set). He leads a hunt and discovers the cave. At this point, the story diverges. One version is the version I chose, in which he orders that gunpowder be used to blow up the entrance to the cave, sealing in the Bean clan. The other has his troops bring the entire clan to Edinburgh for a very public and very nasty execution.

It's not the easiest story to believe, particularly with King James' involvement, and evidence to back it up is said to be sparse. Some argue that the story was created to act as anti-Scottish propaganda in the wake of the Jacobite rebellions. Whatever the case, over the years the story has become part of Scotland's folklore and seems to be one that compels readers. What I found compelling was the idea of exploring Sawney and Agnes' characters within the confines of the existing legend.

THE PIPER'S BOOTS

There was and there wasn't a wandering piper named Willie Munro. All year round, Willie travelled the highways and byways of Scotland, selling his services. He played his pipes in towns, villages and farmhouses, and for weddings, parties and funerals. On many nights his hosts would offer him a bed, and on other nights he simply stopped in at the nearest house as evening drew near. It wasn't an easy life, but it was the only life he knew and he would never have changed it.

It was New Year's Eve, or Hogmanay as it's called in Scotland, and Willie wasn't having a great run of luck. His road had led him to a desolate stretch of the Northeast. There were few farms and no villages thereabouts, so Willie's pipes hadn't been required at any parties. He did the only thing he could do in that situation: he went on walking in hope of finding a place to stay, a bellyful of food and perhaps some willing listeners with a coin or two in their pockets.

Such circumstances weren't unusual. This was all part of the job for Willie. The problem was that it was freezing cold, far colder than an ordinary winter's day in the north. A thick layer of crisp, brittle snow covered the land, and Willie's breath froze in front of him. He could feel little icicles forming in his beard. He walked as quickly as he could to stave off the cold, but he wasn't as young as he once was, and his tired legs could only carry him so fast. Especially with the state of his boots; they were old, tattered and full of gaping holes.

'I'm risking frostbite with these things on my feet,' he muttered as he wrapped his coat tighter about him. 'Hopefully my luck will change and I'll find a warm hearth soon, or else I'll freeze tonight.'

Almost as soon as those words left his mouth, Willie spotted something strange by the roadside up ahead.

He drew closer and saw that it was a pair of boots sticking up out of the snow.

'Someone up there must be listening,' he said. 'A pair of boots, just for old Willie! And good ones, too.'

Willie dug into the snow and found that the boots hadn't found their way there alone. There were feet inside them, and those feet were attached to the body of a man.

'Frozen stiff,' said Willie. 'Poor thing. Must have been another traveller, like me. Well, if he was a man of the road then he must have been a practical fellow. He wouldn't want good boots going to waste.'

Willie took hold of one of the boots and pulled. It wouldn't come off; it was frozen to the man's foot.

You might think that Willie's luck had run out there. But he was an odd-job-man as well as a piper, and he had a few tools in his pack. He set his pack down on the snow, dug out his saw and set it to the man's ankle. It was hard work but soon Willie had sawn right through one ankle, then the other.

'Please accept my apologies,' said Willie. 'I don't like leaving you like this, but I wouldn't have minded if you'd done the same to me.'

Now Willie faced a new problem. The traveller's feet were still inside the boots. As hard as Willie pulled, he couldn't get them out.

'You're making me work for them!' he told the half-buried corpse. 'I'll just have to put them in my pack, feet and all, and figure out what to do with them later.'

Willie stuffed the boots and his saw into his bag. He carried on down the road.

DARKNESS FELL. Willie was still on the road and couldn't remember ever feeling so cold. Thankfully, the moonlight reflecting off the snow allowed him to see his way.

'A farmhouse, a farmhouse, that's all I ask,' said Willie, his teeth chattering.

Finally, he saw light up ahead and sighed with relief. Now he just had to hope that whomever he met was hospitable... but that shouldn't be a problem. Most people were. It was

Hogmanay, besides, and who would turn someone away on Hogmanay?

Willie soon saw a farmhouse ahead, with a barn beside it and half a dozen fenced fields. The farm sat between the road and a snow-mantled pine forest.

He approached the farmhouse and knocked on the door. There was a scraping sound and a moment later, a man opened the door.

He eyed Willie suspiciously, but Willie hardly noticed. He could see past the farmer to his table, where the farmer's wife sat, and oh! What a spread they had prepared! Haggis, bacon, turnips and tatties, ale and whisky... Willie could scarcely contain himself.

'What do you want?' asked the farmer.

'I... well, good evening to you. My name's Willie and I'm a piper. I was wondering if you might have a bed or a seat by your fire for me on this Hogmanay night?'

'Oh, your name's Willie, is it? And you're a piper, you say? How are we to know that's true? Folk who wander the roads can't be trusted. You could be anyone, you could be from anywhere and you might murder us in our sleep if we let you stay. Begone!'

The man was about to slam the door in Willie's face when his wife spoke up.

'Hold on now, there's no need for that! Can't you see the man's half-frozen? He'll die in a ditch if we turn him away. And on Hogmanay! I'll not have that on my conscience.'

The farmer sighed. 'Fine,' he said, glancing back towards his supper. 'He can sleep in the barn. Come with me.'

Willie followed the farmer out to the barn. Inside, a cow lay sleeping in the lamplight.

'It's warmer in the loft, so you'd best sleep up there. Don't even think about stealing anything.'

'Thank you,' said Willie through gritted teeth. 'You're very kind.'

The farmer glared at Willie and left.

Willie looked at the cow which lay peacefully sleeping. It was cold enough in the barn that Willie could see the cow's breath.

That gave him an idea.

A rather wicked idea.

He dug the boots out of his pack and set them down in front of the cow, so that the cow was breathing onto the frozen feet. Chuckling to himself, Willie climbed the ladder to the loft and settled down in the straw to sleep.

WILLIE AWOKE EARLY the next morning. He climbed downstairs. There was the cow, still sleeping. He picked up the boots and, as he had hoped, the cow's breath had warmed them so much that he could pull their previous owner's feet right out.

He unlaced his own beaten-up boots and slipped on the new ones. They were warm and toasty from the cow's breath and fit him near perfectly. He then slipped his old boots onto the traveller's severed feet, tied the laces and set them down beside the cow.

The first stage of Willie's plan was complete. Now on to the next.

THE FARMER'S wife woke up soon afterwards. Her first thoughts were for the piper.

'I'll go out to the barn and see if he wants a bannock for the road. Poor man. We should have let him in.'

Her half-awake husband responded with a snort.

She dressed, went downstairs and left the house. The winter morning was still dark. Shivering, she crossed the farm-yard to the barn and crept inside.

She screamed.

The farmer's wife screamed and screamed until her husband came running.

He followed her gaze. The cow still lay there, looking up at them both with a confused expression. Beside her was a pair of worn old boots. The boots the piper had been wearing.

'She's eaten him, Hamish! The cow's eaten the piper! And all because you couldn't find it in your heart to let him into the house, and on Hogmanay! Oh, we'll go straight to Hell for this, so we will...'

'Get a hold of yourself, woman! Maybe I should have let him in but it's done now. We need to make sure nothing more comes of this.'

'What do you mean?'

'I mean we need to get rid of these boots, and these feet! We'll bury them out among the trees and that'll be the end of it.

No one's going to miss a wanderer like him. He never came here.'

The farmer's wife nodded, her chin quivering. 'Alright then,' she whispered.

The farmer took a spade and, with his wife trailing behind him, he picked up the boots and left the barn. They walked to the edge of the forest, where the farmer looked around. There was no one in sight.

'We'll do it here,' he said, and began digging. He soon had a hole big enough for the boots.

'Is it deep enough, do you think?' asked his wife.

'It's deep enough.' He bent down and tossed the boots into the hole.

'Should... should we say something, do you think?'

'No.'

The farmer refilled the hole with earth and covered it over with snow.

'That's it done and that's the last word we'll speak of it.'

His wife nodded. 'Let's get in and have breakfast,' she said.

They returned to the farmhouse as Willie watched from among the trees.

SOON AFTERWARDS, the farmer and his wife were back at their table. There was more than enough left over from the previous night's feast to see them through breakfast and lunch. They were just setting knife to meat when a sound made them leap up, their chairs flying.

It was the sound of bagpipes.

They flung open the front door. Standing out by the barn, pipes in hand, was Willie McPhee.

'It's... it's the piper's ghost!' said the farmer's wife. 'He's come back for us!'

Pipes wailing, his eyes fixed on the farmer and his wife, Willie began to walk slowly towards them.

'Run, woman!' shouted the farmer. They tumbled out the door and ran off down the road as fast as their legs would carry them.

Willie played until he was sure they were long gone, enjoying the sound of his pipes singing over the snow. Then he went inside, stoked the fire and sat down to enjoy a good breakfast.

He stayed at the table all day, working his way through the food. When his stomach was full and in need of a break, he played his pipes by the fire with a glass of whisky beside him. It was as peaceful a day as Willie had ever passed.

Late in the afternoon, there came a knock on the door.

Willie went to the door and opened it. An old man with glistening, translucent skin stood there. He had no feet.

'You must be the ghost of that fellow whose boots I took,' said Willie.

The ghost nodded.

'Well, you're very welcome by my fire,' said Willie. 'Come inside.'

Being a ghost, the man wasn't able to eat much, but he happily sat and listened to Willie play his pipes. The two of them had a fine Hogmanay ceilidh, and a few days later they each went their own way. *

---

* I thought you might appreciate something a little lighter after Sawney Bean! Stories of ghost pipers are common across Scotland and are often attached to castles. The best known is probably that of the Piper Boy of Edinburgh Castle.

This story is one commonly heard at ceilidhs; I've heard it so many times over the years that I can't remember where or when I first heard it.

THE CURSING OF HILDALAND

Between the Isle of Rousay and the Orkney mainland lies a tiny island called Eynhallow. Long ago, it was known as Hildaland. Though it is small, flat and almost featureless, it is famous in Orkney for having once been the home of the finfolk.

The finfolk are a mysterious race of beings sometimes described as tall, shadowy sorcerers capable of rowing to Iceland with seven strokes of an oar. Female finfolk, known as finwives, are said to be beautiful mer-women who will retain their attractive appearance if they snare a human husband, but become ugly, wizened crones if they marry a finman.

There are stories of finmen, and stories of finwives, and Thorodale reckoned he had heard too many of them.

Thorodale was a fisherman who lived on Rousay with his wife, Helga, and their three sons. When Thorodale travelled to Kirkwall or some other place and told folk he came from

Rousay, they would say, 'You'll have to be watchful, living so close to the finfolk.'

'Och, I've no time for fear and suspicion,' he would say with a shake of his head. 'I've never even seen a finman, let alone been harmed by one. They're probably as scared of us as we are of them.'

People laughed at this, but only a little, for Thorodale was a well-respected man. He had a quiet, dignified way about him and a handsome face, though he hid it beneath a long, thick beard. Though people thought well of him, no one could say they knew him well, as he wasn't one for ceilidhs or long conversations. He belonged to the new Christian religion which was spreading fast across Orkney in that time, but he didn't go around trying to convert people. His only care seemed to be for Helga, whom he would walk with for miles on the Orkney beaches. They would say they were out looking for driftwood, but really, they just liked walking together, enjoying the shriek of the gulls, the pounding of the surf or the vast silence of a still day.

It was on one of these walks that Thorodale saw his first finman.

It was an early evening in April. The sky was a spiderweb of pink and orange and red. The clouds stretched tendrils across the horizon as they danced their slow, unending dance. Thorodale and Helga were walking hand in hand along the southwest shore of Rousay. The Island of Hildaland lay across the sea from where they walked, shrouded as ever in a veil of mist.

They talked of the winter just passed and of work needing done in the summer to come. They spoke of how the boys were growing and changing. Mostly, they walked in silence. The day was so quiet, so still, that every word spoken seemed a stain upon it.

'Call of nature,' said Thorodale eventually. 'Back in a moment.'

He headed away from the shore and up a little path that cut through the dunes, his footsteps sinking into the deep sand. He saw to his business, turned back around and then froze as he heard a scream.

It was Helga.

Thorodale ran for the beach, cursing as he stumbled in the deep sand. He half-ran, half-fell down the path leading to the beach.

Once there, he sank to his knees.

A narrow boat with no sail was making its way out to sea. Steering it was a tall, dark-cloaked, dark-haired man, who regarded Thorodale with a vicious grin as he rowed.

Tied up in the hull, screaming for Thorodale to rescue her, was Helga.

There was nothing Thorodale could do. His own boat was back at home. There were no other boats on the beach and the finman's craft was already disappearing into the distance. *To Iceland with seven strokes of an oar,* he heard a hundred voices whisper in his mind.

Was that where the finman was taking her? To Hildaland, to Iceland, or maybe even to Finfolkaheim, their legendary city under the sea?

All the finfolk tales Thorodale had ever heard crashed into

his mind at once. Submerged cities. Blue cattle. Vanishing islands that no mortal man could ever hope to find.

He had shaken his head and scoffed at all of them. Were they all true, then? He had no idea. Yet one thing he knew for sure: his wife was gone. His heart told him he would never see her again.

FROM THAT DAY ONWARDS, a dark cloud hung over Thorodale's house. His silences that had once been peaceful were now angry; his neighbours feared to run into him. Soon he only saw his sons, who shared his grief, yet even they found him hard to bear. All the work that their mother had done, they now shared out between them, along with Thorodale's work. He did nothing but sit by the fireplace, drinking ale, indifferent to whether a fire was lit. His skin sagged from his bones; if he spoke, his words were harsh and cruel.

His sons took to meeting in the fields and speaking about him in whispers. They feared greatly for him, but didn't know what to do. Eventually they agreed that the least they could do was get him out of the house. Perhaps fishing would take his mind off his grief, if only for a little while; he always used to enjoy it.

'Do you think you could get out fishing today, Pa?' said his eldest one day. 'There's more work than we can do, and we're struggling.'

Thorodale refused, but they had agreed they would keep on

at him until eventually he relented. It took half the day but their plan worked.

'Fine! I'll go, just to be away from you nags.'

Thorodale gathered his fishing gear, left the house, went down to the shore and set out on his boat. He rowed out to sea and cast his line.

Thorodale settled back to wait for a bite. Out at sea, things were as they had always been. The world went on, indifferent to his pain. Gulls and guillemots flew overhead; a school of porpoise swam by, the sun reflecting off their smooth, silvery backs. Thorodale used to enjoy fishing. He had enjoyed being reminded how vast the world was, how insignificant his little life was within it. Yet now all he could think of was finmen, and Helga, who was somewhere out there on the sea, or under it. Or dead.

Which was it? Was she still out there somewhere, suffering?

'Oh, Helga,' he said, moaning as grief clutched his heart. 'Helga.'

Thorodale.

He looked up. Surely he had imagined...

Thorodale. My dear, said the voice again. It was coming from everywhere and nowhere.

'Helga? Where are you?'

Listen to me, said Helga's voice. *I cannot return to you. But there is something you can do for me, and for all Christians.*

'What is it? Tell me, my love.'

Thorodale listened, his fishing rod forgotten in his hands, as Helga gave him his instructions. After she had spoken, a wind whipped at Thorodale and, just like that, she was gone.

THE NEXT DAY, Thorodale set out to sea again. He wasn't fishing today. Instead he sailed south to the Orkney mainland then west around it. He sailed all day until finally he drew into a harbour on the north coast of Hoy.

Here, Thorodale left his boat and set out on foot. He stopped in at a couple of houses to get directions, and by following them, he arrived that evening at the house his wife had told him to find.

It was a little, lonely house at the edge of the Trowie Glen.

It was the home of a spey wife.

A spey wife is an Orkney witch. There were spey wives on every island, though Thorodale had never had dealings with one. He was a Christian, and the speys gave their allegiance to the gods of Asgard. But Helga had told him to come here, so through the door he went.

The spey wife was cooking over her fire. She welcomed Thorodale, bade him sit down and shared her food with him. After they had eaten, she asked him what he desired.

'Revenge,' he answered.

The spey wife listened gravely as he told his tale.

'Will you help me?' he asked once he had finished. 'Will you help me get revenge on the finman?'

'I will do nothing,' said the spey wife. 'But the Allfather might.' She closed her eyes. They sat in silence for a while, the fire crackling.

'You are fortunate,' she said eventually, opening her eyes.

'Odin has spoken. I know what you must do. You know the Odin Stone?'

'Yes.'

'Go there tomorrow. Come the evening, crawl on your hands and knees around the stone, nine times, against the sun. Do the same the next night, and the next. On the ninth night, after your ninth circuit, look through the hole in the stone. You will see your answer there.'

'I am a Christian,' said Thorodale. 'Why would your god help me?'

'The minds of the gods are not ours to know.'

THORODALE CHOSE not to stay with the spey wife that night, preferring to shiver under his boat. As soon as the sky lightened, he sailed north, putting in at Stenness and walking overland. His feet sank deep into the marshy ground; angry skuas swooped overhead as he stumbled upon their nests which lay hidden in the long grass.

After a few hours, he arrived at Brodgar.

Two circles of lofty stone pillars stood on a rise of land between two lochs. Thorodale shivered. Some Orcadians had no problem with visiting such places, but not him. He wasn't superstitious, but the sight of the stones had always given him an ill feeling. It was said that pagans used to dance there and even perform human sacrifices. Perhaps they still did. Yet Helga had bade him visit the spey, and the spey had bade him come here.

There was no one in sight. Thorodale walked across the narrow stretch of land leading to the stone circles. He skirted around them, trying not to look at them directly. Thorodale felt as if they were watching him. Beyond, he saw a pair of outlying stones; his destination. He drew closer and saw that one had a hole in it, a few feet from the ground.

The Odin Stone.

Some Orcadians would come here to gain blessings for infants, or to swear the Odin Oath. To do so was to align with Satan, the ministers said; a man could not ride two horses. It was the old gods, or the true god.

Thorodale sat down to await the evening.

EVENING CAME.

Thorodale stood and approached the Odin Stone.

Nearing it, he fell to his hands and knees. He crawled around it, against the sun, nine times.

All that night and through the next day, Thorodale wandered the fields or slept fitfully, wrapped up in his cloak. He bartered for food at nearby houses and hamlets, the occupants of which regarded him with canny eyes. They had a fair idea what business he was about.

Nine days passed. Thorodale felt half-mad with hunger and cold. As he approached the Odin Stone one last time, he wondered if he should abandon his quest. All of this was so far from everything he had known. So far from the peace he had shared with Helga, leaving long trails of footprints on Rousay's white sand. How could any good come of this?

But then Thorodale thought of the finman. The way he had grinned.

Thorodale fell to his knees and began to crawl.

Nine times he circled the stone.

Finally he crawled to the stone, rose up and peered through the hole.

Thorodale's ritual was rewarded. Whether it was Odin or his own god who spoke that night, he was gifted a vision. One dark enough to sate the hatred in his heart.

THORODALE RETURNED HOME. He gathered his sons around him and told them what he had seen. They were sceptical at first, but as he spoke, they forgot their doubts. His fervour seized them, and they tasted what he had tasted; the siren song of vengeance.

'Will you do it, sons? Will you come with me tomorrow?'

They looked at one another.

'Aye, Da,' said the eldest. 'We'll do it.'

THEY WORKED LATE into the night to prepare. In the morning, they pushed their boat out to sea and made for Hildaland. In the keel sat three baskets of salt and a chest of meal.

They travelled southwest, crossing the narrow strait that lies between Rousay and the Orkney mainland. About halfway across the strait lay a shimmering mass of mist.

Hildaland, home of the finfolk.

'We're getting close!' Thorodale soon called. 'Row, and be ready!'

The boys strained at the oars as Thorodale steered them, eyeing the horizon. He was sure the finfolk would see them coming and divine their intent. But he was ready.

They drew closer. Up close, the mist around Hildaland swirled and glittered like a mass of jewelled serpents. It somehow seemed to be alive and watching them. Their coming would not go unchallenged.

The sea before the boat erupted. A whale rose up, opening its great yawning maw as if to swallow them whole.

'The salt!' roared Thorodale. 'Throw the salt!'

As the whale's jaws closed, turning the world black, they grabbed handfuls of salt and threw them into the cavern of its mouth.

The whale disappeared. The sea was calm, as if the whale had never been there.

'Phantoms and illusions,' said Thorodale with a bitter grin. 'If that's the best they've got, we'll have little trouble today.'

The boys were not so confident. They were afraid to approach the island now that it was close, but they were even more afraid to be on the open water. They gritted their teeth and rowed harder, the boat skimming over the water like a cormorant. Hildaland drew ever closer.

A song danced over the water towards them. Four figures rose out of the sea, surrounding them. Beautiful young women, singing in unison, and Thorodale had never heard a song so enchanting.

The oars slipped from his sons' hands as they gazed at the mermaids, who smiled at them and reached out to take their hands and guide them into the water. But Thorodale resisted their spell; there was no answering song in his heart. He grabbed handfuls of salt from the nearest chest and threw them at the mermaids. They screamed, hissed and spat at him before disappearing into the water.

'Pick up your oars, you fools,' said Thorodale, cuffing each of his dazed sons. 'Only a little way to go.'

They entered the mist around Hildaland. It shone and danced all around them, spectral voices shimmering in the air. Dark whispers, warning them back. But nothing would turn Thorodale back.

They reached land.

'This is it! You know what to do. Out! Out!'

The boys grabbed the meal chests. They leapt into the shallow water and ran off into the mist while Thorodale strode up the beach.

From out of the mist came a monster.

It was at least nine feet tall. Matted, dark fur hung from its body; its teeth were longer than Thorodale's sword. He drew his sword and brandished it at the beast.

The monster roared. It lowered its head, stalking forward, sharp claws slipping from their sheaths.

Thorodale edged back.

'Closer,' he whispered.

The monster leapt at Thorodale. He leapt aside, swinging

his sword and landing a blow upon the monster's arm. It shrieked as the blade sank into its flesh.

Thorodale pulled his weapon loose and danced backwards. The monster advanced, but warily now, clutching its wounded arm close to its body. Thorodale lunged forward, swinging his sword in wide arcs, forcing the monster back. Yet it soon recovered and came at him again. Thorodale struck and missed; the monster swung and caught him across the chest.

Thorodale went down, roaring in agony. The monster's claws had raked deep gouges into his flesh. His sword fell from his shaking hand as blood poured from his wounds.

The monster loomed over him. It roared again, rattling Thorodale's bones as its saliva sprayed his face.

Thorodale saw his chance.

He reached into his cloak, pulled out a cross made of sticky grass and, with the last of his strength, threw it at the monster.

It struck the beast's chest. The cross stuck there, steaming and hissing, the flesh beneath it melting. The monster's wail of pain was terrible even to Thorodale's ears, yet it quickly diminished as the monster shrunk and wilted. Fur fell from its body and it collapsed on top of Thorodale.

He wriggled out from beneath it and got to his feet, gasping for breath, blood pouring from his wounds.

The monster was no longer a monster.

It was the finman who had kidnapped Helga.

'You win, Thorodale,' said the finman. The cross had fallen away with the fur but there was a gaping wound upon his chest where it had struck; he would not live long. 'You win, but you lose. Your wife is no longer in this world. You will not see her again.'

'That is true, finman,' said Thorodale. 'There is no winning for me any more. But all the same, you have lost. Not just your life, but your island. It is ours now.'

'Never,' said the finman. 'You will never take Hildaland.'

'Listen,' said Thorodale, 'and know the truth.'

At that moment, a chorus of cries went up in the distance. It grew and grew, and was soon joined by the pounding of feet and hooves.

A horde of finfolk came streaming out of the mist. Finmen and finwives ran for the shore, their children trailing behind them or clutched in their arms. They shot past Thorodale without giving him a second glance, intent upon reaching the water. Among them raced giant blue cows, bellowing as if in terrible pain. Thorodale and the fallen finman watched as the exodus raced into the water and disappeared beneath it.

As the finfolk left Hildaland, the mist cleared, revealing an island that looked like any other island in Orkney.

'You monster,' hissed the finman. 'This was our place. We had just this one—'

He got no further. As the last stragglers raced past, Thorodale picked his sword up off the sand and buried its point in the finman's chest.

His sons soon reappeared. Horrified by his wounds, they insisted on taking him to the boat, but he refused. Thorodale wanted to see what they had accomplished. So after bandaging his wounds, they set their shoulders beneath his and guided him around the shores of Hildaland.

Just as he had instructed, they had circled the island carrying the baskets of salt. They had each cut into the ground in three places and filled the wound in the earth with salt. Thus Hildaland was poisoned, its magic destroyed.

Thorodale and his sons returned to the boat. They made it back home, watching Hildaland disappear into the distance behind them.

Thorodale never returned to that island. Others did, though. They sang hymns as they burned the homes of the finfolk, built new settlements and sowed the land with crops. It is no longer cocooned in glittering mist.

Yet it does have something about it. A certain, subtle magic. The Vikings named it 'Eynhallow', meaning Holy Island. Christians later built a monastic settlement there, and even today, those who come to walk its quiet shores – for the island is no longer inhabited – often feel a certain atmosphere, something they can't quite explain.

Why? Because one of Thorodale's sons, the youngest, had small hands. He didn't throw quite as much salt into the earth as he was supposed to. Thus the island retained a sliver of its power.

If you ever go there, I hope you will feel it: the ancient magic of Hildaland. *

---

* This Orcadian tale which came to me from Tom Muir is one of the saddest stories I know, both for the events of its narrative and for how it symbolises the passing away of the old beliefs of Scotland.

The island's modern name of Eynhallow is derived from the Norse *Eyin Helga*, meaning Holy Island. The island was home to a monastic settlement which seems to have later been used as a home by the islanders. Eynhallow's tiny population of four families left in 1851 due to an outbreak of disease and it is now uninhabited. There is no ferry to the island but the Orkney Heritage Society organises a visit in July each year.

MALLIE & THE TROW

There once lived in Shetland a couple named Johnny and Mallie. They had three children and lived in a little house close to the sea.

Like many men in Shetland then and now, Johnny earned his living at sea. He would find work on ships bound for Iceland, Faroe and even Greenland, and was often gone for many months. His family missed him greatly while he was away, but his work kept them fed and they enjoyed him all the more when he was home. Mallie kept busy looking after the house and the children, but at night she would imagine Johnny's arms wrapped around her and pray to the Sea Mother to keep him safe.

Year after year passed in this way. Then, one grim October evening, Johnny's ship returned without him.

The captain came to Mallie's house and gave her the hard

news himself: Johnny had been swept overboard during a storm. There had been no chance of recovering his body.

Grief sank deep claws into Mallie, and fear too. Her family had lost their only source of sustenance. The seasons were turning; winter's breath rode the wind. Mallie had no money, and only a chest of meal and a barrel of salted herring to feed her family.

Once that was gone... she didn't know.

Only Tom, her eldest, was old enough to truly understand. They wept together that night while his younger sisters slept.

Winter struck with all its fury. Thankfully there was no shortage of peat for the fire, and they were able to keep warm. Yet their meal and fish dwindled by the day. They ate less and less, until eventually they were down to one tiny meal each day. Their clothes hung off them; the children were pale, their bones ached and they did not grow as they should have done. Mallie ate even less than her children, and struggled to rise from her chair. She retreated to her bed as often as she could, reaching for memories of Johnny that grew ever fainter, ever more elusive. It was hard now to recall his smell, or the rough touch of his beard as he kissed her.

ONE DAY, late in February, Mallie rose from her bed in the cold, dark morning. Every bone and joint in her body ached. She blew on the embers of the fire and slowly crossed the room to the meal chest.

Mallie opened the chest. It was empty.

Next she tried the herring barrel.

It was empty too.

Tom woke up just then and asked for breakfast. Soon the two girls were awake; they were hungry too.

'I'm sorry, bairns,' said Mallie. 'We've no food left.'

The children pleaded for food, then cried for it. Every word and wail tore strips from Mallie's heart.

Finally the girls cried themselves to sleep. At that point, Mallie came to a decision. She put on her coat and said, 'Come on, Tom. We have no food, but others surely do.'

Mallie and Tom left the house. A pale winter sun hung low on the horizon; silvery clouds raced over the sloping moors and restless sea. Mallie took Tom's hand and they set off west along the coast. Half a mile from their home was a little hill, and atop this hill lived their nearest neighbour, an old woman. Her husband had died a few years back, but folk said he had provided well for her. Perhaps she could help them.

They reached the hill and followed the path to the old woman's door. Mallie knocked and the old woman soon appeared.

'Mallie,' she said. 'It's been a while. I was sorry to hear about your Johnny. Are you keeping well?'

'Not so well, I'm sorry to say,' said Mallie. 'That's why we're here.'

Mallie explained how things stood. As she did so, Tom peered past the old woman and into her house. From where he stood, he had a clear view of her pantry.

There was enough food in there to feed all of Shetland!

Tom spied bread, butter and legs of ham. Jam, tea, barley

and wheat, corn and oats. Tom's mouth watered as he grinned. There was no way the woman would ever get through all that herself; surely she would share with them!

'And so I've come to your door,' Mallie was saying, 'much as it shames me, to ask for charity. If you could spare a wee bit of food to keep me and my bairns—'

'Enough!' said the old woman.

Mallie stared at her.

'I've heard enough. More than enough. I won't have beggars at my door. Be off with you now.'

Tom couldn't believe what he was hearing. He was expecting his mother to put the woman right. Instead, with a shaking voice, Mallie said, 'Very well, then. Sorry to trouble you.'

Pulling on Tom's hand, she turned and walked away.

'How could she turn us away?' asked Tom as they walked. 'I saw her pantry. She's got loads of food! Far more than she needs. How could she do that? How could she turn us away when we're hungry?'

'I don't know, son,' said Mallie, shaking her head and wiping a tear from her eye. 'Some folk are just different to others, I suppose.'

THEY ARRIVED HOME. The girls had hoped they would return with food, and when they learnt there was none, they set to wailing. Mallie held them in her arms until they cried themselves to sleep again, then she put them to bed. Tom eventually went to sleep too.

Mallie sat in her chair all that day, watching her emaciated children sleep. With her body empty of strength and her mind full of fog, she wondered what to do. Yet she knew there was nothing she could do. There were no jobs to be had on the island; every family provided for themselves.

Evening fell. Mallie realised she was shivering; the fire was down to embers. It was time to go to bed; she could at least get warm, drift off to sleep and forget it all for a while. But just as she was rising from her chair, someone rapped on the door.

'Who on earth is that?' said Mallie. She rarely received visitors.

Mallie crossed the room and opened the door. Standing outside and looking up at her was a tiny old man. He was about three foot tall, with wizened, leathery skin and eyes that were sharp yet kind. He took off his hat and said, 'Good evening to you. I'm on my way from one place to another and in need of shelter. May I stay here tonight?'

'You're very welcome to bide here for the night,' said Mallie, 'but besides the warmth of a fire, I've nothing to offer you.'

'Oh, don't worry, I'm not fussy. I'll be happy with a peedie bite to eat and a drop of ale.' He stepped past her into the house.

'You really are welcome,' said Mallie as he settled into her chair. 'Very welcome, as is any stranger who comes to my door. But I'm being truthful with you; we don't have anything to eat.'

'Come on now,' said the little man. 'You must have something.'

'Really,' said Mallie. 'We have nothing.'

'I don't believe you.'

Mallie sighed. 'Well, let me take another look at the meal chest. Maybe there's something I missed.'

She opened the meal chest and peered in. It was empty. But perhaps...

Mallie fetched a heavy wooden spoon from her cupboard. Kneeling down by the meal chest, she pressed the spoon to the inside wall of the chest and scraped it up and down. As she did so, flecks of dried meal, dust and cobwebs settled on the base of the chest.

Mallie scraped at the four walls of the chest until a thin layer of sediment had amassed on the bottom. She used the spoon to gather it into a tiny little pile in the centre of the chest, then scooped it up into five bowls.

Next, Mallie went to the herring barrel. There were no fish in there, but she used a cup to scoop up the salty, fishy water, and poured some into each bowl. She then stirred the sediment and fishy water into a thin, brown paste.

'I've managed to make something,' she said to her visitor, placing the bowl in his hands. 'It's not much, but you're welcome to it.' She put the other four bowls on the table and woke up the children. Soon they were all at the table and eating the paste with delight, savouring each mouthful and licking their bowls when they were done.

The little man, though, was more hesitant. He peered at his bowl for a while before taking a cautious mouthful. He grimaced, swallowed it down and ate the rest.

The children finished eating and went back to bed, grateful to have something in their shrunken stomachs.

The little man said, 'Thank you for that. I don't suppose you have any ale to wash it down?'

'Ale? If I had barley, I would use it to make soup, not ale. Will you take some water?'

'Goodness, no! Never touch the stuff. I think I'll just go to sleep. Goodnight.' He curled up on the chair and closed his eyes. Mallie put a blanket over him then went to bed herself.

IT WAS EARLY MORNING, still dark, when Mallie awoke. She climbed out of bed as her visitor rose from his chair, stretched and yawned.

'Good morning,' he said, keeping his voice low. 'I'll be on my way now. Thank you again for your hospitality.'

'I'm not sure you could call it that,' said Mallie. 'But I'm glad to have met you. Stop by any time you like.'

The man bowed at Mallie and put on his coat. As he opened the door, he paused and turned to her.

'That meal we had last night,' he said. 'Was that really all you had?'

'Yes, it was. And I don't know what we're going to eat today.'

The man nodded slowly. 'Well, it takes a kind heart to share the last of what you've got. You have my blessing.' He tipped his hat at her and went on his way.

Tom awoke soon after that. 'We can't eat, son,' Mallie said to him, 'but we can at least stay warm. Go outside and fill the peat basket.'

Tom took the basket outside and soon staggered back in with a basketful of peat bricks. He knelt by the fire and picked one up. It was big, too big for their fire, which Mallie had covered over before retiring the previous night. So Tom broke the brick in half, and when he did so, a curious thing happened.

A shiny coin fell from the brick and landed on the floor.

Tom picked it up.

'Ma... is this gold?'

Mallie took the coin from Tom. She stared at it.

'Tom,' she said, her eyes fixed on the coin. 'Break another brick.'

Tom did so. Another coin fell onto the ground. He began to laugh, and so did Mallie. They each seized another brick, broke them in half and shrieked with joy as two more coins hit the floor. More bricks were broken, more coins amassed, until all the peat was in pieces and they had a glittering heap of gold.

'We can buy food, Ma!' said Tom.

'We can indeed! Go to the shop for me, would you, son? Buy us some meal, and some fish. And some salt, too, and sugar, and meat... oh, buy whatever you like! Buy everything!'

Tom ran off and soon returned laden with food. Mallie cooked a stew and the children danced and sang as its aroma filled the house. Mallie's family ate bowl after bowl of stew until they were almost sick, and still found a little room for bread and jam afterwards. Mallie watched her children eat, their faces smeared with jam, and she cried with happiness.

'We need never go hungry again,' she said to herself. 'What a blessed day.'

As she said those words, she thought back to the little man who had visited her. She remembered his words as he left.

You have my blessing, he had said.

Now her suspicions were confirmed. The little man had been a trowie, and he had truly blessed them.

MALLIE'S HOUSEHOLD was a happy one from that day. She and her children ate five or six meals per day and gradually regained the weight they had lost. Mallie's hair recovered its shine and her eyes regained their sparkle.

That might have been the end of this story. But there are people in this world who take exception to the happiness of others. The old woman in the house on the hill was one of them.

She was on her way to the shop one day when she ran into Mallie and her children. They had smiles on their faces, meat on their bones and a basket full of food. Mallie gave her a polite smile but did not stop to talk.

'How can that be?' the old woman asked herself. 'It wasn't so long ago that Mallie was begging at my door.'

She could have asked Mallie the source of her good fortune, of course, but their last meeting hadn't been friendly. So the old woman decided to find out for herself.

That night, under cover of darkness, she took the road to Mallie's house, sneaked up to the window and peered in. Mallie was knitting by the fire; the two girls, she presumed, were asleep in bed. The boy sat beside Mallie, playing with a straw doll.

She watched for a while, even after the rain came. Eventually, her patience was rewarded. At a word from Mallie, Tom took a peat brick and snapped it in two. Something shiny and golden fell out. Tom put it in a little box before throwing the lumps of peat on the fire.

Gold! There was gold in Mallie's peat. Why? Had she learnt a spell from a spey wife?

Whatever the truth was, the old woman knew exactly what to do next.

She walked home, brewed tea and sat by her own fire, watching the night pass. When it was very late, she put on her coat and went outside, carrying an empty sack.

The old woman returned to Mallie's house. After peering in the window to check that everyone was asleep, she went to the peat stack and filled her sack with as much of Mallie's peat as she could carry.

She dragged her sack home, panting and heaving all the way up the hill, greed lending her strength. Finally she hauled the sack through her front door.

The old woman took some time to catch her breath. She wanted to savour this moment. She wanted it to be perfect.

Once she was ready, by flickering firelight, she reached down, picked up a peat brick and broke it in two.

There fell to the ground... a mouse.

The mouse looked up at her, squeaked in alarm and ran off to hide.

'What? But... that one must be a dud. I'll try another. Yes, this one will work.'

She picked up another brick and broke it. Another mouse fell out.

The old woman cursed and grabbed another brick, then another, then another. Mice rained down and were soon scampering all over the house. A few even ran up her legs. She batted them away as she broke more and more bricks until finally there were none left. She hadn't found a single gold coin; only mice.

Meanwhile, the mice had found the pantry.

Inside they went. Soon they were on every shelf, biting through every bag, devouring her bread, her barley and everything else. She tried to defend her pantry by striking at the mice with a wooden spoon but it was hopeless. By morning, they had eaten everything she had.

The old woman was hungry herself now, with nothing to eat.

There was only one thing she could do.

Once more, she took the road to Mallie's house. She knocked on the door and Tom answered.

He stared up at her. 'What do you want?' he said.

'Oh, hello, young man. Gosh, how you've grown. I was wondering... I mean... I've had a little problem with mice. I don't have any food to eat. I don't suppose... I don't suppose you could share some with me?'

Tom's mouth hung open.

'You... you want us to share our food with you! We came to you when we were starving, and you called us beggars and gave us nothing! Well, that's what you'll get from us. Nothing!' Tom slammed the door shut.

The old woman hung her head. She'd never known such shame.

Inside, Tom turned from the door to see his mother watching him.

'Can you believe that, Ma?'

Open the door, Tom,' said Mallie. 'Call her back.'

'Why?'

'So we can feed her.'

'But she—'

'I know, son. I know what she did. But we're better than that.'

Tom did as his mother asked. Red-faced, the old woman entered the house.

'Sit down,' said Mallie with a smile. 'Whatever we have, you're welcome to it.'

So Mallie, her children and the old woman ate together. It was the first time they'd done so, but it wasn't the last time. The old woman went home later that day with a basket of food, and the next time someone came to her door, asking for help, she treated them with far more kindness than she'd treated Mallie and Tom.

As for Mallie, she went on with her life, watching her children grow. She still grieved for Johnny, of course, but time did its work and she learnt to live without him. Every day for the rest of her life, she whispered her thanks to the little trowie man who had stopped by her house and blessed her family. *

---

* I heard this story from Orcadian storyteller Tom Muir, who heard it from the late Lawrence Tulloch of Shetland. Lawrence grew up in Shetland at a time when there was no electricity on the islands and most people spent their evenings visiting one another and sharing stories. I was lucky enough to meet him once while in Shetland and to spend an afternoon sharing stories with him, including tales of his time as a lighthouse keeper at Muckle Flagga.

You can listen to a recording of Lawrence on the BBC Radio Shetland show *In About Da Night* on Mixcloud. It's well worth listening to hear the beautiful Shetland dialect as well as Lawrence's stories.

THE SWEETEST MUSIC

Fionn and the Fianna were gathered around their evening fires. They had made camp at the edge of a bubbling burn, in a birchwood glen nestled among the mountains of Alba's north. As songbirds sang among the trees and golden sunlight lit the camp, Fionn put a question to his men.

'Diarmuid,' said Fionn as Bran trotted over to lie at Fionn's feet. 'Answer me this. What is the sweetest music of all?'

'Not hard to answer,' said dark-haired Diarmuid with a smile. 'The sweetest music is the sound of a woman's laughter.'

'A fair answer,' said Fionn, stroking Bran's head. He turned to old, thin-limbed Caoilte. 'What about you, Caoilte? What do you call the sweetest music?'

'The sweetest music,' said Caoilte, 'is the bellowing of horns and the barking of hounds as the deer streaks through the forest and the Fianna give chase.'

'Well spoken,' said Fionn. 'What say you, Goll mac Morna? What is the sweetest music to your ears?'

The grizzled, thick-muscled, one-eyed old warrior was sharpening his sword on a whetstone. He looked up at Fionn and growled, 'The sweetest music is the sound of my sword splitting a skull in two.'

Fionn nodded at his old adversary and turned to his son, Ossian, the finest poet of the Fianna. 'What say you, son?'

Said Ossian, 'The sweetest music is the sound of summer rain falling through the forest at dawn.'

'Sweet music indeed,' said Fionn. 'Sweet music indeed.'

Fionn was quiet for a while. Then Oscar, Ossian's son, said, 'What about you, grandfather? What do you say is the sweetest music?'

Fionn closed his eyes.

The stream sang. Roasting meat hissed and spat. Bran shifted and resettled herself at Fionn's feet.

Then Fionn gave his answer.

'The sweetest music,' said Fionn, 'is the music of what happens.'*

---

* This jewel of a story originated in Ireland before spreading to Scotland. I heard it from David Campbell many years ago, and was fascinated by how it reflected Zen poetry and teachings. Compare this poem by the Japanese Zen poet Ryokan, who lived much of his life as a woodland hermit:

Returning to my hermitage after filling my rice bowl,
Now only the gentle glow of twilight.
Surrounded by mountain peaks and thinly scattered leaves;
In the forest a winter crow flies.

Stevens, John, *One Robe, One Bowl: The Zen Poetry of Ryokan*, Shambhala

It's a great story for bringing strangers together and encouraging people to share their passions. Open the story, give one or two example answers then have Fionn ask your companions what they call the sweetest music. There's no need to announce that you're about to tell a story; just start and people will pick up the game.

THE SEA MAIDEN

Long ago, as long ago as forever, a fisherman and his wife lived on a bay on Scotland's west coast. They were happy enough, for the bay was beautiful, the fishing was good and neither of them were troubled by ambition. Yet a single great sorrow weighed on their lives, for they were childless. As the years passed, that sorrow grew and grew until it darkened their every hour.

Of course the wife had been over the hill to see the hen wife, so many times that her legs were as stout as oaks. She went there so often that the hen wife grew tired of her. Week after week, month after month, year after year she came, moaning and pleading and begging for help. She would do anything for a child, she said. Anything.

The hen wife counselled her against such foolish words. She tried to remain sympathetic to the woman. But everyone has a limit to their patience. So one rainy day, when the fisherman's wife appeared at her door yet again, the hen wife told her an old story.

'There is a cove north of here,' she said. 'Your husband will know it. None pass the way willingly, and there are markers to warn the unwary. For in a cave on that cove lives a sea maiden. Young for her kind, yet powerful. She knows spells that were old when the world was young. Send your husband to her and she will put life in your belly. But I warn you, the price will be high.'

The woman walked home through the lashing rain. Her husband arrived home from his fishing and she bade him sit with her.

'There is a way,' she said. 'A way for us to have a child.'

Her husband listened gravely to her story. Of course he knew the cove. He had rowed as close as he dared and seen its grisly sentries. No fisherman would dream of passing that way. But if the hen wife's words were true...

They talked late into the night. By the time they went to bed, they had made their decision.

They would have their child. No price could be too high.

THE FISHERMAN AWOKE before his wife. He slipped out of bed, slipped on his clothes and left the house. Fear and excitement battled in his belly as he pushed out his boat and rowed north beneath iron clouds.

The sea was restless. It seemed to know what he was about;

it tried to turn him around. The whistling wind whispered warnings in his ears. Yet he steeled himself and rowed onwards.

A few hours later, the fisherman spied his destination ahead.

Hunched and gnarled pines stood on either side of the entrance to a sea loch. From their branches hung the bones of birds, men and beasts, woven together into nightmarish shapes. The bones clicked and clacked and rattled in the wind, a death song with a clear message: stay away.

Yet between those grim guardians, the fisherman rowed.

He rowed up the sea loch, dark mountains looming high above each bank. Soon the fisherman spotted a waterfall shielding a cave entrance.

That was the place.

He beached his craft and walked upshore. Skirting the waterfall, he entered the damp darkness of the cave.

Quickly the day's light faded. The fisherman had come prepared with an oil lamp, which he now lit with an ember he carried in a pouch. Dim light splayed across the walls, illuminating a deep, narrow rupture in the rock. He could feel the weight of the mountain pressing down upon him.

The sea maiden was nowhere to be seen.

He set down the lamp.

'Hello,' he called out, wincing at the volume of his voice as it bounced back at him. Lowering his voice to barely above a whisper, he said, 'I'm... I'm looking for...'

A mass of shadows fell on him.

The fisherman cried out as he hit cold stone. Lying prone

on his back, his head throbbing and spinning, he watched in terror as the sea maiden loomed over him.

Her flesh was grey-green and glistening with slime. She had a long, fishy tail which she now wrapped around his legs and torso, crushing his ribs. Her clothes were mouldy rags and the stench of her breath made him retch.

'Pretty man,' she rasped. 'So pretty, but not as pretty as me. That's why you came. You heard stories of my beauty, yes? You came here to give me your love, yes?'

'No.'

Her face darkened. 'Then what do you want, pretty man?'

'A spell.'

The fisherman told the sea maiden his story. 'Can you help us?' he finished.

The sea maiden answered, 'Yes. I can help you. I will quicken your wife. And I only ask for one thing in return.'

'What is it?'

'Lonely is this cave. Nobody to talk to. Nobody to kiss. I want a husband. A man to call mine. If I put a boy in your wife's belly, you will swear that when he comes of age, I shall be his bride.'

To that, the fisherman agreed.

WHEN HE ARRIVED home that night, the fisherman found his wife sitting by the fire, stroking her belly. She wore a smile on her face that he had never seen before.

He put his hand on her belly and smiled the same smile.

Nine months later, a boy was born. Nine years later, their childless days were a distant dream. Their son's name was Rhion. He was fair-haired, fair-faced and kind of heart. He was everything they had ever wished for. And he was utterly ignorant of the fate that awaited him.

The family knew years of happiness together. Yet when those years were gone, they were gone.

On the night before his fifteenth birthday, Rhion's parents sat him down for what they called 'A serious talk'. They told him the whole story, leaving nothing out.

When the tale was told, Rhion said, 'So she's coming for me? Tomorrow?'

'She is,' said his father. 'But you won't be here.'

'Ever since you were born we have prepared for this day,' said his mother. 'Your father has fished from dawn 'til dusk. I have dried the extra catch, sold it at market and put every penny aside. Here is all we earned.' She handed him a bag, heavy with coins. 'Leave at first light. Head inland. Get as far away from the sea as you can. Buy a horse to speed you on your way. And marry another, so you cannot marry her.'

'What about you?'

'Our memories of you will be enough,' said his father. 'We won't see you again.'

There was much weeping and embracing in the cottage that night. At last, at his parents' urging, Rhion stole out into the awakening day. Clutching his coin bag, he took the path leading up the hill behind their cottage. At the hill's crest, he turned to take one last look at his childhood home.

At that moment, he heard a terrible screeching.

Rhion ran.

RHION TRAVELLED INLAND AS FAST as his legs would carry him. He passed his nights on the roadside or else stopped in a village and spent precious coins on bed and board.

After a few weeks of travel, he started enquiring as to where he might buy a horse. He was directed to a nearby stud farm. In exchange for most of the money in his pouch, the horse dealer handed over to Rhion a white mare. She had grey dapples upon her neck and back, and Rhion thought she was the loveliest thing in the world.

Rhion resumed his journey, this time on horseback. The horse dealer had given him some riding instruction, taking pity on the lad who was alone in the world and as green as they came. Yet it seemed to Rhion that the man had wasted his time. The mare seemed to know his mind better than he did. She never fretted or tested him, despite his nerves, and gave off an air of calm which soothed him as he rode. Rhion had been doing his best to stay far from the sea. Now, he trusted the mare to carry him where he needed to go. Whenever they reached a crossroads, she chose a path without hesitating for a moment.

Things stayed that way for a time. Rhion grew thinner and his clothes more ragged as his coin bag grew lighter. Then, one day, he entered a forest which was unlike anywhere he had ever known.

In this forest, nothing lived. No beetles or slaters crawled among the rocks; no squirrels skittered among the trees; no deer barked, no owl screeched, no fish patrolled the streams and rivers.

Well, thought Rhion, *every road has an ending, and surely this forest does too.* So on they went. Yet a few days later, Rhion began to wonder if the forest really did have an end. Still he had seen no living thing; his food supplies were running dangerously low. And most worryingly of all, his mare no longer seemed to know the way. Within the forest, whenever they reached a crossroads, she would halt, whinny softly and scrape the ground with her hooves.

They were lost.

There was nothing to do but carry on. They went slowly, for Rhion and his mare were both desperately hungry by this point.

One evening, they approached another crossroads.

If I don't choose the right path, thought Rhion, *this turning will be my last.*

From atop his horse Rhion spied movement amid the litter of fallen leaves. He dismounted, walked over, bent down and parted the leaves.

It was a raven. Or rather, the remains of a raven. The limp creature in his hands was thin, cold, mangy; little but bones and feathers and... meat. Not a lot of meat. But meat.

Rhion was starting to salivate when the raven croaked and opened its eyes.

'I am meat,' it said. 'Stringy, smoky, foul meat, but meat. Eat me if you want... or... feed me. Share what you have with me.'

It was hard to sympathise with the raven in that moment, given how hungry Rhion was. Yet for some reason he could not have explained, he took a last tiny strip of meat from his pocket, tore it in two with his teeth and dropped one half into the raven's open beak.

The raven swallowed the meat and shot into the air, flying in circles around Rhion.

'Take the path to your left!' it croaked. 'If you need me, call and I will come.'

So Rhion rode that way, his stomach knotted and whining. The next day, feeling even weaker and hungrier, he came to a river. He dismounted to drink and saw on the stream bank a fat, glistening salmon, flapping and slapping itself against the stones.

Rhion could almost taste its tender, pink flesh. But before he could take a step further, the salmon spoke.

'I am meat,' said the salmon. 'Smooth, succulent, juicy meat. You would grow fat as a bull by feasting on me. So eat me... or help me. Throw me back in the river.'

You can't imagine how badly he wanted to eat that salmon. It would have been so easy, so much within the order of things for him to kill it, cook it, feast on its flesh. But instead he picked up the floundering fish and threw it into the water.

The salmon disappeared from sight then burst from the water, leaping high and shouting to Rhion, 'Follow the path uphill and out of the forest! If you need me, call and I will come!'

That was the way Rhion went. He was even more wretched than before, of course, but the salmon's words had filled him with hope, and his mount seemed to sense it; there was a new strength in her step. Up and up they went until the trees thinned out around them.

Rhion left the forest behind. Looking ahead, he saw only mountains. They were as lifeless as the forest; nothing but bare stone in every direction. Yet the raven and the salmon had told him to go that way.

Night fell. Rhion rode on by the light of the silver moon. He might have been on the moon, he thought, so lifeless and empty was this place...

Rhion's thoughts were interrupted when his mare suddenly drew to a halt.

She whinnied, and her whinny was full of fear.

Ahead of them was a shape that Rhion had taken to be just another rock. But looking again, he saw that it was not a rock.

It was a wolf.

A mangy wolf. A starved, skeletal, dead or dying, black-furred wolf.

Rhion dismounted. He walked over to the prone shape, believing he had nothing to fear from it.

He bent down. There wasn't much meat on it. But meat it was...

The wolf opened its eyes and raised its head, exposing shining white teeth.

'I am not meat,' it said, its voice as deep as the mountain was high. 'I am your brother. I once hunted beside you. Feed me.'

'I have no meat,' said Rhion.

'You have meat,' said the wolf, looking past him.

Rhion turned and saw, glistening white in the moonlight, his mare.

Her eyes bulged with fear as she looked from the wolf to Rhion.

Rhion did not want to give his mare to the wolf. He had grown to love her; she was his companion, his guide, his only friend. But his heart told him he would need a new companion on the journey to come.

Rhion stepped aside. The wolf rose to its feet. It stalked forward; the mare turned on her heels but she was too weak for a chase. The wolf leapt at her. His teeth sank into her haunches and she fell.

Rhion forced himself to watch as the wolf set to work, gnawing and crunching and ripping and swallowing. By the time the wolf was done, it was a different creature.

No more was it thin and mangy; it stood as tall and broad as his mare. Grinning at Rhion, its teeth shining like silver swords, it said, 'Climb onto my back and hold on tight. The one you seek lies ahead.'

Rhion did as he was ordered. He climbed up onto the black wolf's back and as soon as he did so his hunger left him. His fear left him. He grinned and laughed as the wolf walked, then ran, then surged forward as swiftly as the dawn through the mountains, sure of its way as they travelled upwards, upwards, ever upwards.

FAST THEY FLEW upon stony roads, all night and all day, climbing higher until there was no higher left. Rhion guessed they had come to the very roof of the world.

At the roof of the world one mountain stood higher than all the others. It looked like it could have split the sky asunder. Beneath it, mountaintops stretched into the distance in every direction, like the rippling waves of the sea.

Atop that tallest of mountains stood a castle. Before the castle, the wolf finally halted.

Turrets bristled above black stone walls that seemed to grow out of the mountain. The castle was a creature of stone that might crack open the world with a shake of its haunches. At any moment it might open a hundred hidden eyes, or so it seemed to Rhion. Drawing closer, he saw demons and devils, dragons and ghouls spewing from the stone walls, warning him back.

'Why have we come here?' he asked the wolf.

'To find your true bride,' said the wolf. 'She is a prisoner inside.'

Over the drawbridge they ran, through the enormous doors that opened to the wolf's howl. Down vast, dark corridors they went, and up staircases so wide that an army might have marched up them without breaking rank.

Finally, the wolf slowed outside an open door. Into the room Rhion rode.

In contrast to the dark, dank corridors, this room was luxurious. A fire roared in the fireplace. Candles burned in golden candelabras and upon a magnificent chandelier. Books lined the walls, their spines as tall as Rhion. An enormous piano stood by a bay window that surveyed the mountaintops and stars. Jugs of ale sat on the table, and beside the fire sat a young woman.

She was staring unabashedly at Rhion, which was understandable, given that he had just ridden into the room astride an enormous black wolf.

'Who are you?' she asked.

'I'm Rhion. Who are you? What are you doing here?'

'My name is Una. I'm doing the same thing I've done all day, every day since the giant who lives in this castle took me prisoner.' She held up a mass of fabric. 'I'm making my wedding dress. On the day I finish it, the giant will force me to marry him.'

Rhion's eyes wandered over the dress. He'd never given much thought to dresses but he could see that this one was extraordinary. His eyes quickly returned to the maiden, though, for he found her far more interesting than any dress.

'I would like to marry you,' he said.

'Good for you. But as I just told you, I must marry the giant.'

'If I were to rescue you from the giant, would you marry me instead?'

'Well, if it's you or him... but how are you going to do that?'

Rhion wasn't sure how. He hadn't a clue, really. But he knew who to ask.

He looked over at the wolf, who had stretched himself out on a rug.

'How can I defeat the giant?' asked Rhion.

'I know only this,' said the wolf. 'To win the maiden's hand, you must kill the giant. To kill the giant, you must destroy his heart. But the giant does not keep his heart in his chest. He keeps it hidden in some secret place, known to none other than him.'

'How can I find out where it is hidden?'

Before the wolf could answer, the floor shook. Rhion and the wolf quickly hid themselves and a few moments later, the giant strode into the room.

'There you are, my sweet thing,' he said to Una. 'You'd better be working hard on that dress. I grow impatient to—'

'Darling!' Una leapt up and ran across the room. 'I'm so glad to see you home. Come, sit down, put your feet up. You look so tired. Can I get you an ale?'

'Er, well, yes,' said the giant, looking puzzled. He sat down in an enormous armchair and took the jug of ale that Una offered him. 'You're being very nice to me today.'

'Well, I missed you,' she said.

'I missed you too,' said the giant, finishing the ale.

Have another,' said Una. 'I imagine you walked a long way today. Can I give you a foot rub?'

'That would be lovely,' he said, finishing his second ale and pouring himself a whisky as Una set to work. She pulled the giant's socks off and sat down to rub and pummel his gnarled, crusty feet.

'Ooh, that's lovely,' he said.

'Giant?' she said.

'Yes.'

'I was wondering. People tell so many tales of you. The great and terrible giant, the one who cannot be killed, for his heart is hidden somewhere unknown to anyone. It would be so awful if anyone was ever to find your heart and kill you. I would be devastated, left alone without you in this brutal world. Would you tell me where it is, so I can help ensure no-one ever finds it?'

'Now, that's not information I've ever shared with anyone before.' He sighed. 'Yet you are good to me. And they say that trust is important between lovers.'

'It is, it is,' said Una, rubbing harder. 'And I love you so much.'

'Hmmm... well, in that case, I suppose I can trust you. There is an island in the middle of Loch Affric, thick with birch and pine trees. On that island there is a pool, and at the edge of the pool is a duck's nest. In that nest is an egg, and my heart is in the egg.' And with that, the giant fell asleep.

Rhion and the wolf leapt from their hiding places. Rhion climbed onto the wolf, promised to return soon and shot out the door. They tore through the castle then across the country, arriving at Loch Affric just as the sun rose behind the mountains.

'Can you swim?' Rhion asked the wolf.

'No.'

'Neither can I.'

'Then fly,' said the wolf.

Rhion understood. He called out 'Raven!', and the raven swept down from the sky.

'Climb upon my back,' said the raven, alighting on the stony shore and growing in size until he was as large as a horse. Rhion dismounted the wolf, mounted the raven and took to the sky. The raven carried Rhion over the water to the island, and there he crept through the trees until he saw the pool.

There was the nest. There was the duck in her nest, balanced atop an enormous egg.

Rhion crept around the edge of the pond. His feet sank into the soft, squelchy, mossy ground.

The duck watched him approach.

'Never mind me, duck,' murmured Rhion. 'There's a good duck. I'm just wandering by...'

The duck burst into motion, flying away over the pool and out of sight. As it did so, it knocked the egg out of the nest and into the pond.

Rhion approached the edge and peered into the water. The pool was deep. Very deep. He knew this because he could see the egg down at the bottom, giving off a faint, spectral light.

Even if Rhion could swim that far down, he would never make it back up. He would drown. The egg was lost.

Unless...

'Salmon!' Rhion called out.

He waited. Nothing happened. Perhaps the salmon was too far away to hear him...

The salmon came shooting through the air, landing with a mighty splash in the pond. It swam to the bottom of the pool and then back to the surface, the egg in its mouth.

'Thank you! Thank you!' said Rhion.

'My debt to you is paid,' said the salmon. It dived down and then leapt from the pool, through the trees, disappearing from sight.

Rhion returned to where the raven awaited him. It carried him back to the waiting wolf.

'My debt to you is paid,' said the raven before flying away.

Rhion rode the wolf back to the giant's castle. They rejoined Una and the giant just as the giant awoke upon the floor, his vision spinning and his head throbbing. Una still sat beside the fire, her dress in hand.

Climbing unsteadily to his feet, the giant fixed his gaze on her and frowned. 'You gave me too much ale, woman,' he said. 'A wife should know better...'

Something in the corner of his eye caught his attention.

He turned and saw a young man sitting astride a black wolf, watching him with a broad grin upon his face.

In his hand was the giant's beating heart.

The giant turned pale.

'Give that to me,' he said.

'Maybe I will,' said Rhion. 'Or maybe I won't. Maybe I'll do this instead.' He gave the heart a squeeze.

The giant cried out and fell to his knees. 'Please! I'll do anything...'

'Anything?' said Una.

'Anything!' gasped the giant.

'In that case, release Una,' said Rhion.

'What? No! She is to be...'

Rhion squeezed the egg again, harder this time.

'Ow! Take her! Take her, just give that to me!'

Rhion ceased squeezing the giant's heart, but he did not hand it over either.

'I have an idea,' he said. 'You will release Una. I will take her away from here and you shall not pursue us. In return, I will give you your heart back. But you are not to keep it in an egg, underneath a duck.'

'Where do you want me to keep it?'

Rhion pointed. The giant groaned, prompting Rhion to begin juggling the heart between his hands.

The giant growled at Rhion. 'Very well,' he said.

The giant stiffened his fingers and with a mighty roar, plunged them into his chest. He took hold of his ribs and pulled them out, two by two, until his chest was gaping open, revealing an empty space where his heart should have been.

Rhion threw the heart. It landed in the empty space in the giant's chest. The giant pushed his ribs back into place, smoothed out his tattered skin, wiped off the blood on his sleeve and smiled.

'Will you stay for tea and cake?' he asked.

AFTER AN ENJOYABLE MORNING EATING, drinking and gossiping with the giant, Rhion and Una mounted the wolf and left the castle. They took the path through the mountains to the once-dead forest and saw that it had returned to life. Squirrels scampered, deer barked and songbirds crowded the branches.

'So, about marriage...' said Rhion as they lay among the grass in a green meadow, the wolf stretched out beside them.

'Of course,' said Una, who had been more than impressed by Rhion's actions so far. He seemed like good husband material. 'But do you want to keep wandering as you have done?'

'I don't think so. I'm ready to settle down somewhere if you are.'

'I've always wanted to live in the west, beside the sea,' said

Una. 'To look out over the waters and dream of Tir Na Nog. To maybe catch a glimpse of the Cailleach washing her plaid in the Corryvreckan. Would you be happy in the west?'

Rhion didn't like the sound of that. He still feared his past, which he hadn't got round to sharing just yet.

'Let's go to the east,' he said. 'The west isn't all it's cracked up to be. The weather's dreadful.'

Una agreed and they set off east.

AFTER A LEISURELY JOURNEY up and down Scotland's east coast, Rhion and Una found a shoreside village where the people were friendly and the sea full of fish. They built a cottage at the edge of the village and set about building a life together. The wolf stayed with them.

All was well, and the story might have ended here. But one day, as Rhion and Una strolled along the shore, the sea maiden shot out of the water, wrapped her tail around Rhion and pulled him kicking and screaming into the sea.

Una stood motionless. It had happened so fast that she could barely comprehend it. But as her breathing slowed, the truth sank in. Something had taken her beloved Rhion away from her.

Una heard a growl behind her. She turned to see the wolf watching her.

'What happened? Who was that creature, who stole my husband from me?'

The wolf told her Rhion's full tale. Rhion had always been

afraid to tell it to her, for he feared to face it himself. It was easier to keep silent and pretend that there had never been a sea maiden.

'I wish he had just told me,' said Una when the tale was told. 'What can I do?'

'You must make a bargain with her. Give her something in exchange for your husband. You have something she wants.'

'What is that?'

'Something that will help her to win her own husband. A husband who truly loves her.'

Una thought about this for a while then smiled. Of course,' she said.

Later that day, Una returned to the shore. She walked to the water's edge and called out to the sea maiden, singing a special song that the wolf had taught her.

The water stirred and the sea maiden emerged.

'What do you want?' said the sea maiden

'To offer you something in exchange for Rhion.'

'Rhion is mine,' said the sea maiden. 'I made Rhion. I put him inside his mother's belly. I made him for me, to love me, and he betrayed me. But I have him now, and I will never give him up...'

Her words faded away as Una fished something from her pack and held it up to the sunlight.

The sea maiden stared, enraptured. She slithered forward, reared up on her fish-tail and reached out to stroke it. She gently took hold of the dress, hissing in wonder at its beauty. Finally, she slipped it over her scaly, rag-clad body.

'Go now,' said Una. 'Find one who loves you.'

The sea maiden disappeared below the water. A few moments later, Rhion burst from the water, flew through the air and landed on the sand with a thump.

Rhion and Una walked home hand in hand. The wolf retuned to the forest, for its debt was paid. And here the story truly does end.*

---

* This story is for the most part based on a story from *Popular Tales of the West Highlands* by J.F Campbell, also called The Sea Maiden. It's a long and complex story which is entrancing at times and at other times very hard to follow. I've simplified it and blended it with elements of the closely related Norwegian story of *The Giant Who Had No Heart in His Body*.

The ogre or giant who keeps his heart outside his body is a common folklore motif which appears in stories throughout the world; it seems to touch something very deep in us.

You can listen to Scottish storyteller Ryan Martin tell a version of The Sea Maiden on his Finding Folklore Podcast.

THE BAOBHAN SITH

Four young men once lived in Coylumbridge, which sits by the River Drurie at the edge of the Cairngorm mountains. Their names were Jamie, Callum, Alasdair and Ranald, and they were keen hunters. Their favourite place to hunt was the vast Rothiemurchus forest, where countless deer lurked among the shadows of the endless pines.

One autumn day, they set out hunting on horseback. They rode east for several hours into the forest, following well-known paths. Though they could have hunted closer to home, they enjoyed ranging widely and seeing far-off corners of the forest.

It was late afternoon when they sighted a stag among the undergrowth. They spurred their horses forward and the hunt began. The four friends worked like a pack of wolves, steering the stag this way and that as they tightened their net. But hunting is hard, the stag was fleet-footed and it finally broke free of their net, disappearing into the dusk.

The hunters didn't take it too hard; that was simply the way it went some days. They circled their horses and Callum passed round a flask of whisky.

'We came a fair way east before we sighted the stag, and he led us further east,' said Ranald. 'It'll be a long ride home, and I'd wager there's rain on the way.'

'We needn't head home tonight,' said Alasdair. 'I know a bothy south of here. It's a cosy wee place with benches and a fireplace. Why don't we pass the night there?'

'I vote we stay at the bothy,' said Callum.

Jamie and Ranald were happy to go along with the plan. They didn't fancy a long, wet ride home. So the hunters followed Alasdair as he led them through the forest to the bothy.

They arrived within the hour. The bothy stood on a bank beside a stream, offering a fine view over the forest to the mountains beyond. It looked like a perfect spot to pass the night. They tied up the horses just as the first raindrops fell, and headed inside.

It was cold inside, but dry. The custom when using a bothy in Scotland is to leave a stack of firewood ready for the next visitor, and somebody had done just that. Ranald got the fire going and they dug in their packs for the bread, cheese and dried meat which they always carried. It turned out Callum and Alasdair both had whisky on them.

The four hunters ate while passing round the flasks. After they had finished eating, they began telling stories. Local gossip mingled with ancient stories of giants and gruagachs, interspersed with plenty of jesting and laughter.

'I've had my fill of stories for now,' said Callum in time. 'I fancy some music.'

All eyes turned to Jamie. He was a fine singer and fiddler. Jamie usually carried his fiddle in one of his saddlebags, for lazy afternoons by the loch or for evenings such as this one.

The only problem was that he was a little shy.

'Give us a song, Jamie,' they said.

'Ach no, you don't want to hear a song from me.'

'Aye we do! Come on now.'

It went as it always did until Jamie relented. He gave them a song, then a second, then a third. He was hard to get going but once he did, it was hard to stop him, especially if he had a few drams in him.

'Now for some tunes!' said Alasdair eventually. Jamie was in full swing now; without further encouragement he went out to retrieve his fiddle, uncased it and put bow to string. He played bright and cheery tunes as his friends cheered, clapped and poured whisky down their throats.

'Well,' said Ranald eventually, 'this is as fine an evening as I've had in a while.'

'Couldn't be better,' agreed Alasdair.

'Oh, I'm not so sure about that, lads,' said Callum.

'What do you mean?' asked Alasdair.

'I mean that it could be better,' answered Callum, a mischievous look entering his eyes, 'if we had some female company.'

'Er, hold on,' said Jamie. 'I don't think you're supposed to say that...'

At that very moment, the door to the bothy opened.

Into the bothy walked four young women. They wore green

dresses which accented their voluptuous curves and dark, waist-length hair. They halted in the centre of the bothy and smiled at the four dumbstruck hunters.

'We were just passing by,' said one. 'We saw firelight in the window, and heard fine music, and thought perhaps to come in and pass the night with you.'

The hunters could not believe their luck.

'Of... of course,' said Ranald, regaining his composure. 'Of course you can stay here. It's a bothy, after all, everyone is welcome. Would you like something to eat?'

'You're so kind,' said another of the women. 'But we don't want to eat. We want to drink and we want to dance.'

Callum and Alasdair almost fell over themselves as they rushed to offer the women a dram. The women took the proffered flasks and threw their heads back as they drank.

'Music now!' said one of them. 'Music!'

'Come on then, Jamie!' said Callum.

'I don't know,' said Jamie. 'I'm tired, and my throat's a little sore...'

'Don't be daft!' hissed Ranald, shooting Jamie a murderous look. 'Sing! Sing! Sing!'

The others took up the chant, clapping their hands and stomping their feet.

'Sing! Sing! Sing!'

Jamie didn't want to sing.

He'd heard tales of men who wished for female company when out in the wilds at night. Strange and terrible creatures could be drawn by such words. Sure, these women looked harmless enough. But why were they wandering through the forest at night?

'Sing! Sing! Sing!'

It's just superstition, he told himself. *Just stories.*

Jamie drew breath and began to sing.

The company cheered. Each of the women beckoned to a hunter, and soon three couples danced on the bothy floor. The fourth woman tried to catch Jamie's eye, but he avoided her gaze, looking instead at the floor or the fire as he sang.

He gave them a few merry ditties, then took up his fiddle. The dancers loved this and swung one another wildly, stamping and clapping. They danced ever faster, and Jamie could not help but match them.

Faster and faster the company danced. Harder and harder they stomped their feet. Everyone was grinning and laughing, singing along at the top of their voices.

> Diddly dee, da-diddly dee,
> Diddly dee, da-diddly dah...

Jamie noticed that the fire was burning hotter and hotter, even though nobody was feeding it. The flames leapt and danced; sweat poured from his brow; he felt himself grow giddy.

> Diddly dee, da-diddly dee,
> Diddly dee, da-diddly dah...

Faster and faster the dancers danced. Jamie's fiddle-arm was aching but he kept going, as if the same force that stoked the fire had hold of him.

All the while, the fourth woman tried to catch Jamie's eye.

Jamie continued to avoid her gaze. He studied the floor, the fireplace, the forgotten whisky flasks. But as he grew more tired, his concentration began to flag. Was she still looking at him, he wondered? Or had she given up?

He risked a glance.

Their eyes locked together.

She grinned and beckoned him to her.

> Diddly dee, da-diddly dee,
> Diddly dee, da-diddly doh...

Jamie put down his fiddle.

> Diddly dee, da-diddly dee,
> Diddly dee, da-diddly doh...

The world faded away as he stood and walked towards her. There was nothing but her eyes. Her eyes.

She opened her arms to him.

In that same moment, the other three women threw back their heads and howled.

The hunters laughed and howled too.

The women dancing with Callum, Alasdair and Ranald each drew back a hand. They swung at their partners' necks with swift, slicing motions.

The hunters ceased singing. Blood spurted from their

throats, spraying the room and soaking the women. Alasdair, Callum and Ranald fell to their knees and the women leapt on them, pinning them to the ground. They put their mouths to the hunters' necks and drank.

The last woman standing licked her lips and snarled at Jamie.

Jamie threw himself at her. He knocked her to the ground and before she could recover, he turned and ran out the door.

He crashed through the door and looked around for somewhere to hide. The horses! They had crowded together, sensing the threat, and by instinct Jamie hid himself among them.

Jamie looked back towards the bothy. From out of the door slunk a grey wolf. It saw him, bared its teeth and ran at him. But when it neared the horses it pulled back.

The wolf circled the tightly packed horses. They stamped and whinnied, eyes wide with fear, but did not scatter. The wolf's eyes were fixed on Jamie, and they were eyes he recognised well.

Jamie stayed there all night as the wolf circled him, never looking away for a moment. In time, the light of morning crept into the air, illuminating the mountains and the dark forest.

As Jamie crouched among the horses, watching the wolf watch him, he had plenty of time to reflect. The stories he'd heard weren't just stories. The women weren't really women. They were Baobhan Sith, creatures drawn to any hunter out in the wilds who wished aloud for female company.

If only his friends had known. If only he'd told them.

Finally, three more wolves emerged from the house. They called to the fourth wolf with sharp yips, jerking their heads in the direction of the tree-covered foothills of the Cairngorms.

The fourth wolf gave Jamie a last glare and a last growl before turning and joining its companions. They loped away into the trees and were soon lost to sight.

It was a long time before Jamie found the courage to leave his hiding place among the horses. He couldn't bring himself to go into the bothy, so he untied the horses and headed home without looking inside. Eventually he returned to recover the bodies of his friends and give them a proper burial. He retrieved his fiddle too, but never found the will to play it again.

He never sang after that night either. Instead he told stories of the Baobhan Sith, so that no other hunter would meet the same fate as his friends.*

---

* What better way to finish than with shapeshifting vampire fairies?

Baobhan Sith is pronounced 'bavan-shee' (similar to the Irish banshee). This story is not widely told in Scotland, although the Baobhan Sith have inspired numerous visual artists, fantasy writers and game creators, including Raymond E. Feist. This story was recorded as The Hunters & The Maidens in C.M. Robertson's *Folklore from the West of Ross-Shire* and was later picked up by Donald Mackenzie in his *Scottish Folklore & Folk-Life* and by Katherine Briggs in her *Encyclopaedia of Faeries*.

Robertson's version has the events taking place at a sheiling between Loch Droma and Braemore, and he offers a few variations as to the events and where they took place, which suggests that the story may once have been more widespread. I chose to set my version in the Rothiemurchus forest, in the shadow of the great Cairngorm massif, as I felt the setting matched the atmosphere of the tale.

AFTERWORD

Thank you for joining me on this journey. In a time when a handful of myths are endlessly recycled in popular media, it's very rewarding to share some lesser-known folklore. Though it is tragic that in Scotland we have very few stories of our ancient gods and no text akin to Ireland's *Book of Invasions* or the Welsh *Mabinogion*, we do still have a vast body of folklore, only a fragment of which is contained within these pages. These stories are precious, a window into the world of our ancestors, and it's my great honour to share them with you.

As ever, if you enjoyed the stories, I'd highly recommend you do some further exploration. Use the footnotes to find other versions of the stories you like best. Listen to them told orally, on *House of Legends Podcast*, the audiobook version of the title, or elsewhere, and savour the differences rather than worrying about which version is 'correct'. Tell them yourself and see how they live on your tongue. Just to read or listen to the stories is to feed the fire of the tradition, to help keep it burning for future generations, so thank you for tending the flames.

I've got some other books if you're interested. *Irish Mythology: The Children of Danu* and *Finn & The Fianna* are the next two books in this series; they retell the Mythological Cycle and Fianna Cycle of Irish mythology. My book *The Shattering Sea* is the first volume of *The Orkney Cycle*, a mythic fantasy epic which is the most popular book among my dedicated readers.

You can also train as a storyteller with me online or join one of my mythic immersion retreats in the Scottish Highlands. There's lots on offer; the best way to keep in touch is to join my mailing list at houseoflegends.me/landing-page, which gets you my free ebook, *Silverborn*.

One last thing: the mythology market is being swamped by low quality, A.I-generated books. These titles are usually written by anonymous 'authors' or by named authors who put out a dozen new books each month. Watch out for them.

If you'd like to support me and vote for a future in which books are written by real authors, the best way to do so is to leave me a review on Amazon. I really appreciate your support!

Wishing you many good tales around many fires.

Daniel Allison

THE DREAM OF ANGUS

A SAMPLE STORY FROM IRISH MYTHOLOGY: THE CHILDREN OF DANU

The Tuatha Dé Danaan never loved anyone so much as they loved Angus.

They loved him for his kindness, his generosity, the bounty of his feasts. Yet mostly they loved him for the way he made them feel. To stand in his presence, to look into his eyes, to hear him sing was to feel loved. To know that whatever troubles one had would soon pass. He made people feel loved and made people love one another, leaving a trail of happiness, friendship and new romance in his wake.

Hundreds of Tuatha were hopelessly in love with golden-haired Angus. Yet Angus had never been in love himself. That is not to say he never fancied a woman, or shared a kiss or a night of passion. Yet his heart had never opened so far as to fall in love.

That changed one night at Brú na Bóinne.

Angus was asleep in bed. He woke up to the sound of a harp being plucked. He sat up and saw a woman sitting on the end of his bed. She wore a cloak of white feathers. Her hair was white, her skin pale, her eyes as black as a crow's wing.

She was the most beautiful woman Angus had ever seen.

He opened his mouth to greet her and found he could neither speak nor move. He could only lie still and listen. So he did.

He listened as she played and sang for him, gazing into his eyes all the while. It seemed like hours or even years passed in which she played. However long it was, it was more than long enough for Angus to finally fall in love.

Then he woke up.

Angus shot up in bed. It had been a dream. Yet she had seemed so real. And this awakening in his heart, how could he feel it if she had not been real?

He had to get back to her. That meant he had to get back to sleep.

Angus lay back and closed his eyes.

Sleep would not come.

Eventually Angus gave up trying to sleep. Instead he dressed and took his twin swords and spears to the practice yard. There he duelled all day with everyone who would face him, thinking to tire himself out and be sure of sound sleep that night.

It worked. Night fell, Angus went to bed and, despite his excitement, quickly fell asleep.

The white-cloaked woman was waiting for him.

Again she played and sang for him while he lay abed,

entranced. When Angus finally woke up, it pained him to leave her, yet he was full of joy. He somehow knew he would see her again the coming night.

He was right. Angus saw her that night, and the night after that, and every night. It was always the same dream, and Angus never spoke a word to her. Yet he felt he came to know her all the same.

This went on until one night, a year and a night since the first visitation, Angus went to sleep and did not dream.

'It doesn't matter,' he told himself when he awoke. 'It's only one night. I will see her again tonight.' Yet she did not come that night, nor the night after. By that time, Angus knew in his heart that when he next dreamed, he would dream alone.

Angus plunged into despair. He stayed in bed day after day, scarcely rising to eat or bathe. His mother, Boann, grew greatly worried and asked him to tell her what was the matter. He could not even bring himself to speak. Boann sent for healers, but none who came found anything amiss with Angus.

The Dagda had been on a tour of the country, visiting the halls of far-dwelling friends. He arrived at Brú na Bóinne, and Boann explained the situation to him. They talked at length before reaching a decision together.

They would summon Diancecht.

Neither of them had any great love for Diancecht. It was said that he had murdered his own son, and that he had fled the Well of Slaine when Bres attacked it at Moytura. Yet no healer in Eriu had more experience than him.

Diancecht no longer wandered the roads. He kept to his own hall, where he need not face the dark looks many sidhe would give him. Yet he could be lured from home with promises of coin. Thus, a messenger left Brú na Bóinne laden with silver and gold.

Several days later, the messenger returned, Diancecht walking behind him.

The white-bearded healer entered Brú na Bóinne. He met Boann and the Dagda and allowed them to guide him to Angus' bedchamber.

They entered. Angus was lying in bed. His skin was pale, his eyes empty of expression. He stared up at Diancecht, who studied him for a moment, then laughed.

'Why are you laughing?' asked Boann.

'I am laughing because you paid dearly for me to diagnose what should be obvious to everyone.'

'And what is that?'

'The lad is in love.'

'Don't be ridiculous!' said Boann. 'This is far more serious than lovesickness. I would know if my own son was in love—'

Angus interrupted her. 'He's right. I am in love. My lover has left me, and thus I have no will to live.'

Diancecht laughed and laughed until Boann ordered him out of the chamber.

'Now, son,' said the Dagda. 'You might have told us this sooner, but at least we know now. So give us the whole story.'

Angus relayed the tale of his dreams to his parents. When

he was done, Boann said, 'It's clear what must be done. We must send scouts out across the country, to search every glen, hill and shore for this girl of yours.'

Angus nodded. 'Thank you,' he said.

Messengers left Brú na Bóinne soon afterwards, in search of the woman with the swan-feather cloak.

Weeks later, the Dagda entered Angus' bedchamber and said, 'I have good news for you, son.'

Angus sat up in bed, his malnourished bones creaking.

'One of our scouts went to Tipperary. She climbed into the high hills and reached the Lake of the Dragon Mouth. There she met the druid Bov, who claimed to have knowledge of your lover. Bov bids you go to him there.'

Angus leapt out of bed. Hurriedly he put on clean clothes and left Brú na Bóinne, shielding his eyes from the sun; he had not seen it for weeks.

He travelled south across the country. It was spring and Banba was coming alive all around him. Flowers bloomed in the meadows and red squirrels bounded through the trees. Angus swam in waterfall pools and ate fruits and berries off the branch. He waved greetings to strangers and felt his old spirits returning as Tipperary drew closer.

Finally Angus reached the Lake of the Dragon Mouth. It was a small, almost circular mountain lake, ringed by dark cliffs. Not far from the bank was a little hut, and in that hut Angus found Bov awaiting him.

Angus and the white-bearded druid sat down upon deer hides. Bov poured ale for Angus, stoked his peat fire and said, 'I know the maiden you seek.

'Her name is Caer. She is the daughter of Ethel, a druid well-renowned in these parts. Yet as powerful as Ethel is, his daughter is more powerful.

'When Caer came of age, Ethel wished to see her married. She refused every man who courted her, which led her father to rage and threaten her.

'Caer took matters into her own hands. She came here to this lake, which has always been a favourite haunt of hers, and cast a spell.'

'What did this spell do?' asked Angus.

'Since the casting of the spell, Caer's life follows this order. Every first year, she is bound to the shores of this lake. She cannot leave it. Every second year, she takes the shape of a swan and flies across Eriu in a company of fifty swans. It is at Samhain that she turns.'

'So Caer believes that no man will wish to marry a woman who is either bound to a lake or flying free as a swan.'

Bov nodded. 'And I know what you're thinking, lad,' he said, his expression hardening.

'You're thinking that you're the famous Angus Óg. The man whom every maiden in Eriu swoons over. This woman went to the trouble of visiting you and singing to you in your dreams, every night for a year and a night. You're thinking that if you can only talk to her, she will change her mind. She'll break her own spell and go off with you as your bride.'

Angus nodded.

'I thought as much. You're wrong, son. So very wrong. That might be what any other woman would do, but not this one. Not Caer. Her will is strong; she will not change her shape or her ways for you.'

Angus sat in silence for a while, searching the flames of the fire, before meeting Bov's gaze.

'We'll see,' he said.

Six months remained until Samhain. During that time, Angus did not return to Brú na Bóinne. Instead he walked the length and breadth of Eriu. Wherever he went, people recognised him and asked him what business he was about. So the story soon spread that Angus Óg was gathering ingredients for a spell; one which would break Caer's enchantment and make her his.

Angus gathered quartz from the cliffs of Donegal. He hunted for owl feathers in the woods of Slieve Bloom. He filled his bag with bone, fur, stone, seed and claw, until Samhain drew near and he turned for Tipperary.

Angus approached the lake at sunset, beneath iron-dark clouds.

He was not alone there.

The cliffs surrounding the lake were packed with onlookers. Tuatha and even Gaels had come from across Tipperary and throughout Eriu to witness the working of Angus' spell.

Angus approached the water's edge. He waded in until he was knee-deep.

He waited.

Dusk inched towards night.

In the day's dying light, fifty-one swans flew towards the lake. They were bound in pairs by silver chains at their necks, and the lead swan wore a chain of gold.

They landed on the water. The swan with the gold chain paddled away from the others and towards Angus.

She cast off her swan form and became a woman with white hair, black eyes and a white, swan-feather cloak.

The watchers strained to hear as Angus cleared his throat and chose his words, which he found surprisingly difficult.

'I... er, I mean... I am Angus.'

'I know,' said Caer.

'Yes. Well... I am going to cast a spell.'

'Then cast it.'

Angus reached into his bag. Raising his trembling hand high, he scattered its contents over Caer, over himself and over the surrounding water.

Angus spoke the words of his spell, and became a swan.

Caer smiled. She spoke druid-words and became a swan again too. She and Angus beat their wings, rose into the sky and flew away into the night.

Angus had indeed set out to break Caer's spell. Yet as he walked the roads of Eriu, he came to realise that before he asked her to change her ways for him, he should learn her ways. If she wished to be a swan, he would be a swan too. If she wished to live by the lake, he would dwell there too, for a while at least.

Angus and Caer lived as swans for a time, and they lived by the Lake of the Dragon Mouth for a time. Eventually Caer tired of that life, and she and Angus left the lake, in their sidhe forms, as husband and wife. They dwell together now in Brú na Bóinne, but often leave home to fly as swans across the land they love.

ACKNOWLEDGMENTS

I want to say a very big thank you to Donald Smith and Daniel Abercrombie at The Scottish Storytelling Centre for working so tirelessly to keep the tradition alive and vibrant.

To my Myth Singers students, thank you for continually showing me new trapdoors in stories I thought I knew.

Thanks to everyone at Martial Arts Academy for being in my corner and giving me so much fuel for the fight scenes.

Fiona Herbert, thank you for the power of your elf eyes once more.

Angus King, thanks for being the best narrator I could hope for.

Oak and Ash crew, thank you for making the dream of full mythic immersion in the highlands come true.

Finally, thank you to every elder who encouraged me to learn and pass on the stories they told me. This book wouldn't exist but for your kindness.

ALSO BY DANIEL ALLISON

CELTIC MYTHS & LEGENDS RETOLD

Scottish Myths & Legends

Irish Mythology: The Children of Danu

Finn & The Fianna

THE ORKNEY CYCLE

The Shattering Sea

Silverborn & Other Tales

HOUSE OF LEGENDS PODCAST

House of Legends Podcast brings you powerful myths and legends told by storytellers from across the world.

Stories are told by Daniel and his guests, and Daniel also shares readings from his books.

Listen on Apple Podcasts, Spotify or wherever you get your podcasts.

FREE DOWNLOAD OFFER

As the winter winds shriek and their family sleeps, Grunna and Talorc sit at the hearth-fire, telling the tales of ancient Orka. Stories of trowies, silkies and even the mysterious Silvers.

I'm offering *Silverborn* as a FREE ebook exclusively to my readers' club, the House of Legends Clan. By joining you'll get regular updates from me and exclusive previews and offers. You can join the clan at houseoflegends.me

ABOUT THE AUTHOR

Daniel Allison is a *USA Today* bestselling author, oral storyteller, storytelling coach and Muay Thai fighter from Scotland. He hosts the *House of Legends* podcast and is the author of *Scottish Myths & Legends I & II, Irish Mythology; The Children of Danu, Finn & The Fianna* and *The Orkney Cycle*.

Myth Singers, Daniel's online Celtic Storytelling Apprenticeship, provides a unique training platform for emerging storytellers throughout the world. He leads mythic immersion retreats in the Scottish Highlands.

Daniel has performed throughout the world, from the jungles of Peru to Thai villages, Hebridean hilltops, Indian theatres, Arabian markets and global festivals. He divides his time between Scotland and Thailand.

Printed in Great Britain
by Amazon

57330298R00178